Becoming Sir

Becoming Sir

ISBN 13: 978-1494748586
ISBN 10: 1494748584

Dedication

To the awesomeness that is my husband and daughter. They are loved beyond anything I can describe in words. Their humor keeps me entertained and inspired, and their discipline keeps me in line (most of the time).

Becoming Sir

Acknowledgements

To family, friends & coworkers who keep me entertained,
inspired & who can never be replaced.

To the following amazing, responsive & speedy beta
readers for their keen eyesight & insight: Becki W., Yvonne L.,
Monica M., Terrie A., Lita T., Gabby B., Christina M. &
Dorothy R.

To Gwen from Rebel Books Chicks & Terri from My Book
Boyfriend for their significant contributions & invaluable
feedback (& whom I'm seriously girl crushing on)

To the best fans an author could ask for & loyal readers
whose kind words keep me going.

To the readers & lovers of The Art of D/s Trilogy who
encouraged me to write Sawyer's story.

http://houseslut.tumblr.com

Epigraph

"There will be a few times in your life when all your instincts will tell you to do something; something that defies logic, upsets your plans and may seem crazy to others. When that happens, you do it. Listen to your instincts and ignore everything else. Ignore logic, ignore the odds, ignore the complications and just go for it." – Judith McNaught

Prologue

Sawyer's eyes rested on his face in the mirror. What was reflected back was someone he didn't like, but that he had come to accept; someone cold, hard, and murderous. His dark, ominous eyes held a note of desolation that was hard to hide, and his handsome, scruffy face looked older than his true age of thirty-eight.

His eyes flicked to the sink as he washed the last of the blood from his hands, the crimson swirling into the abyss of the drain pipe. He hoped he had just killed for the last time. Three times he had murdered in the name of loyalty to his friend, confidant and business partner, Dylan Young and his wife, Isabel. There was no doubt in his mind that he would do it again if push came to shove, but he prayed to a God he doubted existed that it would never come to that again. Sawyer had his fill of death and was put off by how easily he found it to take another person's life. He would be content if only the murders of these three people were on his hands, but there were many more than that. Dozens. Who the hell was he kidding? The number was far more than that and he damned well knew it. He was good at killing and that was one of the many reasons the CIA had hired him.

His breath caught at the sudden and sharp stab of pain that shot through his chest. The gunshot wound emblazoned over his heart was still on the mend and the bullet still lodged near his aorta. Lifting his shirt, a fresh blood stain soaked through the gauze bandage reminding him of his own mortality. He had come so close to losing his life it was frightening to think about.

After his beloved wife Serena had died so many years ago, nothing mattered to him, not even his own existence, but with Sonya in his life, he felt a sense of responsibility to her, as well as to Dylan and Isabel. They all needed him and it was both touching and terrifying to face the reality that so many people relied on him. What if he failed them? He couldn't bear the thought.

He made his way from the bathroom to the kitchen and found the cleaning supplies he needed to create the mysterious concoction that would eliminate all traces that he, Dylan and Isabel had been in the house. It was just another of the many tricks of the trade he had learned from his days with The Agency. Clearing his mind of everything but the task in front of him, he mixed the ingredients. After he finished, he found some latex gloves with the housekeeping supplies and went about the undesirable and tedious chore of setting up the crime scene.

What a fucking mess. Images of Isabel standing over her father, Emilio Ibanez, at point blank range invaded his thoughts. The distressing words she had spoken, begging him to explain his abuse of her and his heartless response about hating her and never having wanted her.

Sawyer wasn't sorry in the least for having taken Emilio and his henchman Simons lives. That abusive son-of-a-bitch Emilio was a menace to his family and society, and they both deserved to die for all the shit they had done, not only to himself, but to Dylan, Isabel, her mother, and God only knows who else.

As if it was second nature, Sawyer finished staging the scene and typed out a suicide note and letter of admission of guilt on Emilio's behalf for his actions against Isabel's mother and for murdering Simons. It was only a partial lie at best seeing as Sawyer had been the one to deal the final blow with a deadly shot to Simons' heart. He had simply carried out his revenge on Simons and finished what Isabel had started. It only seemed appropriate after Simons had wounded Sawyer in almost the same spot only days before.

Nearly two hours after the whole ugly fiasco had played out, Sawyer's job was complete. He walked out of the house feeling satisfied and met Dylan and Isabel back at the car. He climbed into the driver's seat and Dylan moved next to him.

"Is it done?" he asked with hooded eyes.

"It's finished," Sawyer responded, his mellow baritone voice edged with control.

"I'm starting to think this will never be finished. I'm so tired, Morrison." Dylan's voice was distant and the sincerity in his tone tore at Sawyer's heart.

He peered over the back seat to see Isabel in a crumpled heap, sleeping soundly. He reached over and pushed her wavy and tangled blonde hair from her blood spattered face and ran his index finger over her leather and diamond collar fastened securely around her frail neck. She looked like a sad, delicate, corrupted angel.

"I promise you, Young, one way or the other, it's over. You and Isabel need rest; lots of it. Take as much time as you need and leave the business to me. I'm here and I'm not going anywhere."

Dylan leaned his head back and closed his eyes.

The drive back to the airport was short. Sawyer attempted to lift a still sleeping Isabel from the back seat, but the pain was too much. Dylan gently pushed him aside and lifted Isabel into his arms and carried her onto the jet. Seating himself next to them, Sawyer became engrossed in watching Dylan and Isabel. They were such a beautiful sight; Dylan holding onto Isabel as if nothing else in the world mattered to him, and Isabel resting oblivious to the world in his wearied arms. Their love was so pure and intense; Sawyer couldn't help but feel a twinge of jealousy. He wanted what they had; he wanted to command and own his own submissive like Dylan; he longed for the kind of devotion that they shared.

As if reading Sawyer's thoughts, Dylan spoke without taking his eyes off of Isabel. "You can have this kind of love, too, Morrison," he spoke softly, running his fingers over Isabel's lips and then through her hair.

Again with this. Sawyer recalled his previous conversation with Dylan about the BDSM lifestyle. Yes, he wanted to experience that kind of powerful love and commitment with Sonya, but how would she feel about it? Would she take the same interest in it that he had? He held out hope that she would.

"Yes, I want it, too," Sawyer replied. "Show me, Young. Teach me."

Chapter 1

"Are you ready for this, Morrison?"

Sawyer was halted by Dylan's iron grip on his shoulder just before they made it to the entrance of the Dark Asylum club. His expression stilled, his mood instantly growing serious. No, he wasn't ready. He had been putting this day off for months; making excuses and avoiding it like the plague.

Close to a year had passed since he had taken Emilio's life, and with Dylan and Isabel being mentally rested and stable, they were back into full swing and pushing to get Sawyer's Dominant training started. But Sawyer liked routine. As the head of a major security corporation and now equal partners in Young Security Corp., he thrived and relied on knowing exactly who, what, when and where. He hated the unknown and that's exactly what he was facing – unfamiliar territory.

Even though he had been studying and going over the basics of Domology for just over a month, he still felt ill-prepared for the meat and potatoes part of his education to commence.

When Dylan's mouth opened, Sawyer swiftly cut him off. "Is this where you give me the *'this is the first day of the rest of your life'* speech?"

Dylan smiled benevolently as if dealing with a temperamental child. "No, but I can if you'd like."

Sawyer's eyes darkened with insolence and his jaw tensed. "I'd rather you didn't. I'm already nervous as fuck."

Slapping Sawyer on the back lightheartedly, Dylan shook his head as he reached for the door. "You nervous? I find that hard to believe. If it makes you feel any better, I'm certain this is what you were destined for."

"I'm not completely convinced of that yet," he countered.

He wished he had the same confidence about his future as Dylan did. Was he really destined to be a Dom? He wasn't so sure. Yes, he was attracted to submissive women and had even fantasized about them, but that didn't mean anything. A lot of men were and they weren't Doms. On the few occasions he tried to be dominating in the bedroom he had been harshly rebuffed and chastised, and had quickly put those inclinations aside. Work was the only place he was allowed to exert his control and he had come to accept that.

With a light shove, Dylan pushed Sawyer through the door and into the club. He was immediately hit with the smell of rich fragrant oil and leather. He had been in the club before when securing it for Dylan and Isabel, but never past the main entrance.

As they entered the large, dimly lit social area, he took in his surroundings; white Christmas lights adorning the bar, painted red brick walls, and an assortment of kinky memorabilia like whips and canes hanging everywhere in addition to vintage photos of scantily clad women in leather and lingerie. The smell was sensual and pleasant, the ambiance warm and inviting. He even spotted a few of Isabel's erotic paintings hanging proudly near where the manager and owner were seated.

The usual sounds of sexy activity were absent and only the lull of music to the tune of Beethoven's Piano Sonata No. 14, Moonlight, could be heard. Between the muted lighting that was casting murky shadows across the walls and floor and the sounds of Beethoven, the atmosphere took on a somber feel. Sawyer's eyes scanned the room as he counted the number of people mingling and made a mental note of the location of all exits. It was innate for him to always be on high-alert and his former CIA training was always running in the background.

A few people were seated at the bar, one of them being the club owner, Kerian. Luckily, he was engrossed in a lively conversation and completely ignored both him and Dylan. The last thing he needed or wanted was fanfare and a welcoming party. Dylan motioned for a tall woman who was seated at a table and she promptly approached them, carrying herself confidently.

"Mr. Young, Mr. Morrison," she bowed her head. "It's my pleasure to meet you," she offered her small hand to Sawyer. He took her hand into his and gently squeezed it. When the woman didn't make direct eye contact, Sawyer grasped harder, trying to prompt her to look at him, but she kept her eyes to the floor. Slowly and gracefully, she lowered herself to her knees, making for an awkward situation. He stood immobile and addressed Dylan.

"I'm not sure I'm comfortable with a woman on her knees in front of me," he spoke unconvincingly, his eyes never leaving the woman.

When she timidly peered up at him, he was stunned by her beauty. She had long, straight, hazelnut-colored hair that hung around her face and shoulders and flowed down her back. She was wearing a sheer lace halter dress that accentuated her curves and large breasts. She wasn't thin. In fact, most might consider her on the heavy side, but it made no difference, he was instantly attracted to her and found it difficult to take his eyes off of her. The woman's bright eyes, light skin and cream-colored frock were a stark contrast to the darkened room, and the way they glowed from the overhead lighting reminded him of a bright winter day.

"Are you sure about that?" Dylan asked.

True to form, Dylan was reading Sawyer's body language and it was maddening. Sawyer hesitantly looked away from the gorgeous submissive to eye his friend. He had an eyebrow lifted and an easy questioning smile played on the corners of his mouth. Sawyer managed to shrug, doubting the believability of his own statement.

Directing his gaze back to the enthralling femme fatale in front of him, he leaned down slightly, pressing his index finger under the curve of her chin. "I want to see your eyes."

When he spoke, he was surprised to hear his own authority resonate through. His statement left no room for concession and she slowly raised her head. When her ultra-marine eyes met his, she wet her crimson lips nervously. Sweet Christ... those eyes and ridiculously long lashes. Even in the darkened room they glowed. Like something otherworldly or paranormal. Perhaps she wasn't really human. Maybe she was a Goddess or demi-God... or...

"You're beautiful," he inadvertently whispered. He shook his head at his lusty remark and forced himself to pull it together. "Tell me your name, Snowflake."

"Sarah," she smiled radiantly, her eyes scanning his face.

"Are you here to teach me how to be a good Dominant?" he asked, squatting in front of her as he swept a strand of hair away from her eyes, tucking it behind her ear. He hoped she would teach him. He wanted to learn from her.

Sarah dropped her chin to her chest and let out a sigh of pleasure. "Yes, Sir. If you find me worthy, I would like very much to help you."

There was a gentle softness in Sarah's voice and Sawyer was struck by the sheer sincerity of her joy. The idea of her eagerness inexplicably energized him and he was unable to deny the spark of excitement at the prospect of having a willing woman under his command. Any previous hesitation he had melted when she leaned into his touch and purred.

"So tell me, Morrison, what kind of Dominant do you want to be?" Dylan asked from above.

"The kind that I was born to be. The absolute fucking best."

Chapter 2

"That's the Sawyer I know," Dylan nodded with poise.

Sawyer stood, helping Sarah off her knees, unable to look anywhere but at her. There was something about her that spoke to him; her softness, delicateness and, most undeniably, her submissiveness. Even though he had been drawn to submissive women, he had always attracted headstrong females, like Sonya, and had never been confronted with this type of female; one who craved a man's domination.

Sonya. Guilt pierced his heart at the thought of her. He missed her touch, her raspy voice, and poignant gray eyes looking back at him. He blinked long and hard and hesitated as the trio walked to a private room, dropping Sarah's hand in the process.

Sarah turned to face him, a look of confusion settling on her full, round face.

"If you would be more comfortable with someone else, I won't take offense," she remarked softly.

Sawyer couldn't resist smiling at her. He felt more than comfortable with her. In fact, he wanted nothing more than to caress her nude body and to feel her soft skin pressed against him. Her meekness stirred something primal within him, and he wanted to find out what it truly felt like to control a woman simply with his touch or command.

"No, you aren't the issue," he tried to put her at ease.

Dylan guided Sawyer aside and gave him an inquiring look.

"I have someone else on my mind," he answered before the question was asked.

"Sonya?"

He nodded and looked over Dylan's shoulder to see the most exquisite incandescent eyes watching him.

Dylan spoke in soft tones. "I know you miss her, but you're doing the right thing. If it's meant to be, she'll wait for you."

"And what if she doesn't?" Sawyer's voice was barely a whisper and he hated how desperate he sounded. He detested what Sonya had done to him – to make him feel again; to love again. When Serena had died, so did all of his feelings. That is, until Sonya.

Dylan gave a firm squeeze to his shoulder, but said nothing. There was nothing he could say and Sawyer knew it. It was now or never and he knew that, too. He wanted this, truly wanted this. Having done his homework, he knew what the lifestyle meant and what pleasures it could hold. But all the books and Google searches in the world could only go so far. He needed to experience BDSM to understand it.

He was tired of sitting in the shadows and watching Dylan and Isabel, desiring what they had. He wanted his own life; his own experiences; maybe even his own submissive some day. He had hoped Sonya would be that woman for him. Hell, she seemed passive enough in the bedroom. But life had a cruel way of dealing shitty cards to Sawyer. Just when he had gotten comfortable with Sonya and told her of his wants, she had backed away, leaving him to journey down this path on his own.

Sawyer squared his shoulders. *Sarah.* He liked the way the name formed on his lips unconsciously.

"I'm fine," he croaked out in a hoarse whisper.

Making their way to private quarters, he was confronted with lush surroundings and a room nothing at all like he had imagined. The leather furniture was worn but plush and comfortable looking; the walls a dark shade of chocolate brown with gold accents, and a hand woven rug placed in front of the couch added a touch of exoticness. The smell was mouth watering and strangely reminded him of his travels to Burma – spicy with floral undertones.

Dylan seated himself in a large oversized chair next to the couch while Sawyer sat at the end of the long davenport. Sarah stood waiting, her eyes resting on Sawyer's mouth. Patting the space next to him, she dutifully seated herself. It was charming that Sarah had waited for his invitation, and his mouth curved into a stupid grin.

"You have a breathtaking smile," Sarah commented.

Suddenly feeling uncomfortable and constricted, he coughed nervously while shifting in his seat and loosening his tie. He wasn't fond of compliments, they made him uneasy.

"My apologies for speaking out of line, Sir," Sarah quickly apologized.

Sawyer's eyes zoomed in on her expression. Her cheeks were a vivid shade of pink and he had obviously, though inadvertently, embarrassed her.

"You don't ever need to apologize for speaking your mind," he replied with a tinge of astonishment in his voice.

Sarah's look of shame quickly turned to uncertainty, and her eyes darted from Dylan to Sawyer and back.

"I think you'll find Mr. Morrison isn't going to be like most Dom's you've encountered, Sarah," Dylan stated with a light chuckle. "For one, he's new at this and fairly easy going given the right circumstances. Secondly, he's not full of himself and despite his gruff and unapproachable countenance; I think you'll find he's quite gentle."

Sawyer bristled and winced. Who the hell was Dylan calling gentle and easy going? For fuck's sake, he had the blood of countless men on his hands. No, he wasn't conceited, but that's because he had come to accept who he was – murderer and all. He sat forward and almost voiced his sentiments but stopped himself for fear of scaring the pants off of Sarah. Then again, he did like the image of a pantless Sarah. He smiled to himself, sat back and fidgeted with the lapels of his suit jacket, his eyes shimmering with the vision of the thick beauty in her best lingerie and kneeling at his feet.

"He also has a wicked sense of humor, if he ever decides to grace you with it," Dylan continued.

Sawyer shot Dylan a harsh look. He was at it again. Couldn't he keep a thought in his head without Dylan honing in on it? "Oh, Christ, can we get started with this?" Sawyer grumbled.

"Okay. Ask away," Dylan laughed, clearly amused at making him uncomfortable, his cerulean blue eyes bright with amusement.

Directing his comment to Sarah, Sawyer asked, "How long have you been into this lifestyle?"

She answered without hesitation. "I'm 33, so just about ten years."

Ten years was a long time; almost as long as Dylan. Nodding his head, he asked his next question. "What interested you in this kind of life?"

Lacing her fingers together in her lap, Sarah kept her eyes on her hands. "My partner at the time. We learned about BDSM together and eventually married."

Shocked that Sarah would help train a Dom while being married, he kept moving right along, but found it strange that a man would be willing to share his life partner in such an intimate way.

"So your husband is okay with you teaching other men about this sort of thing?"

Sarah shook her head and when she spoke again, her voice was more tender and soft, almost a murmur. "My Master is gone, Mr. Morrison. He died well over a year ago, but I believe within my heart he would want me to share my knowledge with others. I know he would. He was an amazing man; firm, but loving."

Sawyer sat silently. He had touched on a sensitive area and was taken by Sarah's candidness. When he didn't immediately respond to her, she lifted her face.

"I have only had one Master, Mr. Morrison, but please don't let that deter you from allowing me to teach you. We were an active part of this club and have taught many. My grieving process has been long and it's taken a lot for me to come back without my Sir, but I sincerely want to rejoin the community and help others find the kind of happiness that I once had."

The heartrending look on Sarah's face leveled Sawyer and he unconsciously reached out to touch her cheek. Her eyes were glassy but she resolutely held back her tears. She was a strong woman, he could see that. She knew the terrible loss of a loved one and they shared that common bond. Sawyer couldn't help but wonder if that's why Dylan had chosen her and what other commonalities they shared.

"I'm not deterred in the least, Snowflake. I, too, know the loss of true love."

"I'm sorry to hear that," she blinked rapidly.

Sawyer did his best to sound strong. "It was a very long time ago."

Reaching out, Sarah placed her hand on his. "It's a lie when people say time heals. No matter the length of time, the pain never really goes away, does it?"

No, it didn't. Sawyer had never gotten over losing Serena. Time had simply moved forward and some days were better than others. Even when he met Sonya, Serena was still in the back of his mind. She always would be. He nodded his agreement and they exchanged a bleak forced smile.

Moving on with his questions, he asked, "In your opinion, what makes a good Dominant?"

Sarah looked uneasy with the question but pondered her answer thoughtfully.

"I'll answer you, but please keep in mind that every submissive has different needs. For me, a good Dominant is someone who is comfortable with themselves and accepts who they are, and what their needs and their submissive's needs are. He is a leader and not a follower. There are so many things, Mr. Morrison. It's a difficult question to answer. Perhaps I can think more on this and get back with you as my thoughts form into something more logical being as I'm feeling a bit flustered at the moment."

Sawyer touched Sarah's arm and noted that her breathing quickened.

"Why are you flustered? Am I making you uncomfortable?"

Sarah's face flushed and she averted her eyes to the floor. "Can I speak openly?"

Sawyer found Sarah's question strange, but gave his approval. "Of course."

"Because of you, Mr. Morrison, but it's not discomfort that I'm feeling. It's been a long time since I've been this close to a man who wasn't my Sir. I thought I would be better composed, but I'm finding myself aroused by your curiosity and dominance, yet, I'm feeling incredibly guilty at the same time. Perhaps another submissive would be better suited for you," she stammered out.

Sawyer leaned in and guided her to look at him. "My dear Snowflake, I understand about the guilt you're feeling. I'm not looking to replace your husband. My apologies. Your *Master*. I simply want to learn from you. There is no one at this time that is better suited to show me the ropes than you. And if you're not comfortable calling me Sir, then by all means, keep calling me Mr. Morrison. It has a nice ring and if I can speak freely, I find it nothing less than charming coming from your mouth."

Sarah's eyes lit the dim room and her mouth parted with a sharp intake of air. "A true Dominant also knows the value of the spoken word. His words are chosen carefully with full awareness of their consequences, and he respects their power. And your words, Mr. Morrison, hold great power."

Sawyer's core temperature rose and he feared that Sarah would be offended by his obvious attraction to her.

Dylan stood and calmly spoke. "I'll leave you two to discuss more on your own. At this stage in the game, only conversation is allowed, Morrison, but Sarah knows the rules of engagement."

Without saying anything more, Dylan excused himself.

Sawyer immediately turned his attention back to Sarah. "There are so many questions I had planned on asking today, but now faced with the situation, I find myself at a loss for words."

Relaxing into the soft leather, Sarah began talking openly. "Since I'm not sure what you've read or been told, I'll tell you what submission is to me and probably most, if not all submissives. It's more than a sexual experience, Mr. Morrison. It's a bond so powerful that it contains the very soul of the submissive. A man's domination and acceptance of the gift of submission is the greatest expression of love I believe there to be."

Sudden synapses began to fire in Sawyer's brain. This woman sitting in front of him knew so much more than him. It seemed everyone around him did. Dylan, Isabel… how could he have not known about this his entire life? With his eyebrows pinched together, he tried to formulate an articulate question to ask, but he still found himself unable to speak.

Sarah leaned back, exhaling with tension. "I'm preaching. I don't mean to. Tell me what interested you in becoming a Dom."

"Dylan and Isabel."

"Yes, they're an interesting couple, aren't they? I remember Dylan back in his hey-day when he was training submissives. It's beautiful to see how he's changed for Isabel."

"Yes, they are interesting. I remember him, too. He was quite cocky. Not to say that he still isn't."

"You work with him, right?"

"Yes. Actually, we're not just business associates anymore; I keep forgetting that. I worked for him for so long that it's strange being equal partners now."

Sarah's faint smile broadened. "Congratulations on that. You must be proud of yourself."

"Proud? No, I wouldn't say proud. It was sort of forced on me. I am grateful, though. It means a bigger paycheck. Even though, with more money comes more problems, I'm told." Suddenly aware of his rambling, he cleared his throat. "I'm bragging when I don't mean to."

"A humble Dom is a respected Dom, Mr. Morrison. And you weren't at all bragging."

***

The rest of their conversation was informative and friendly, though Sarah did most of the talking. Sawyer found himself appreciative of everything she had shared and her openness. When he looked at his watch, more than two hours had passed. The time had flown and Sawyer didn't want their conversation to end. He had enjoyed Sarah's company.

Heading back to the social area, he was greeted by Isabel.

She was beaming and her toothy smile reached from ear-to-ear. "So how was it? Did you like Sarah? I picked her. Isn't she a doll? Oh, Sawyer, tell me everything!"

"Jesus, Isa, let the man breathe," Dylan chastised.

"I picked her. I just want that to be said. I know Dylan will try and take all the credit on that."

"You also picked Sonya, remember?" Dylan huffed.

"That was just mean," Isa pouted.

Sawyer seated himself next to Isabel at the bar. "She was very nice. Thanks, Isabel. You did a good job; even picking Sonya."

Dylan rolled his eyes and gulped down his tea. "Yeah, yeah. Let's get this party started. I'm itching to whip a certain someone," he tugged on Isabel's hair.

"Yes, it will be a whipping good time. See what I did there, Dylan? *Whipping* good time?" she giggled, mocking his constant lame wordplay jokes.

Dylan lifted a threatening eyebrow at Isabel. "Are you making fun of me?"

Isabel immediately remembered her place. "Sorry, Master."

Though they were switches in the privacy of their bedroom, in public, Dylan was the Master. Only once had Dylan given her the reins in public and that was in Paris on their honeymoon. In Denver, at their club of choice, he dealt out the punishment and pleasure.

Sawyer had never actually seen them *perform* before and nervous apprehension began to creep up on him. He knew the kinds of things they did from the private footage that was leaked to the media by Isabel's father. It was hard getting the images from those exploits out of his head, but seeing their activity up close and personal... he wasn't sure he could go through with it. Isabel was a masochist to Dylan's sadist and even though what they did was consensual and supposedly safe and sane, Sawyer was never fond of the idea of doling out pain to a woman. To a man who deserved it, sure, but not a woman.

Dylan and Isabel disappeared for a few minutes to get things set up when Sarah reappeared.

"I thought I'd stay to watch Dylan and Isabel. Have you seen them scene before?"

Sawyer lifted his eyebrows in acknowledgment and smiled. "Yes and no."

"A man of few words."

The double meaning of Sarah's statement wasn't lost on him and though her tone was playful, the implication was anything but. The expression on her face gave away the frustration she was trying to disguise, and it wasn't the first time a look or comment like that had been directed at him. Both Serena and Sonya had told him numerous times he was too emotionally distant.

"Communication, Mr. Morrison. We need to work on that with you. It's a very important part of being a Dom."

"Well aren't you the officious little submissive," he raised his eyebrows.

Sarah's eyes widened and her mouth opened. "I didn't mean that to be disrespectful."

Shaking his head, he placed his hand on her shoulder. "I didn't take it that way. You're right. I do need to communicate more. Hopefully you can help me work on that."

She immediately let out a sigh of relief and Sawyer fought the urge to pull her close and plant his mouth on her fire-engine red pouting lips. He was starting to like this new role and the effect his words had on Sarah.

Chapter 3

Dylan laid the leather across Isabel's bare stomach in one quick motion, leaving a red streak on her supple, pale skin. She was dressed in only tight-fitting, waist-high shorts and a satin bra, and he was stripped down to his black slacks and barefoot. The setting was intimate with only a handful of onlookers in the small niche. Nina Simone, *Sinner Man*, played softly while Dylan moved in rhythm to the beat.

Sawyer was mesmerized by the way Dylan's eyes were trained on Isabel as he moved around her stealthily, all the while power and dominance exuding from every pore as he took control of her.

Sawyer had feared he wouldn't be able to stomach the scene, but it was proving hard to look away from. No, he still didn't like the idea of causing someone as beautiful as Isabel pain, but just because it wasn't his kink, he wasn't going to judge someone else on their preferences.

Isabel's amber eyes fluttered open and closed, and her tongue slicked across her mouth causing an obvious erection on Dylan's part. Her body swung hypnotically from the suspension rig, the chains jangling noisily. As Sawyer's probing brown eyes took in the details of her body, unwanted lascivious thoughts popped into his head, filling him with guilt. He never felt a physical attraction toward Isabel, but seeing her so compliant and captivatingly submissive stirred his sexual desires. He looked away, trying to contain his unwanted physical reaction.

"I'm neither a masochist nor a sadist, Mr. Morrison, but I try to keep an open mind with regards to all things sexual. May I politely suggest that you do the same?" Sarah whispered into his ear.

Focusing on her, his mouth formed into a tight smile. "It's not that I'm being closed-minded. It's just that I'm feeling..." he stopped himself.

She squeezed his bicep as she continued to lean into his ear, her breath felt on his cheek.

"Oh, I see. It's normal to feel aroused. It's a natural response to what you're seeing and just shows you have a healthy libido and imagination."

Her electrical touch took his mind off of Isabel and he was thankful for it. Feeling better after Sarah's reassurance, he turned to watch the scene again. He watched as Dylan circled around Isabel, flicking the whip across various parts of her body as she squealed out her approval and pulled against her restraints. Sawyer just didn't get it. Why would someone want to be hurt in such a way or cause pain to someone you love?

Dylan's wild eyes suddenly darted to Sawyer and he motioned for him. It was a complete what the fuck moment for him and his body froze. Dylan's eyes moved to Sarah and he nodded, prompting her to take Sawyer's hand and guide him to the center stage.

"You're up, Sawyer," Dylan stated.

A knot rose in his throat and he shook his head adamantly. He didn't want any part of harming Isabel, regardless if it was something that she got off on. He backed away and put his hand up. "Don't ask me to hurt Isabel. I won't do that. I can't."

Isabel's feminine voice resonated over the music. "It's okay, Sawyer. Dylan won't let you hurt me beyond what I can handle. I trust you implicitly, as does Dylan," she panted out, still winded from Dylan's whipping.

Maybe Isabel trusted him, but Sawyer wasn't sure he trusted himself. What if he liked it? What if hurting a woman appealed to him?

"Try to forget all the social norms you've been spoon fed, Sawyer. Push all the things you've been told about sadism out of your head and the stigma associated with it, and go with what you feel. You'll never know if this is something you like or not unless you try it," he spoke firmly. "Watch me. Like this: relax your wrist and pace your movements slowly." He demonstrated what he had done before and lightly snapped the cat-o-nine tails on Isabel's glistening right thigh. "Your motions should be smooth and fluid; the weapon a part of you; like the talons on an eagle. You can do it, Morrison, and don't worry; neither I nor Isa will be offended if you're turned on."

Dylan's prompt and statement caused Sawyer's defenses to slowly subside. Hesitantly taking the whip in his left hand, his palms became clammy and a trickle of sweat ran down between his shoulder blades. He couldn't believe he was really going through with it. Dylan stood back, giving him room to wield the calfskin. Closing his eyes, he drew in a long steady breath through his nose and blew it out his mouth. *Just focus, Morrison*, he repeated to himself.

Bringing up the cat midair he paused, his eyes taking note of the light sheen of sweat that had built up on Isabel's petite form, but finally snapped the end of the leather across her stomach lightly; so light there was no reaction on Isabel's part. Even though it had barely touched her, something about what he was doing just didn't feel right. He did it three more times over her thighs just to make sure he wasn't being too quick to call judgment, but the same feeling was there, or lack thereof. Sure he felt in control, but there was no excitement in what he was doing and no sexual arousal. The only thing he felt was that it wasn't for him. But the way Isabel was responding, Sawyer became aware that it wasn't only about his needs, but hers.

He moved behind her and as he slowly became more comfortable with the whip, he stroked her body at a more rapid pace until Isabel's moans became louder. When he sensed that Isabel was near orgasm, he looked to Dylan who promptly came over and fingered her to release. When everything was said and done, he dropped the whip to the floor with a resounding thud and a prevailing sense of relief filled him.

Turning to face Dylan, he let out a loud sigh of relief and spoke. "Thanks for the invite, but that," he gestured with his head to the cat lying on the floor, "is not for me."

Ella Dominguez

Dylan smiled knowingly as he unshackled Isabel and cradled her in his arms. "So you're not a sadist. I guessed as much. Even still, Isa thanks you for going through with it. Isn't that right, pussycat? Now be a good girl and thank Sawyer."

Isa was still in her subspace high, her body shivering as she turned to face Sawyer, instantly doing as her Master had asked.

"Thank you, Sawyer," her voice shook and her teeth chattered.

Dylan carried Isabel away, murmuring his praises in her ear while Sawyer began to pace the floor, stunned with everything that had played out. If Young assumed he wasn't a sadist, then why the hell did he insist he whip Isabel? Was this some sort of fucked up test of his resolve?

While Dylan delivered aftercare to Isa, he became more irate with every passing minute. When Dylan finally approached, Sawyer huffed, "If you suspected I was no sadist, why the hell did you make me do that?"

"Because now you know for yourself and you'll never wonder again."

God, Sawyer hated when Dylan was right. He was so damned smug about it, too. He shook his head and his mouth ruffled into a sarcastic grin. Typical, fucking, Young.

***

Back at his condo, Sawyer showered and made himself dinner. The afternoon had been more stimulating than he had expected and his earlier reluctance now seemed completely unwarranted. Sarah's luminous eyes flashed in his mind. She had the most seductive shade of blue he had ever seen, like a blue flame sky. Perhaps it was just the club setting, but he couldn't stop thinking about her. His cock began to harden as his mind wandered to all the things he wanted to do while staring into those eyes. Suddenly the flame of desire was doused by guilt.

Tired of thinking of Sonya and the what if's, he picked up his phone and dialed her number. He hadn't spoken with her

29

in nearly a month, but he needed to tell her everything that had happened.

"Sawyer," she answered.

"Lady Sonya, how are you?"

"Busy. We're getting ready for a show at the gallery. Have you spoken with Isabel? She's agreed to supply four paintings, but I haven't been able to get in contact with her. I think she's still mad at me."

Sawyer smiled. Isabel had initially set the two up and she had voiced her displeasure with Sonya's decision to put things on hold and her less than enthusiastic attitude toward all things BDSM. Isabel was protective of him and though it was often annoying at times, it was also nice knowing that she cared. Of course, it was her protective nature that had gotten her into the whole mess with her father over a year ago.

Sonya's voice became distant as he recalled that horrible night again; Isabel confronting her father and the shit storm that came after. He often wondered what would've happened if he and Dylan hadn't shown up that fateful night. That would've been an even worse mess to clean up than simply killing Emilio and Simons. As fragile as Isabel's psyche was, he had no doubt she never would've recovered if she had taken the same action herself.

"Are you still there?" Sonya asked, breaking through Sawyer's thoughts.

"Yes, I'm here. It's just good to hear your voice. If Isabel agreed to four paintings, I'm sure she'll follow through with her commitment, but I'll have her call you to verify."

"I've missed you're voice, too," she sighed, her once loving tone gone and replaced by something else; distance and dejection.

Had so much time passed that she had gotten over him already? Feeling forlorn at the thought, he let out a long slow breath.

"I went to the Dark Asylum today." As the words left his mouth, his nerves tensed.

There was a quiet pause before Sonya responded blandly. "So you went through with it then. How did that go?"

"It was interesting and... educational, to say the least. I learned a lot in one day. I wish you had been there to learn with me."

"We've been through this. I'm not ready for... *that*. I'm not even sure I ever will be. That *lifestyle*... it's just so..." she answered in a grudging tone.

He interrupted before she could say the judgmental words he hoped she would never say. He wanted to live the lifestyle with her... if only she would consider the possibility. "Please don't, Sonya, don't do that. Don't judge."

"I'm sorry. I'm trying not to. I know how much it means to you. I also know how important Dylan and Isabel are to you. I just hope they're not influencing you to do something that goes against who you really are."

Sawyer shook his head. The conversation was turning out to be a replay of what they had discussed months before and the unwelcome tension stretched ever tighter between them.

His voice took on a strong, disciplinarian tone. "I'm not easily influenced, Sonya, and no one can make me do anything I don't want. But you already know that, don't you?"

She remained silent, not answering and the chill between them seemed to grow. Damn her silence. It was only one of a few things about her that drove him insane.

"Answer me, please," he urged her.

"You won't like the answer I have for you." Now her voice was curt and patronizing.

"Can we not do this? I just wanted to talk to you; to tell you that..." he debated whether or not to speak his true feelings but remembered what Sarah had mentioned about open communication. "I want you to be a part of my life and this new experience."

He could hear a soft gasp of surprise on the other end of the phone. "Sawyer... wow."

Chuckling at her response and also surprised by his own admission, he countered, "Yeah, I know. It's a lot to take in isn't it? I'm trying to be more open. It's one of the things that I learned today."

"I see. What else did you learn?"

Sonya suddenly became interested and Sawyer cheered up when he detected thawing in her frigid tone. "That I'm not a sadist."

"Well that's good to hear," she laughed incredulously. "Did you ever have any doubt about that?"

"Honestly, yes."

"Oh. Well... I don't quite know how to respond to that. Did you ever want to hurt me?" she asked with anxiety in her soft voice.

"No. Did I ever lead you to believe that I wanted to?"

"No. Never. It's just strange that you weren't sure." It was hard not to detect the note of bewilderment in Sonya's tone.

"If you knew my past, not really," he stated, suddenly realizing his almost admission.

"I don't know about your past. You never shared anything. Or have you forgotten about that?"

Reeling from the sting of Sonya's statement, he shook his head and sighed. "No, I haven't forgotten."

He sat wordless, waiting for her next response. He almost wished she would ask about his past so he could be free from his secrets and not be forced to do it on his own, but she didn't. After sitting for more than a minute in silence, Sawyer spoke with hopefulness in his voice.

"Can I see you? I'd like the chance to talk you into coming to the club with me."

Sonya let out a heavy sigh and he could hear the sound of her moistening her lips. Would she go? The silence was deafening and his heart sank.

"Maybe. I can't make you any promises right now, but this new, more open Sawyer is definitely an improvement, so... we'll see."

Chapter 4

When the weekend rolled around, Sawyer felt animated despite Sonya's refusal to go to the club. He held on to the hope that she would soon change her mind. His heart ached at the thought of continuing his journey without her, but he was prepared to do it, no matter how heartbreaking the thought was. He had to. He owed it to himself to explore this part of his life.

New things were on the horizon for him. Even with the possibility of facing a future without Sonya, he couldn't help feeling optimistic. The last time he had felt this energized was when met Sonya. Before that, it had been years.

He owed Isabel a big thanks for everything she had brought about. Namely the changes she had inspired in Dylan that in turn made him discuss his love for her and his lifestyle choices. It was strange to think of the Dylan *before* and the Dylan *after* Isabel. It was two completely different men. He wondered if Dylan realized that.

Also, he owed her a great debt for introducing him to Sonya. Although things hadn't worked out the way either of them had wanted, Sonya had brought him emotionally back to life and awakened the feelings he had buried alongside his wife.

A gift was definitely in order to convey his deep gratitude. The image of her body hanging from the suspension rig flashed in his mind. He hoped he hadn't hurt her too badly the previous day when he whipped her. He reminded himself to ask her when he saw her.

Sawyer arrived to work later than usual after stopping to get something for Isabel and found Dylan looking more stressed than usual.

"What's the problem?"

Looking up from his desk, Dylan's eyes flickered with annoyance. "You don't want to know. I knew it was too good to be true," he commented somberly.

"What is it now?"

"Someone is contesting the disbursement of Emilio's estate. They want an investigation into his death."

Sawyer frowned with cold fury. Emilio Ibanez. Again. Even dead he was wreaking havoc on their lives. After his death, it had come out that he surprisingly had no will and so all money and property was to be released to his only living family member, Isabel. The amount his sizable estate was worth was staggering, in the hundreds of millions.

Sawyer quickly became irritated. "Who?"

"A business partner. Fuck, Morrison. We don't need this kind of stress. Not with us trying..." he snapped his mouth closed and cut his statement short as if he had inadvertently spoken.

"Trying to *what*?"

The look on Dylan's face was intense, as if he were holding onto a secret. He shook his head and stood, moving towards the large bank of windows and gazing out at the Denver cityscape. Something was obviously eating at Dylan, but he was avoiding talking or thinking about having to deal with the shit that was about to go down.

"Tell me," he demanded when Dylan refused to elaborate.

"Trying to get pregnant," he whispered.

Sawyer stumbled backwards towards the large chair in front of Dylan's desk and sank into it. He was under the impression Isabel couldn't have children after the physical abuse she had endured at the hands of her father. Dylan had told him as much. But how? And what the fuck?

"You let me whip Isabel knowing that?" he barked when he got his wind back. Dylan swung around to face Sawyer with an astonished look on his face. "And you? You whipped her, too. What the fuck were you thinking, Young?"

"Calm down. There was no chance of any harm being done. Don't you think we've done our homework about that? Jesus, give us some credit," Dylan responded defensively with a haughty toss of his head. "And I wouldn't have allowed to you to do anything that would seriously hurt her," he added.

Sawyer felt slightly better, but not much. The fact was he still felt nauseous at the thought of lashing Isabel with even the remote possibility of her being pregnant. "I thought she couldn't conceive," he forced himself to say.

"She couldn't, but she underwent extensive fertility treatments and surgery, and we've been really lucky."

One corner of Dylan's mouth twisted upward and he was suddenly beaming, but Sawyer was hurt he was the last to know.

"Why didn't you tell me sooner?"

"In case... you know... anything should go wrong."

That was understandable but it still didn't alleviate the sting. Fucking, Emilio Ibanez; he always had the worst timing to rear his cruel head. Though in all honesty, Sawyer wasn't worried about the investigation. He had confidence in his cleaning skills and knew a probe of Emilio's death wouldn't yield anything of great value. The only thing he dreaded was that the news media would be all over it.

After Isabel's father had died and everything came out about his past and abuse of Isabel, the media storm around them had been intense and stressful. It had only recently started to die down, and now this bullshit would only renew the public's interest in the couple. No doubt the sexually explicit videos of them that were leaked would resurface again and make their rounds as well.

Dylan had been Denver's Golden Boy and most eligible bachelor for years. He had piqued the public's interest and made his way into the City's Heart when he was orphaned at 14 after his wealthy and respected parents were heinously murdered. They took even more interest in him when, at the age of 16, he had been emancipated as an adult and was recruited by the NSA at age 17 after hacking into several government agencies.

But people were fickle and the community had turned against him when they had found out about his sexual proclivities and taste for sadism. Luckily, his business reputation preceded him and wasn't affected, but the exposure, along with everything else that had happened at the hands of Isabel's father had taken its toll on the couple. Sawyer had done what he could to help them out the only way he knew how – by protecting them from further threats. He wished he could've done more, like shielding them entirely from the harsh scrutiny of the media. Everything had spiraled so far out of control, all any of them could do was put their heads between their legs and wait for the tempest to pass.

With his eyes downcast, Dylan sat on the edge of his desk, scanning the floor. His muscular shoulders heaved with his breathing and he shook his head but remained quiet. When he finally spoke, his voice was low and troubled.

"Fuck."

"I know you won't listen to me, but you really have nothing to worry about. The powers that be won't find anything," Sawyer spoke with cool authority.

Dylan's eyes shot up to his. Squaring his shoulders, he cleared his throat. "I'm not doubting your abilities, Morrison; I just want to make that clear."

He stood in response and slapped Dylan on the back, a hint of humor touching his mouth and dark eyes. "Of course you're not. You know better than that, don't you?"

Arching a sarcastic eyebrow at Sawyer, Dylan scoffed, "One day of training and you think you're all that?"

"I've always been 'all that,' Son, or have you forgotten Guam?" he snickered low and throaty.

Dylan rose from his chair and the two tall, broad-shouldered and solid alpha men stood eye-to-eye, glaring at each other before both bursting into laughter. Sawyer was only six years older than Dylan, but he had always felt like a father-figure or older brother to him.

"Fucking, Guam. How could I ever forget? Damn, Morrison, we've been through some jacked up shit together, haven't we? How old was I - twenty?"

"I don't recall how old you were, but I do remember you being smug as hell. I'll never forget your face during our first firefight when I made my first kill in front of you. I thought you were going to shit your pants."

"Actually, I'm pretty sure I did," Dylan chuckled, walking around to the back of his desk.

Sawyer grinned thinking about their first outing together. It was the summer of 2002 and the heat and humidity were unbearable when they first met in Guam. Dylan was working for the NSA and Sawyer, the CIA. The mission was a joint agency effort to capture a group of suspected foreign terrorists and one of Dylan's first times out as a field agent. He was a cocky little-shit-rookie, but by far the smartest man Sawyer had ever met. Who the hell was he kidding, Dylan was no man then. He was merely a boy pretending to be a man.

They bonded over the incident and kept in touch over the years. Having no siblings or family of his own, he had always felt an inexplicable sense of responsibility for Dylan and took him under his wing, each of them sharing the knowledge and skills that they learned over the years.

Sawyer was also orphaned at a young and impressionable age and so he felt a connection with him. They had grown up in completely different environments – Young surrounded by wealth and Sawyer's early years in a lower/middle-class home in Baltimore. But it made no difference; they were both survivors with dark and tortuous pasts. He knew all of Dylan's dark secrets, even those about his parents' death, and in turn, he had shared his unpleasant past with Dylan. They were joined at the hip so-to-speak and there was no other person in the world that he trusted more.

After Sawyer's parents had died in a tragic car accident when he was six years old, he was transferred to an orphanage in Phoenix and lived the remainder of his youth in and out of various foster homes throughout Arizona. He had been exposed to every kind of piece of shit there was imaginable, including bullies, pedophiles, drug dealers and crack-whores, but he came out stronger for it and managed to fight off every one of them on his own and without the help of anyone. It was his cold detachment, strong self-preservation skills, and driving intelligence that had garnered him a job with the CIA and made him such a good field agent and assassin.

He had felt tremendous pride when Dylan had ventured out on his own and opened his own national security business, and felt an even greater honor when Dylan had offered him a job, even knowing he had been disavowed by the CIA for his drinking problems.

The alcohol. Sawyer winced at the memory. It had come after Serena's death and gotten out of control. Thinking back, he still felt the sting of dishonor for his failures as an agent; a job he took great pride in. Luckily no lives had been lost due to his drinking on the job. If they had, he didn't dare think about what he might've done to himself. He was a wreck back then; miserable, depressed and angry at the world for having taken his beautiful and kind wife in such a cruel way. Fucking cancer.

Sawyer walked back to his office, still thinking about Serena. He hadn't thought about the details of her death in almost eight years. He had pushed the horrible memories of her leukemia and treatment to the recesses of his mind, not wanting to dredge up how frail and sick she had gotten in her last days, and how sad and fragile his once strong wife looked as she laid in his arms and took her last breath. He had never loved anyone more. She was his first and last true love; his one and only.

He wondered how Sarah's husband died. Was it an unkind death, too? For her sake, he hoped not. He didn't know her well, in fact, he didn't know her at all, but he could sense she had a caring soul. Like Dylan, he had a keen sense of judgment when it came to people and what he sensed about Sarah, he liked very much.

He smiled thinking about Dylan and Isabel being parents when Emilio suddenly came unbidden to his mind. He immediately logged onto his computer and checked into what was going on with his estate. It turned out not only Emilio's business partner was interested in his money but several people, though no one else was moving forward legally to contest the disbursement. It was no surprise that Emilio had screwed over so many people and now they were all swarming around like maggots on rotted flesh wanting their share.

Lunch came and went and his thoughts were scattered – Serena, Sarah, Sonya; domination, submission; Isabel and Dylan as parents. His attention was redirected when he received a phone call from an unknown number.

"Mr. Morrison? It's Sarah. I texted Isabel and she passed your number along to me. I hope you don't mind that I've called you."

Sawyer was glad to hear her voice. He had been thinking about her all week and looked forward to speaking with her again.

"Not at all. I've been thinking about you," he admitted.

Sarah cleared her throat anxiously. "Have you? Good things, I hope. I've been thinking about you as well and about your questions. I've had plenty of time to write out my answers and I was hoping we could meet again. There's a munch planned for tonight and I thought it would be a good opportunity for you to meet some of the other members at the club."

"Munch?" The word elicited all sorts of dirty thoughts.

Laughing, she explained. "It's a get together; food, friends, conversation - that sort of thing. I would be honored to attend with you, if you'll have me."

Adorable, darling, Sarah - her submissiveness was alluring. "I'd be grateful if you'd let me tag along, Snowflake."

"May I ask you something, Mr. Morrison?" she asked with bemusement in her voice.

Sawyer shook his head. He didn't know if he would ever get used to a woman asking permission for everything. "Of course."

"Why do you call me Snowflake?"

He hadn't even realized he had been calling her that. Glancing toward the window, the Denver day was cloudless, vivid and clear, the burnt oranges, rusty reds and saffron yellow colors of the leaves scattered across the landscape. Fall was nearing its end and Sawyer wondered how long it would be until the first snowfall. He cherished winters in Colorado.

"Because winter is my favorite time of year. I grew up the majority of my childhood in Arizona and I love the change of season," he answered. "Your face was so bright the first time I saw you, and the added color of your eyes and the way your skin glimmered under the lights... you reminded me of a beautiful snowflake." As soon as the statement spilled out of him, he regretted it. The whole open communication thing was foreign to him and made him feel weak, and the silence on the other end of the phone only added to his discomfort. "I apologize. If me calling you that makes you uncomfortable, it won't happen again," he replied when she didn't immediately respond.

"Please, Mr. Morrison, there's no need to apologize," she said quietly. "I adore the name you've chosen for me. I'll meet you at the club at six. Is that satisfactory?"

He heaved with relief. "Yes, I'll see you then."

***

Sawyer anticipated an interesting night. He wasn't a people person and dreaded being forced to be social. It was bad enough he had to do it for his job, but in private? No thanks. Even though he knew it was good for him, it didn't make him any less uneasy. He had no idea what the dress-code was to a function with a deceptive name that reminded him of oral sex, but decided to dress casually in dark jeans and an arsenic black suit coat with a white collared shirt underneath.

Looking at himself in the mirror, he ran his fingers through his silver-frosted, coffee-brown hair. It was overgrown and in sore need of a cut so before showering, he took the clippers to it, tapering the sides down and leaving the top longer. Having been out in the field for so many years with The Agency, he had learned the finer points of surviving on his own, and that included cooking and cutting his own hair, and a few other unmentionable and unsavory skills as well.

When he pulled up to the Dark Asylum, Sarah was waiting out front for him. He waited in his car for a moment, watching her interact with some of the others as they made their way in. Her round face and kind smile was kindled with a sort of passionate beauty. What made a woman like her tick? He wanted to probe the depths of her psyche and find out what kinds of things she liked and disliked. She had stated she was neither a sadist nor masochist, so exactly what were her turn-on's?

Meeting her at the door, her eyes scanned his body and a smile stole onto her eager face. When their eyes met, Sawyer felt a shock run through him.

"You look spectacular, Mr. Morrison" she said with a rasp of excitement in her voice and her eyes sending him a private message. Reaching a hand out, she touched his forearm.

"Likewise, Snowflake. Shall we?" He opened the door and guided her through, but not before noticing a spark in her eyes at his nickname.

Once inside, Sawyer and Sarah were greeted by several people, including the club owner, Kerian, and Derrick, the club manager. There were conversations and introductions, and from the sounds coming from the rear of the club, even a few scenes being played out in the back rooms.

Sawyer made his way around the club, taking it all in. It was such a strange environment to be in and so far out of the ordinary 'vanilla' life as they called it. Yet everyone that he came into contact with was well-mannered and engaging.

He noted that Sarah remained respectful towards him at all times, never leaving his side or speaking out of turn. Though she remained acquiescent to all the Doms, she was particularly attentive to him which he found enthralling. She seemed to relish his small touches, but he remained mindful of where he placed his hands, not wanting to cross any lines or make her feel uncomfortable.

Half-way through the night, Dylan and Isabel showed up. Dylan's mood was noticeably serious and it was hard not to miss Isabel's red swollen eyes even though they both tried to put on a care-free façade. Sawyer could only guess the reason why.

Hating to see anything but joy on their faces, he pulled them aside to a quiet room and sat them down, wanting to reassure them that everything was going to be okay.

"You two look a mess," he announced to the pair.

Isa's bottom lip began to tremble and Dylan wrapped a shielding arm around her shoulders. Sawyer wanted to put Isa at ease and tell her that he had taken care of everything, and there was nothing to worry about, but he and Dylan had decided it was best she didn't know the gory details of her father's demise. She simply thought Emilio had killed himself and written the letter of apology to Isabel on his own. It was the closure she needed to move on with her life, and Sawyer was more than happy to provide it.

He had often wondered if Isa suspected anything or if her mind had just clouded over the facts of that dreadful night and had accepted what he and Dylan had told her to save her own sanity. He would never know.

Despite knowing Dylan felt guilty about lying to Isabel, Sawyer had convinced him that if Isa knew the complete truth, it would only make matters worse and most likely, she would have a mental breakdown. Some things were best left unsaid, especially when it would do no good for the facts to be known.

"I don't want my father's money..." Isa began. "Those people can have it for all I care, but Master says I deserve it after everything Papa put me through. Tell him, Sawyer; tell my Master it's best to just let sleeping dogs lie and move on," she pleaded with tear-filled eyes.

Dylan pulled Isa close and fingered her chin, staring at her sternly. "You know better than to challenge my authority and decisions, and Sawyer isn't going to change my mind. That money is yours to do with whatever you want. After what that man put you through..."

"Please, Sir, *please*..." she continued to beg, looking to Sawyer for help.

"Young is right, Isabel. I'm sorry."

Isa sharply looked away from them both as if she had been betrayed by the two Doms. "I don't want it. It will only serve as a reminder of everything he did to my mother and the both of you."

It was just like Isabel to not even think about what that son-of-a-bitch had done to her. For fuck's sake – he had beaten her to the point of being unable to have children and nearly killed her husband. They both deserved the money.

Dylan shook his head and blinked long and hard. "This discussion is over, Isabel Young. That money is yours. If you want to give it away or burn it when everything is said and done, that's fine, but for now, things are moving forward as planned."

Sarah moved to the far end of the small room, uncomfortable with what was playing out in front of her. Sawyer reached for her hand and pulled her close, feeling the sudden need to protect her as well, though he wasn't sure what he was defending her from. She hid her face in his chest, but reached a hand out to Isabel and squeezed her shoulder in a gesture of submissive solidarity and acknowledgement of Isabel's frustration and pain.

Isabel attempted to scoot away from Dylan but his strong grip pulled her back by her waist.

"I didn't make this decision to hurt you, Baby Girl. I love you..." He paused, before burying his face in her hair. "Oh, hell," he waivered. "We don't need the stress; not with the possibility of a baby coming." Isabel shot Dylan a look of surprise for telling their secret. "I told Sawyer today," he confessed with an apologetic look and Isa's alarmed eyes softened.

"It's wonderful news, Cookie. You two deserve to have a family," Sawyer smiled down at Isa, knowing that she found the nickname he had given her sweet.

Isa immediately returned his smile. She had been through so much only to come through it stronger, she was the toughest cookie he knew, all 5'2" of her. Hell, she even stood toe-to-toe fearlessly against Dylan in an epic show down of wills at one point. Even in the face of Dylan's fierce dominance and threat of punishment, she didn't give an inch. She was a Domme through-and-through when the situation called for it, as well as a submissive, and it was a beautifully sexy and frightening thing to witness.

Isabel nuzzled into Dylan's neck when she heard his voice soften. "I'm sorry for doubting your decision, Master. I know you love me and only want the best for me," she purred.

Dylan's hand snaked up to her neck and he planted a passionate kiss on her mouth, their tongues mingling endlessly. Sarah and Sawyer both watched with affection as the couple displayed their love for one another unabashedly. Sarah's hand came up and rested on his chest directly over his heart, making his pulse thud rapidly against his chest wall. He wasn't sure Sarah even realized what she had done as her eyes stayed focused on Dylan and Isabel. He reached his hand around her back and gently tugged her long hair, forcing her to direct her attention onto him. With the smacking sounds and panting of Dylan and Isabel's rapidly intensifying make out session, Sawyer planted a firm kiss on Sarah's forehead.

Her eyes closed and her mouth parted, a soft breath barely heard. When Sawyer pulled away, her eyes fluttered open, the neediness and confusion hard to miss in her penetrating eyes. He studied her thoughtfully for a moment, sensing she wanted more but was afraid to ask, and perhaps even feeling guilty for thinking about it. He decided to remedy her indecision by taking the initiative of offering her more.

"Would you like another?" he lifted an eyebrow at her. She nodded slowly, still unable to voice her desires. Yanking her locks harder and wrapping his fingers deep into her mane at the nape of her neck, he ghosted his mouth over her cheek, trailing small delicate kisses along her jawline. He wanted to invade her mouth and to feel her tongue gliding over his teeth, but he could feel her hesitation when her body stiffened. Stopping just shy of her lips, he left a single wet kiss on the corner of her mouth. Everything around them faded out and only Sarah's blue irises shone in the romantically lit room. She blinked rapidly and focused on Sawyer's mouth, her nails digging into his chest as if insisting on more.

Unexpectedly and softly, Isabel moaned out. Sawyer's eyes darted towards Dylan and Isa. They were oblivious to him and Sarah, and were sprawled out on the small love-seat. Isabel's skirt was hiked up over her shapely hips, her hands pinned high above her head, and Dylan's face was buried in her exposed pussy. Guiding Sarah out of the room, they left them to their privacy.

Sarah reached into her pocket pulling out a neatly folded piece of paper. "Before I forget, here are the answers to your questions, but before I give it to you, I'd like to add a little more."

"Thank you, I'll read your responses tonight..." Sawyer trailed off, curious what she was going to share with him.

Sarah promptly seated herself at a small table and feverishly wrote more on the paper. Remembering that she had mentioned a demonstration was going to be held on sensual sadism, he scanned the room for the couple who were going to give the demo. The subject was intriguing and sounded like something he might like to investigate and research further. After several minutes, Sarah refolded the piece of paper and handed it back to him, a light of desire illuminating her cobalt eyes. He gripped her hand and walked toward the back of the club.

"I was hoping to watch the scene with Elizabeth and John."

The corners of Sarah's mouth rose ever so slightly. "Sensual sadism interests you? It's very fascinating to watch. I've always wanted to try it. What I mean to say is: I have to a certain degree, but my Sir and I never really had the chance to delve into it fully before he…" she broke off midsentence. "He was mainly into bondage and a few other things." Her mouth snapped closed and she swallowed hard. "I'm sorry. I mean you no disrespect by dwelling on my former Master. This is about you."

Sawyer shook his head in disagreement and framed her face in his large palms and focused on her stunning eyes. "It's good for you to talk about your experiences with your husband. And this isn't about just me; it's about us and what we can learn about one another."

She sighed and said nothing more as they walked in silence to the farthest and smallest back room. The setting was extremely intimate even though it was crowded with people wanting to watch Liz and John in action.

Sawyer and Sarah stood at the back, peering over heads to get a glimpse of the average looking couple. He was glad to see people of various shapes and sizes, many with less than perfect bodies exposing their flaws for all to see. It made the experience that much more real to him. The people he was surrounded by were everyday individuals with normal jobs, mortgages to pay, and kids in school. He could be next to a schoolteacher or a local dentist for all he knew, people who were living the life of an ordinary person by day and a kinky lifestylist by night. It was comforting knowing that everyone around him was seeking their own nirvana on some level. He glanced around the room, wondering if he was in the presence of any other killers like himself or people trying to put their haunted pasts behind them and move forward like he was.

The couple introduced themselves and John gave a brief description of what was going to take place while Liz lit a scented candle and loaded a CD on a nearby portable stereo.

The aroma of jasmine soon filled the small space and the relaxing sounds of Enya filtered over the speakers.

John guided Liz by the shoulders to a long padded bench and undressed her slowly, skimming his fingers casually over her skin. He planted small kisses along her spine followed by raking his nails down her back. Liz's body shivered and the sounds of her rapid breathing overtook the room. Tugging down Liz's red thong gently, he tossed it aside when she stepped out of it. With her bare ass exposed for everyone to see, he harshly smacked it, making her yelp out. There were soft giggles heard throughout the audience as everyone enjoyed John taking her by surprise. She laughed, too, and hid her face in her hands, embarrassed by her outburst.

John then moved directly behind Liz and pulled two long, wide strips of burgundy-colored leather from his back pocket. The first he bound tightly over her eyes, the second he looped around her wrists in front of her. Next, he helped her to lie on the bench where he lifted her hands above her head and fastened the wrist binding to a hook above her. He taunted and teased Liz, pacing his movements and touching her purposefully but without rhythm. Tormented by his soft strokes, she began to pull her knees up to her chest, so John reached over to a small table and brought over two more bindings of soft rope. He then bound each of her ankles to the legs of the bench, rendering her unable to resist his touches.

Sawyer was captivated by what he was seeing. Despite the term 'sadism' being used, there was going to be no pain involved at all in the scene before him. Moving stealthily, someone from the back of the room pushed their way through the crowd and brought John an ice cooler of goodies, piquing Sawyer's interest even further.

John quietly lifted the lid on the cooler and pulled out a frosted pink glass dildo and a thick, square of chocolate. Sawyer grinned when he saw the objects, his mind racing with his own ideas of what to do with them.

Looking at the crowd, John cunningly smirked and raised a finger to his lips, signaling the crowd to not let on to the frozen surprise in store for Liz. A fine mist rose from the faux cock revealing how frigid the item was. The man who was acting as an assistant lit a tall, deep yellow wax candle and waited for further instruction, and Sawyer suspected it wasn't for lighting purposes at all.

John allowed her to smell the sweet treat before touching it to her lips. She smiled and poked her tongue out to lick the candy that was placed flat against her mouth, but John swiftly pulled it away, teasing her and making her lift her head in response. She nipped at the air until he finally placed the chocolate between her teeth.

"Hold it steady. Do not eat it until I say so," he ordered.

With his free hand, he pinched and tweaked her nipples and leaned down and bit into one hungrily. She attempted to squeal but when the chocolate slipped, she clamped her teeth harder around the soft candy. Arching her back, she pushed more of her breast into his mouth while he circled his tongue around her taught nipple.

Gently, he slid the dildo past her shimmering pussy lips, impaling her and taking her by surprise. She tried to moan out from the sensation but John's mouth crushed down onto hers, stifling her blissful cries. He eased the glass shaft in and out as visible goose bumps covered her torso and thighs. John raised his head slightly, taking a bite of the nearly-melted chocolate. The sweet treat oozed down the sides of Liz's mouth and he slowly licked every bit of it off of her before finally allowing her to finish the remainder of the candy. When she glided her tongue along her mouth, John quickly engulfed it, smashing his mouth down onto hers and sucking at her tongue greedily.

"My Lizzy Girl," he whispered against her mouth. "Your taste is even more delicious than this chocolate."

Sawyer tried to imagine how wonderful the cool sensation felt on her pussy while John's hot tongue caressed the inside of her mouth, and what John was feeling by giving her such pleasure. John released Liz from his kiss and reached for the burning candle. Tilting it slightly, the flame flickered vividly in the darkened room as the melting hot wax dripped onto Liz's puckered brown nipples and areola. She mewled and thrashed her head back and forth as he continued to fuck her with the cold dildo all the while trailing the searing wax along her large round belly and down to her fuzzy mound.

Sawyer began to feel the building sensation of arousal between his legs when Sarah suddenly reached over for his arm and gripped his forearm tightly. As difficult as it was to look away from the sensual scene playing out, he pried his eyes away and looked to Sarah whose sparkling eyes were fixed on John and Liz. Sex-appeal was dripping off of her and it was obvious that she was just as turned on as he was. Sneaking an arm around her waist, he pulled her flush against his body and kissed the top of her head. She smelled clean and feminine like linen and musk, and the heat emanating from her scorched his senses.

Sawyer began to ponder all kinds of sensual torture he wanted to inflict on Sarah. Leather, feathers, prickly things, fiery and chilly things, things with rough textures to drive her senses mad... His mind was spinning with all the different possibilities. Velvet, lace, silk, denim... everyday items in abundance could be used in all sorts of salacious ways to bring a woman satisfaction and in turn, gratifying his need to see her squirm and beg for more of his touch.

He closed his eyes and leaned into Sarah's ear. When he whispered, his words were decisive and unyielding. "Someday, Snowflake, when we're both ready, I'll pleasure you in the same way."

Chapter 5

Settling into his large leather recliner, Sawyer opened the note that was printed on pale pink stationary, anxious to read Sarah's thoughts and answers to the plethora of questions he had left her to contemplate.

"Thank you for allowing me to share my knowledge and opinions with you, Mr. Morrison.

The first thing I want to put out there is this: Submission is a gift and just because a woman is allowing you to take control of her doesn't mean she owes you anything. I know dominating a submissive is an exciting and powerful thing, but please don't let your ego get the best of you or your role as a Dominant go to your head.

Now on to the questions! A Dominant to me, is someone who is courageous and not afraid to defend himself or his loved ones. He is also not afraid to admit fear and faces it head on.

Self-effacing, well-informed and hard-working are other qualities that define a Dom.

A sense of humor and ability to laugh at oneself is a must in a Dominant personality and a quality I think is underestimated, but that's just my personal opinion.

Most importantly, a Dom is generous, loving and respectful to not only his submissive, but all women. He is gentlemanly in public, but playful in private and a savage in the bedroom.

I found this amazing quote from wrightwilliams.org: A true Dom has a firm hand, a firm mind, a firm gaze, a firm grip, and a soft heart. I couldn't have said it any better so I won't try to.

I think you'll find that a submissive requires more time and affection than your everyday woman. She needs her Dom to continually seduce consent from her and give her what she's afraid to ask for because pushing her limits will set her free from fear of the unknown.

As for what a sub needs, I can only speak for myself, but I crave and need structure and rules, as do most subs, I'd imagine. It sounds like a lot to take on, and it is. But then again, a submissive is giving up a piece of her soul when she offers herself to a Dom.

I'll leave you with this last thing. Everyone's needs and kinks are different and there are a million ways to live this lifestyle. All you can do is live it in a way that satisfies you, but live it honorably because it's a great responsibility being a Dom and not something that should be entered into lightly."

Feeling enlightened, Sawyer laid the piece of paper down in his lap and leaned his head back against the chair. There was also the feeling of nervous energy coursing through his veins. Open communication, in theory, was fascinating, but to actually put that credo into action was intimidating to think about. He had never been fully open with anyone, including the love of his life, Serena. Not even Dylan. Yes, he had spoken of his past, but not all the horrid details. Could he bring himself to admit his past and all of his sins to someone? He wasn't really sure he could.

He had done atrocious things; murderous, vicious, bloody things. So bloody. He shivered at the thought of the all the blood on his hands. He had seen the light go out in many men's eyes and been the cause of it; men with wives and children and people that no doubt loved them. Inwardly he had accepted his culpability because he could justify every single life he had taken; they were, after all, evil men. But to admit it out loud to another human being was completely unthinkable. He would have to trust someone entirely in order to share that kind of information and there wasn't anyone that he completely trusted, and that included himself.

Trying to take his mind off of Sarah and the inevitability of divulging his transgressions, he decided to look into Emilio's probate dispute and everything surrounding his business partners. After nearly an hour of digging around online, he found the person's name that was at the root of the Young's anxiety. Perhaps he should pay the greedy douche a visit and try and convince him that it was in his best interest to leave things alone. Bad idea. A threat probably wouldn't go over well with someone with no scruples.

Sawyer grabbed his phone and speed dialed Dylan.

Picking up after the fourth ring, Dylan sounded out of breath. "Jesus, Morrison, you have the worst timing. I'm trying to impregnate my sub over here."

He cleared his throat, feeling a bit embarrassed for interrupting Young's baby-making time.

"Call me when you two are finished," he said getting ready to end the call.

"Just tell me why you called. I enjoy keeping Isa waiting," he chuckled.

Sawyer could hear Isa's soft moaning and he wondered what kind of scene they were playing out.

"I have this idea about what to do regarding Emilio's will. It's a little on the shady side and a bit old school, but I think it will work in getting his business partner to back off."

Dylan's voice rose an octave and he suddenly sounded animated. "Old school? I'm all ears."

"You're all hard cock, too. Please, sugar, get off the phone and give it to me..." Isa whimpered more loudly.

"You hear that, Morrison? I have a disobedient sub on my hands who doesn't know how to follow a simple rule. She knows her voice distracts me but still she persists on speaking when she's been told not to. I think a reminder on the virtues of silence might be in order. What do you say, Morrison? Ball-gag or her wet panties stuffed in her mouth?"

Sawyer heard the distinct sound of skin-on-skin and Isa yelping. Stunned by what he was hearing and the unwelcome but amusing vision of her hand-printed red ass glowing from her verbal offense, Sawyer couldn't help but smile. Dylan was a true sadist.

When he didn't immediately answer, Dylan continued. "Isa is waiting for your decision and so am I. I'm leaving it up to you how I should deal with this wanton little slut I call my wife."

"Dylan Nathaniel Young!" Isa shrieked in the background.

Sawyer mulled the question over. Ball-gag or panties... he liked the idea of both if he was being honest with himself. But for Isa? She did have a tendency to speak her mind when it was probably best she just keep her mouth shut, but a ball-gag seemed a bit harsh for her minor offense.

Choosing the lesser of two evils, he finally answered, "Definitely panties."

"Excellent choice, my friend." Dylan spoke away from the phone, low and muffled. "Sawyer has decided your fate, little one. It's to be your cum-soaked panties stuffed in that sassy mouth of yours." Redirecting his question to Sawyer, Dylan asked, "Any other suggestions?"

Sawyer answered without hesitation. "Make her beg to cum."

Dylan burst into wicked laughter. "So you like the begging, do you?"

"I like the fantasy of it."

"Well tomorrow night, your fantasy will become reality; I'll make sure of it."

Chapter 6

Saturday had come and gone, and Sawyer had discussed his plan with Dylan over lunch. They tweaked the details and came to the agreement that an extensive background check followed by a shady blackmailing scheme was in order. Dylan was initially hesitant only because he knew what it felt like to be on the receiving end of such a scheme, but Sawyer had convinced him it was the only way to go if Isa was to get what she was owed.

Sometimes Dylan just needed to be nudged in the right direction. Of course, Sawyer was smart enough to know that letting Dylan think it was his idea was the best way to go. Isabel had figured that out, too, but once mentioned that she needed to stop topping from the bottom because it took away from Dylan's dominance. At the time she made the comment, Sawyer didn't understand its meaning, but now, he understood fully what it meant.

After his extensive research into BDSM, he realized Sonya was the queen of topping from the bottom, even if she didn't know what it meant. There was no denying that Sawyer liked that she was strong and independent, but it had always aggravated him how she would try to manipulate his actions and emotions by playing coy or sweet in an attempt to get what she wanted. He made a conscious decision while he was driving home that he would not allow a woman to do that to him again. He liked being in control and though he didn't mind sharing power with Dylan when it came to business, being controlled by a woman or his submissive of choice in the bedroom and in the privacy of his own home was not going to be tolerated.

Sawyer's nerves were on edge for the upcoming nights' activities. Dylan had hinted at there being a new sub in the picture and he was curious as to what kind of woman he would be dealing with.

As he was getting ready, a text message chirped over his phone.

SarahH: 5:22 PM: I hear you're going to scene tonight! I'm so excited for u! I'm extremely disappointed I won't be in attendance to watch the show but please let me know all the juicy details. Have fun!

Upset that Sarah wouldn't be there to lend a hand or participate in whatever Dylan had planned, he wondered why Sarah had chosen not to go.

S.M.: 5:25 PM: Is there a reason you won't be there?

SarahH: 5:27 PM: Late shift at work. :(I'll be with u in spirit. I'll be available to answer any questions u may have throughout the night and I'll do my best to be quick with my responses.

S.M.: 5:29 PM: Quick? What are you suggesting? I'm a man of great stamina and QUICK is not a word in my vocab. Slow, methodical and precise are, however.

SarahH: Oh, my. That's going to be one lucky sub tonight. *panting*

S.M.: 5:33 PM: I hope she feels lucky and not experimented on. I must admit to feeling a bit apprehensive seeing as Young hasn't fully disclosed the plans.

SarahH: 5:34 PM: Just be true to yourself and your wants, and try different things. Take in everything around u, smells, sounds, ambiance, and burn them into your memory so u can replay them over and over like a movie. Cameras aren't allowed in the club, but maybe Isa can paint me a naughty image of you in action. I hear she's good at that sort of thing. ;)

S.M.: 5:35 PM: She is. I'll suggest it to her. I'll keep you informed throughout the night. Be vigilant at work and we'll speak later.

SarahH: 5:37 PM: As u wish, Mr. Morrison. U be safe as well. :*

Sawyer thought it odd that Sarah was excited to hear of his experiences with other women, but the openness that

Sarah urged from him was beginning to kindle a fire within him. Would he have sex with this new sub or would there just be playtime? Sawyer hadn't exactly been keen on the idea of being pleasured in front of a group of people, but having watched multiple scenes it put his mind at ease a bit.

Damn Sarah's work for keeping her from being with him. Shit, he didn't even know where she worked. Irked with himself for not having sought that information out, he texted Sarah back.

S.M.: 5:45 PM: Where is it exactly that you work?
SarahH: 5:48 PM: Rocky Mountain Mental Inst. I'm a medication aide.

Sawyer's stomach did a flip-flop. One of Dylan's many ex-lovers was being held there, and the very same woman who stalked him and Isabel and set forth a chain of events that led to Isabel's kidnapping, attempted rape and shooting. Sawyer thought back to when he had paid the head-case a visit and how acidic her reaction to him had been. He had been disgusted to find out she had been one of the players who had leaked the Young's sex videos to the public. That woman was a prime example of psychotic bitchery at its best. And Sarah was working in the same building where she was being housed because of her mental instability and murderous tendencies.

Sawyer quickly felt protective of her, knowing if she ever found out that Sarah was in contact with Dylan, Isa and himself, she would stop at nothing to exact her revenge for her perceived loss of Dylan and her hatred for Isabel. Sawyer regretted not having permanently taken care of the lethal cunt when he had the chance.

S.M.: 5:50 PM: I know the kind of people that are being treated there. You're safety means everything to me.
SarahH: 5:58 PM: Thank u for your concern and kind words, but there's no need to worry. Almost everyone at that

facility is dangerous in some way and it's just part of the job. Unfortunately I have no control over it.

Like hell there wasn't any reason to worry. If Sarah knew how dangerous Dylan's ex was, she might think differently. He wasn't in the mood to try and explain everything. He would deal with the situation immediately on his own knowing that the ultimate decision was out of Sarah's hands anyway.

S.M.: 6:05 PM: Understood. We'll speak later.

Sawyer promptly retrieved his files on Dylan's psychotic ex via remote access and the physician whom he had spoken with the night he visited the institute. The man had been very receptive to Sawyer and was sympathetic to Isabel and Dylan's problems. Hopefully he could help.

He called the man's personal cell phone, hoping the physician remembered him.

"This is Sawyer Morrison. We met last year," he stated, getting right to the point.

"Yes, I remember you - tall, dark and dangerous. And very well put together, too, I might add."

Sawyer was thrown off balance by the psychiatrist's comment. "Thank you. I'm calling about an employee at the Institute named Sarah Henderson. I can't express how important it is that Sarah has no contact with the person who attacked the Youngs."

"I see. Well, I'll do what I can. May I ask why?"

"It's a bit difficult to explain, but... she's an acquaintance and I'm concerned for her safety."

"You're going through an awful lot of effort for just an *acquaintance*," the physician remarked.

"She's actually more like a friend."

"A girlfriend?"

Why the hell was this guy so interested in Sawyer's personal life? "Not exactly. She's one of my subs," he stated frankly.

"Just my luck. Ah well, I'd be happy to try and help out. Keep me in mind if you ever decide to take on any male subs," the man sighed, defeated.

Sawyer had been hit on by a man and was at a loss for words. The doctor was quite handsome and well-to-do from what Sawyer remembered, and he felt strangely proud to have attracted him, regardless of whether or not he wanted to get pegged by him.

"If I ever decide to swing that way, I'll keep you in mind, Dr. Phillips." Sawyer chuckled.

The man laughed and ended the conversation pleasantly, and Sawyer drove to the club.

***

Once inside, he was met by Dylan and Isabel.

"Thanks for the panty treatment, Sawyer," Isabel pouted.

Sawyer grinned proudly in response. "Anytime Young needs help deciding your punishment, I'd be happy to help out, Cookie." He was okay with helping decide, so long as he didn't have to be the one actually handing it out.

Isabel opened her mouth to respond but quickly snapped her mouth shut when Dylan squeezed her arm. "Not here, Isa. Show Morrison the same respect you show me in this club. Is that understood?" he spoke in his fiercest disciplinarian tone.

Isa's eyes averted to the floor. "Yes, Master. My apologies, Sawyer. I'd be honored if you had a decision in my punishment," she answered obediently, even though he could hear the distinct attitude in her voice.

"That's better, but not much," Sawyer said as he rolled his eyes at Dylan.

Dylan lifted one side of his mouth and nodded in agreement. "There's someone I want you to meet. Her name is Kate, but around here we call her Sam."

Sawyer thought it was an odd nickname. Isabel's eyes shot up to Dylan's and she smiled impishly. "You're evil, Dylan."

"What? Sawyer needs to experience all types of submissives, not just the dutiful ones."

"What's that supposed to mean?" Sawyer asked.

"Kate is known for being..." Dylan paused thoughtfully, scratching his chin before continuing. "Quite a handful. Let's see how you deal with her. I've set up a scene for the two of you tonight. I'm a man of my word and I trust when all is said and done, she'll be begging you to be either fucked or punished."

He doubted that very much. He had never had the urge to punish the female persuasion. Pleasure them, most definitely, but never reprimand them physically. Except, of course, for a few of Dylan's wretched exes.

Dylan motioned for Kate and handed Sawyer a piece of paper. When the woman approached, he was impressed with her looks. She was tall with wavy, shoulder-length auburn hair, had the body of a porn star and looked like she loved being fucked in dishonorable ways. Perhaps even punished.

"Mr. Morrison," she nodded gracefully. "I'm looking forward to finding out what kind of Dom you're going to be."

"So am I," he countered.

They all walked back to a large, bright room where several people were already gathering behind a dark tinted viewing glass to watch the inexperienced Dom's first scene. It reminded him of the seedy parts of town he had experienced in his youth and watching people fuck as he looked on anonymously. He stood glaring at them, nervous butterflies starting to build in his stomach. He wasn't keen on a group of strangers watching him fumble around and/or make a fool out of himself. He ran his palm over his face and lowered his head.

"I chose this room so that we could dim the outer lights and the crowd is out of view. In the meantime, make your sub your only point of focus," he heard Dylan over his shoulder.

Easier said than done. He sighed to himself, revolted at the thought of exposing his cock to a group of unknowns.

Pushing past his anxiety, he walked over to a table where a dozen or so items were laid out, many of which he was familiar with only by having read about them. He picked them up, one by one, touching them and studying them. He wished Sarah were by his side, explaining how each of them felt on a woman's body.

Kate sauntered up next to him while he read over her hard and soft limits, making herself a little too comfortable for his tastes and rubbing herself against him like an animal in heat. She reached for a thick wooden paddle and fingered it.

"I like this very much. And this too," she commented, pointing towards a large purple butt-plug. Pushing gently past Sawyer she continued to grab several of the implements, her actions quickly grating on his nerves. He gripped her upper arm firmly and held her at bay.

"I'll take your wants into consideration. Now let me finish reading."

Her eyes widened infinitesimally and she smiled mockingly. "Yes, *Sir*," she snickered.

"Undress and seat yourself over there, please," he nodded toward an oversized wooden chair with a padded leather seat and restraining points on each of the legs and arms.

He wasn't sure what he wanted to start with so waited for Isabel to join him. When she moved next to him, she began talking about the items he had set aside.

"The tawse can be sharp and painful, but it also feels fantastic when used gently. It warms up the skin nicely. Even though this flogger is small, it packs a punch. See how the ends are knotted? They really bite," she waggled her eyebrows up and down.

He quickly put the flogger back. *Bite* wasn't the sensation he was going for.

"Feathers are nice and playful, and can be used to build up to more intense play," she continued. "So is this double-sided paddle. One of my first experiences with Dylan he used a double-sided paddle on me. Each of the contrasting sides offers a wonder of sensations."

Isabel's eyes drifted off as if thinking back to a fond memory. He heard Dylan clear his throat from behind.

"Focus, Isa."

"Yes, Master. Your expertise in these matters is better than mine," she stated, stepping aside, letting Dylan take over.

"For experimental items, these will do just fine," Dylan nodded.

When Sawyer turned to face Kate, her toned and muscular body was gloriously naked, her bronze skin glowing under the yellow-gold lighting. It was hard for him not to appreciate such a fine specimen even if she wasn't his type. Sitting in the chair, her legs were spread wide as she fingered herself.

Dylan motioned with his head toward Kate. "Did you give her permission to do that to herself?"

"I most certainly did not."

"Deal with it," Dylan instructed.

Sawyer grabbed a pair of fur-lined leather cuffs and strode over to her, gripping her wrist and pulling her fingers out of her glistening pussy.

"Enough of that," he grumbled.

She poked her tongue out and attempted to bring her fingers to her mouth, but his strong grip didn't allow her to. He swiftly pulled her hand down and fumbled with the cuffs before securing one of her hands to the shackles.

When she softly giggled at his mishandling of the restraint, his eyes shot up to hers. "You only get to laugh at me once," he snarled, staring directly into her eyes.

With the speed and agility of a man who meant his words, he strapped her other wrist down purposefully, cinching the cuff to an appropriate but secure fit, and tugging on the restraint to test its stability causing Kate to gasp out at his harsh, sudden movement. The smile quickly faded from her face and one side of his mouth curled upwards.

"I'm a fast learner, Kate," he smirked.

Kneeling in front of her, the smell of her musky perfume and pussy wafted past his nose, urging him forward, and he felt the sudden impulse to tease her. He leaned down and licked the inside of her thigh just above her knee while his hands secured her ankles. She closed her eyes and whimpered as he nibbled his way up the inside of her thigh, bucking hips the closer he got to her pussy.

"Lick me... more," she demanded, her voice breathy and needy.

He didn't like being told what to do, even if he was new at it. "You'll get more when I see fit," he stood boldly.

Her red glossed lips formed a perfect pout and he began to wonder how they would feel wrapped around his cock.

He moved back to the table and with Dylan's assistance, decided on a bit of sensual torture for the brazen submissive. He decided first to instruct her to keep her eyes closed, wondering how well she could follow instructions. She complied and he began by sweeping the feathers over her body. First over her nipples causing them to harden and then finishing them off by pulling them to a point with his fingers. Next, he dusted the feathers over her cheeks causing Kate's eyes to pop open.

"Tsk, tsk. I said closed," he said smoothly with no expression on his face.

Her mouth curved into a cynical frown. Standing back, his hands fell to his side. He meant what he said. When he stood motionless glaring at her, she gave in and closed her eyes.

Dylan then handed him the tawse next and Sawyer began to slap the stiff leather over the tops of her breasts and thighs, pinking up her skin. He liked the way it felt in his hands; firm and unyielding.

It would be too easy for him to get overambitious with his efforts and he worried he might be delivering too hard of blows, so before he continued, he asked "Color?"

"Green. Keep going."

Damn if Kate, aka Sam, wasn't a challenging submissive.

"Flick your wrist more, Morrison. Even if you're not a sadist, it's good to remember that pleasure can originate from pain. You just need to moderate the amount of pressure delivered based on what you're trying to achieve. Do you have anything to add, Isa?" Dylan glanced over his shoulder.

"Just that aftercare is a requirement, not an option, especially after an intense scene."

Sawyer paused, contemplating both of their instructions. He had to trust what Dylan was telling him and believe that he wouldn't steer him in the wrong direction, and neither would Isabel.

Kate writhed, her skin squeaking against the leather and her breathing becoming louder as he flicked his wrist with his next delivery. Beads of sweat began to build on his temples as he paced around her, flicking the tawse in rhythm with the music that Isabel had picked, *Breathe* by Breaking Benjamin. It was a good choice and the deep bass began to vibrate underneath his feet, sending shock waves to his ball sack and making the experience more arousing.

Kate was doing a good job of keeping her eyes closed until he moved to the table to grab his next tool. He looked over his shoulder to see one of her eyes open, peeking at him. *How hard was it to follow a simple order?*

He gave her an uncompromising look. "Eyes closed. I won't say it again."

Both of her eyes opened defiantly to his remark as she glared at him with burning, reproachful eyes. "Or else *what*, Mr. Morrison?" She asked with a heavy dose of sarcasm in her voice.

"Yes, or else *what*, Morrison?" Dylan asked with raised eyebrows. "A submissive must learn to follow your commands and any and all threats must be followed through, or else what's the point?"

Dylan's point was valid. What was the fucking point if not to exert his power?

Irritated with Kate trying to push his limits and question his authority, he stood between her splayed legs. Leaning down, he ghosted his mouth over her ear. Slowly, he brushed his fingers up the inside of her thigh until he reached her pussy. He eased his fingers inside of her causing her to moan out. Pumping his fingers more rapidly, he could sense that she was quickly building up to an orgasm.

Pulling his fingers out of her, he replied coolly in an attempt to disguise his impatience, "Or else you don't get the pleasure of sucking my dick."

His voice was thick and mellow, and Kate's mouth dropped open, her eyes bravely meeting his. He wasn't sure if the jaw-drop was due to shock or to say something, but he promptly shoved his juice soaked fingers into her gaping mouth to shut her up.

"If you want to come, you'll simply suck my fingers and keep your comments to yourself. Is that understood?"

Her tongue twisted around his fingers and she said nothing more. Sawyer's power was greater than he had imagined and the implication of her compliance sent waves of excitement through him. His cock hardened and his head swam with desire. Feeling a little more comfortable in his Dom skin, he decided to venture out and try something a little more risky. Reaching for the flogger, he looked to Dylan.

"Keep your stance in mind. This time, don't flick your wrist. Use a figure-eight motion in smooth, flowing movements. Instruct Kate not to move. She already knows this, but hearing your voice and your commands is soothing to her and reassures her of your authority."

Sawyer nodded and did as he was instructed. Kate's tanned skin reddened under the leather strips and her belly looked like a beautiful piece of art. When he had his fill of flogging the statuesque beauty, he moved to the table for something different. Again, Kate's eyes opened to sneak a peek.

He had enough of her unruliness. Swiftly, he unshackled her and hauled her into his beefy arms. As he carried her to the spanking horse, she wrapped her arms around his neck, smiling smugly as if she had gotten her way. He had never felt the urge to punish a woman, but if anyone deserved it, or asked for it, it was the sexy brat known as Sam.

He gently stood her on her feet and pointed toward the bench. She stood motionless as if she didn't really believe he would go through with it.

"I want that ass in the air. *Now*," he ordered with narrowed eyes.

"As you wish, Sir," she whispered, her eyes gleaming brightly.

As she quickly laid her lean body over the bench, he suddenly felt like he had been had. Perhaps this is what she had wanted all along. He looked back to Dylan who was smirking and then to Isabel who was shaking her head. He motioned for Isabel who speedily moved next to him.

"Why do you call Kate, Sam?"

Tip-toeing up to his ear, she quietly answered, "I'm glad you asked. Sam stands for smart-ass masochist."

Now it all made sense. Kate was intentionally trying to push his buttons. She wanted to be spanked and even though he felt like she deserved it, he wasn't about to give into her petulant and manipulative ways.

His eyes darted back to Dylan and gave him a critical stare. *Fucking, Young.* Leave it to Dylan to make his first scene a frustrating one. Isabel stood next to Dylan and they both smiled stupidly at him, waiting for his next move.

He walked over to Kate and stood to the side of the bench. When she heard his movements, her perfect, firm ass rose in the air.

"You deserve to be spanked, there's no doubt about it," he spoke just loud enough for her to hear.

"I do. I've been a very bad girl," she sighed.

He rested his hands on his hips and glared down at her. "You'd like that, wouldn't you?"

Her ass lifted higher. "Yes, Sir, I would."

"Well, then, a spanking is exactly what you're *not* going to get." Kate's head turned to the side and she had a look of bewilderment on her face. "Do you know why?" No response. "Because it's my decision what kind of pleasure and punishment you'll get tonight." Her bottom lip nearly hit the floor and he felt a sense of prevailing dominance in taking the reins. "Now, say it. Say: *you alone are the master of this scene, Mr. Morrison.*" He skimmed his fingers lightly over her ass. When she didn't immediately answer, he squeezed the smooth flesh of one of her cheeks, digging his fingertips into her browned skin. "Say. It."

Even though his voice was cold and exact, she squealed out and panted, but still refused to comply. She was stubborn if nothing else and he wasn't going to put up with it. He pushed his fingers into her and pumped them in and out rapidly while alternating stimulating her clit.

"Tell me what I want to hear, Kate, and I'll let you come," he breathed out, husky and ragged as he continued his assault on her pussy. Several minutes later the wet sound coming from her body became louder, and as her pussy began to swell with come, he felt a distinct quivering of her inner muscles. Abruptly he pulled his fingers out and clamped onto her ass.

"Oh, God," she mewled with the need for release.

"No. Mr. Morrison," he announced sternly.

When his fingers dug deeper yet in the flesh on her ass cheek, she finally gave in. "You're the Master of this scene, Mr. Morrison."

When he spoke again, his voice was tender, almost a murmur. "Do you want to come tonight?"

She nodded her head exaggeratedly.

"Speak," he stared at her with glacial eyes.

Her eyes came up to study his face. "I want to come, Mr. Morrison."

Ella Dominguez

He slid two fingers back into her dripping folds. The scent of her aroused femininity was clouding his brain and his cock stiffened painfully. Easing his digits in and out little by little, he leaned into her ear and nipped her lobe. "I didn't hear a *please* with that."

Lowering her lids, she responded obediently. "Please."

"I knew you could be a good girl if you just tried," he cooed in her ear.

He had missed the taste of a woman. Removing his fingers, he licked them then quickly replaced them and vigorously fingered fucked her again, seeking out the spot he had been reading about for months. Sawyer was a man who believed that knowledge was power and he had not only done his homework on BDSM, but everything about a woman's body that he could find. He had taken notes and studied for this day. He had even experimented on Sonya who was unknowing that she was his first. He had gotten an excellent response from her and was amazed at how much he enjoyed pleasuring a woman in such a way.

When he found what he was looking for, he tugged at her G-spot, delighting in the rough patch that was making Kate practically crawl out of her skin. The real thing was far better than any picture or video.

Her eyes fluttered open and closed, and shone brightly with lust and wanting. Her moans became louder and she thrust her ass into his palm, wanting more of the bliss that he was giving her. He pulled his hand back, leaving her uncomfortable and needy once again.

"Now beg for it," his voice rang out with finality.

She thrashed her head as if fighting the urge to give into the inexperienced Dom, but when he licked the nape of her neck and nipped her shoulder blade, she gave in, her words spilling out of her fervently.

"Please, Mr. Morrison, make me come. Please, oh, God, please..." She whined, her voice shaky.

The front of his pants cooled with the wetness of his pre-come and he pushed his fingers back into her, pulling and tugging at her pussy viciously. She had given him what he had been dreaming of and he would reward her for it. Kate cried out and her body began to tremble. At the height of her orgasm, he yanked his fingers out and swiftly smacked her ass, giving her what she had wanted all along, but only when he had desired to do so, and leaving a glorious handprint on her bottom. She screamed out and almost fell off the bench from her orgasmic spasm, but he caught her and pulled her into his arms.

"Kate, my delicious, unruly Kate..." He spoke softly, his voice breaking with deep huskiness.

Her eyes focused on his mouth and clouded with some undefined emotion. "Allow me to pleasure you, Master Morrison. I want to taste you, too. Please?"

Feeling satisfied with his performance, he accepted her offer of repayment for having allowed her to come and watched with contentment as she fell to her knees to work his cock with gratitude. Any previous doubts he had about being a Dom pooled at his feet along side his pants.

He was a Dom and there was no turning back.

Chapter 7

Sawyer stood in the shower, washing the red gloss off his cock. Kate had proved herself quite skillful in getting him off. Smiling at the thought of her pouted lips gliding over his rigid shaft, Sawyer wondered what other pleasures awaited him at the Dark Asylum. He had never felt so in control as when he heard Kate beg for his touch.

With water droplets still in his hair and on his shoulders, he wrapped a towel around his waist and made his way to the kitchen to make something to eat. Kate had sapped him not only of cum, but of energy, and he was famished.

The time was just after ten when his phone chirped with a message from Sarah. He had been thinking about her safety and wondering when he would see her again.

SarahH: 10:06 PM: Since I didn't hear from you, I take it you were in your element? ;)

S.M.: 10:07 PM: Not fully, but I'm getting there.

SarahH: 10:08 PM: Would you be comfortable sharing the details?

Sawyer chuckled at Sarah's response. She was always polite, even during texting.

S.M.: 10:10 PM: Of course. Young set up a scene with an exasperating and very frustrating woman nicknamed Sam.

SarahH: 10:11 PM: Funny! How was that?

S.M.: 10:13: PM: Funny? I'm glad you find amusement in my agitation. It was testing but rewarding.

SarahH: 10:15 PM: I didn't mean to make fun. Please forgive me?

S.M.: 10:16 PM: I will, after I'm satisfied with your efforts to make up for that little remark.

Sawyer could think of a few ways she could coax forgiveness out of him, namely allowing him to bury his face in her large breasts and suck at her puckered nipples. He smiled at his vulgar thought, but regretted having sent the message. He knew Sarah was still having intimacy issues and he didn't want to push himself on her with inappropriate remarks. Before he could apologize, his phone rang.

"Snowflake...," he answered.

"I just wanted to hear your voice, Mr. Morrison. It's difficult to decipher the meaning and tone of text messages sometimes and..."

"About my remark, I apologize if I crossed the line."

"Oh, I see," she sounded disappointed.

"Have I crossed the line?"

"The 'line' is still something we're getting acquainted with. But no, you haven't crossed it. I'm at work so I can't talk long, but I'm very eager to hear more about your evening."

"Well, if you're okay with hearing the details, I'd be happy to share," he replied with astonishment in his voice.

"Yes, please share. I wish I had been there..."

"It couldn't be helped. Young and Isabel were very supportive, so it's all good. I made good use of the tawse and short flogger, and also..." he hesitated, unsure if he should reveal all the juicy details.

"Yes?" Sarah urged.

"Some orgasm denial," he stated, unsure of how she would react.

To his surprise, her voice deepened with arousal. "That sounds delicious. You were very busy. What was your objective for the night?"

"I wanted to hear a woman beg. It's been something I've always wanted but never had the balls to try and make happen."

"I'm positive you're not lacking in the testicular region, Mr. Morrison. From what Isabel has told me, you're quite a force to be dealt with in your professional life and I suspect behind closed doors as well."

Sawyer wondered what else Isabel told Sarah. "Being commanding at work and being dominant in the bedroom are completely different things, especially when the women I've been with were conservative. Not to say I wasn't to a certain degree."

"I understand. Back when I was living Vanilla, things in the bedroom were just standard fare, but once the walls came down, that's when my Master and I let our true secret desires be known. If no one initiates it, then how can it be accomplished?"

"I've been wondering lately if I had known about BDSM with my wife, if she would've agreed to it. I guess I'll never know."

Sawyer became quiet thinking about Serena. The love they had shared was beautiful and pure, but the lies he had to tell her to keep the nature of his work confidential had always eaten away at him. Even with Sonya, though not to the same extent. He cared deeply for Sonya, even loved her, but it wasn't the same kind of affection he had felt for his first love, Serena. He often wondered if he would ever feel that connection with someone again.

"There are so many things I wish I would've done with my Master before his time on this Earth was finished, but it does me no good to dwell on it, and it won't do you any good either. I'm just glad for the time we shared."

"I couldn't have said it better, Snowflake."

"So did you get what you wanted? Did you make Sam beg?"

"Oh, she begged," he commented, his voice purposely low and seductive.

"Did you reward her?"

Sawyer laughed as if the answer were obvious, "Yes. I'm not a sadist, Sarah."

Sarah sighed and giggled. "Good, I'm glad to hear that. I hope she satisfied you, as well."

He couldn't get over discussing his sexual experiences with a woman he might possibly have intimate encounters with. He paused, deciding if he should answer.

"Communication and honesty, Mr. Morrison; I can handle whatever you tell me. After all, you belong to the BDSM community, not me."

"Interesting way to put it, but I belong to myself."

"I'll have to politely disagree with you. When you're in training, you belong to your teachers and the community which has accepted you. This journey can't be undertaken alone. Not if you're going to make a real go at it and be successful. Hey, wait. You're trying to get out of answering me, aren't you? Fess up, Domly One!"

Sawyer threw his head back and laughed loudly. He liked the title Domly One. And Master, too. Hell, even Sir. "Yes, I was rewarded."

"Good. You deserve to be pleasured. I only wish... anyway, I should get back to work."

"Practice that which you preach, Snowflake. Speak your mind." He wasn't about to let Sarah's half-statement go unnoticed.

She sighed and fumbled with the phone. "I wish it had been me," she whispered.

"Do you really?" he asked, wishing he could see her face as he was unsure of her tone.

"Yes and no. Yes, because I want to experience all of you and no because..."

He understood where her angst was coming from; she was still grieving. So was he. He had never gotten over his wife's loss. Hell, he barely made it through intact. It didn't matter how many women came after her or the time that passed, he would never get over her and he didn't expect Sarah to fare any better, especially considering how intense her bond with her Master was.

"You don't have to say anymore. Someday when you're feeling comfortable, you will experience all of me. We have plenty of time to get there."

"Thank you, Sir."

Sawyer was taken aback at Sarah calling him Sir. She hadn't done it since the first time they met. "I hope you're not calling me that out of some sort of misguided sense of obligation."

"You've earned the title Sir by being respectful and patient with me, and I never do or say anything out of obligation to those who don't deserve it."

***

With Sarah still on his mind, Sawyer readied for bed. He made plans to meet with her the following Friday for dinner at his place and he looked forward to talking more about BDSM and her experiences. He couldn't deny that he also wanted to see her for more than just business. It was her eyes that he was most looking forward to seeing. And her curves. And her smile. He shook his head and chuckled at himself. All of her.

After changing into sweat pants and a t-shirt, his intercom buzzed. Looking at his wall clock he wondered who would be visiting him after 11:00 p.m. He began to reach into his briefcase for the handgun that he kept for protection when Sonya's voice came over the speaker. He hadn't spoken to her since making his offer of taking her to the club and was surprised at her late-night visit.

She entered his large condo and promptly began to pace the living room, making Sawyer feel uneasy. She was keyed up about something and clearly had something on her mind though he couldn't imagine what was so important to discuss at such a late hour. His imagination was in overdrive trying to read her agonized expression.

"We need to talk," she stated, her brows drawing together.

Without saying anything, he motioned her to the sofa where she sat on the edge, not making eye contact or removing her coat.

"What's wrong, Sonya?" he asked, standing in front of her, his hands on his hips.

"How serious are you about this whole BDSM thing?"

An eyebrow shot up and he stared down at her warily. "What do you mean?"

A secretive smile softened Sonya's lips and she batted her eyelashes up at him. "I mean is there a chance that this is just a passing phase or that you'll change your mind?"

The question was a stab at his heart. A muscle quivered in Sawyer's jaw when Sonya grabbed his hands and ran her thumbs over the tops of them. She was at her old trick of topping from the bottom and a flicker of irritation coursed through him. It was strange how obvious it was to him now that he knew there was a name for her actions.

"My mind has been expanded by these new experiences and can never go back to the old dimensions that it once was, Sonya. So, no, it's not a passing phase. Where are you going with this?"

Crestfallen, she whispered, "I've started seeing someone this week."

Sawyer seated himself next to her not immediately knowing how to respond. He was filled with hurt, anger and jealousy, but knew he had no right to be considering he had his fingers buried in another woman's pussy and her lips wrapped around his cock only hours before. But that was different. He was scening and learning to be a Dom for both their benefit and had no emotional attachment to Kate.

"I'll fight for love, but I won't compete for it," he stated bluntly, his eyes stabbing into her.

She blinked rapidly and her mouth popped open. "I'm not asking you to compete."

"Then *what*? Are you asking for my permission?" he snarled with quiet emphasis.

Hers eyes darted to his and she huffed, her low silky voice holding a note of sarcasm. "Of course not. I don't need your permission."

Perhaps he was getting a little too used to Sarah asking for his approval for everything because Sonya's words quickly agitated him. He liked being asked for consent.

He leaned back and crossed his arms. "Then why are you telling me about it?"

"Because I care about you and need to know if there's still a chance for us."

Reaching out, he touched her arm. He wanted there to be a chance if only…"I want you to come with me to the club, Sonya."

She shook her head and looked away, her face suddenly turning grim.

"If there's a possibility that someday soon you'll reconsider, I can wait for you. But there are things I need to tell you, first."

She turned her body towards him, her eyes rounded. "Like what?"

It was go time. He still cared for Sonya, even loved her on some level, and he knew that if things were going to work out for them, he had to come clean of all his past offenses and do as Sarah had told him – honestly communicate.

"My past," he said with the certainty of a man who could never be satisfied with living withdrawn anymore.

Sonya swallowed loudly and licked her dry lips tensely. "You've never wanted to talk about it before."

"I know, but I told you that I'm working on being more open."

She began to pick at her acrylic nails fretfully. "What kind of things do you want to tell me about?"

"Things I did when I worked for the CIA. Things I'm neither proud nor ashamed of."

Her gray eyes suddenly grew dubious. "If you're not ashamed of them, then why wait to tell me?"

Sawyer considered his words carefully before answering. "Because they're the sort of things that people are judged harshly for."

Shifting uncomfortably, Sonya shook her head. "Sawyer, wait… I'm not sure I want you to tell me. I mean, we've done okay without me knowing. Can't we just start where we left off?"

"You mean with secrets and dishonesty?" he asked incredulously.

"I was never dishonest with you," she came back with.

"But I was dishonest by keeping secrets from you. I did the same thing with my wife and it was wrong. I don't want to live that way anymore." His face was bleak with sorrow and his statement never more heartfelt.

Sonya snapped, her normally elegant face contorting into something unattractive and her body stiffening. "This is ridiculous. This whole BDSM thing has gotten out of control and those people at that club are brain washing you. You're fine just the way you are, Sawyer Morrison, and some things are best left unsaid!"

"You're never going to the club with me, are you?" he asked softly when he came to the realization that Sonya had no interest in living the kind of life he wanted to live.

"Please, Sawyer. Those people..." she pleaded.

"Stop. Those people have taught me more about myself in the last few weeks than anyone has in the last twenty years. I want to share that with you," he told her with conviction, silently praying that she would change her mind.

Looking away as if disgusted, she let out a pitiful sob. "I just can't. I want you, but not like that. I've seen Dylan and Isabel's videos. I don't want to bow at your feet and be whipped and leashed," she choked out.

Sawyer clenched his jaw and struggled to maintain an even, conciliatory tone. "Is that all you think BDSM is? I'm not Young and I'm not asking you to be Isabel. I have different needs and wants than they do, but you'll never know what those needs are because you're too afraid - like I was; like most people are of what they don't know."

"What they do is disgusting," she said in a voice that seemed to come from a long way off, her statement finally piercing his composure.

When Sawyer responded, there was an edge to his voice and his tone became chilly. "What Isabel and Young have is beautiful and sincere, and there's nothing disgusting about it."

Sonya's tear-filled eyes scanned his face earnestly. "I know you hold them in high regard and near to your heart, but they've manipulated you into thinking this is all okay when it's not. They've influenced you..."

"Enough," he warned as he stood. She had no right to point fingers when it came to what she perceived as manipulation and there was no way in hell he would allow her to speak so harshly about the people whom he considered family.

She nodded in agreement and pushed herself off the couch angrily and answered in a rush of words, "You're right; it is enough. No one can say I didn't try to change your mind. I thought by telling you I was seeing someone else you might see things differently, but I can see this is going nowhere."

Gripping onto her upper arm, Sawyer pulled Sonya back just as she made it to the door.

"So you lied about seeing someone?" Blinking rapidly, her cheeks reddened and her eyes averted his gaze, giving away her guilt and he felt like he had been punched in the stomach. His mouth set into a straight line. "So who's doing the manipulating now?" She swallowed hard and her eyebrows pinched together in shame. "It's not your place to try and change my mind about my decisions. It never has been," he rebutted in a clipped voice that forbade any further discussion.

A tense silence enveloped the room and they stood staring into each other's eyes for several awkward moments. It really was over. Sawyer couldn't grasp the reality of it fully until he saw the empty look in Sonya's eyes. She wasn't going to change her mind. Not now. Not ever.

Tired of the silence looming between them like a heavy mist, he loosened his grasp on her arm and grabbed her face fiercely; kissing her like it was the last kiss of a dying man. And that's exactly what it was – the final kiss of a man whose heart had died a little. Their tongues danced inside each other's mouth briefly and the familiarity of her taste tore at his heart. Sonya's body softened and a stray tear rolled down her cheek. Pulling away, he stared down into her sad gray eyes and swept away the hot tear with his thumb.

Sawyer's voice dropped in volume and faded to a hushed stillness. "No matter where life takes us, I'll always be here for you if you need me."

Sonya stepped out of his reach and opened the door. With one last withering look over her shoulder, Sawyer inhaled a deep breath. Only when the door closed behind her did he let it out. It was over. It was really fucking over.

Chapter 8

The week had been difficult for Sawyer. Things were finally over with Sonya, and even though he hadn't had a lot of contact with her for many months, it didn't make it any easier to accept. Based on the way she had reacted and her harsh criticism about things she knew nothing about, Sawyer could understand on some small level how Dylan and Isabel must have felt facing everyone's cruel and judgmental words when their private lives were aired for the world to see.

He coped with Sonya's loss the way he did when he lost Serena; by keeping his head down and busying himself with work. The only difference this time around was he didn't rely on Jack Daniels to help him forget his pain.

The task of digging up all the dirt he could on Emilio's business partners was a welcome chore, and it was proving to be worthwhile. The main culprit in contesting the disbursement of Mr. Ibanez's funds had some pretty nasty skeletons in his closet that might persuade him to rethink his decision.

After a meeting with a potential new client, Dylan sauntered in grinning from ear-to-ear.

"Boy, have I got plans for you tonight, Morrison."

Sawyer looked up, less than amused. "Oh?"

"A friend from out of town called and he's paying us a visit. He's impatient to see me and Isa's stomping grounds. When I told him about your training, he was excited to offer his assistance. He's a master of the bullwhip and..."

"What the hell?" Sawyer swung his head back further to look at Dylan and grunted with utter disbelief. He had been practicing with the short flogger at home for a week on his bedroom wall and had just gotten comfortable wielding that, but a bullwhip? No way. No way in hell.

Sawyer glared at Dylan. "I hope that's a joke. I've barely learned the basics of working the flogger. You can't expect me to move onto something like a bullwhip this soon."

Dylan pushed his dark hair off his forehead revealing the roguish gleam in his light blue eyes. "Oh, simmer down. It won't kill you to give it a try. You don't have to slash and burn to enjoy the whip. Just ask Isa. She was scared out of her mind when she first saw it, but now... just mentioning it gets her all hot and juicy. Anyway, we'll take it slow."

He rolled his eyes and huffed. Surely not slow enough for his tastes. And damn if those two weren't like two peas in a pod. Hot and juicy over a bullwhip? It was unimaginable. "I'd say you two were a match made in heaven, but somehow that doesn't sound quite right. You're more like a match made in kinky purgatory."

Dylan laughed heartily. "Damn straight we were made for each other. Isa has even wielded it herself."

"No shit? Isn't it longer in length than she is tall?" he chuckled.

Dylan paused, his eyes becoming unfocused and his voice drifting off as if thinking back on some fond memory. "It didn't stop her from whipping my ass."

Sawyer stared back with complete astonishment on his face. "You let her whip you?"

"It was our honeymoon and she was going through some difficult shit. I knew she was struggling for control, so yeah, I let her whip me. And it was fucking amazing."

He would never *ever* get used to the idea of Dylan being a submissive. He had never actually witnessed it but knew that behind closed dungeon doors, they were both switches.

"So who's this friend?" he asked, changing the subject quickly.

"Luke Bastille. He's an interesting character. Anyway, I thought we could practice at home a bit before going to the club later. Isa's all wound up about it and has an impromptu dinner party planned with some fun in the dungeon for dessert. Maybe Sonya would be more comfortable experimenting at our place instead of the club."

He sighed and shook his head. "That's never going to happen. Besides the fact that she's not even remotely open to anything BDSM, we ended things Saturday night."

Dylan pinched his eyebrows together and looked genuinely cheerless. "Shit, Morrison, I'm sorry to hear that. Well, I'm sure Sarah would love to join you. Isa would probably like that better anyway."

"Yes, I'll call her right now. Thanks, Young, for everything."

"Don't go getting all sappy on me, bro," Dylan rolled his eyes.

"Bro?" Sawyer asked, raising his eyebrows at Dylan.

"Don't you know? You and I are embroiled in a bromance."

Sawyer's body stiffened and his voice rose in surprise. "Don't I have a say in the matter?"

"No and neither do I, it was Isabel's assessment of the situation. But you know it's true. You can't quit me," he added with a slight smile of boldness.

Walking over, Dylan punched Sawyer in the arm nearly knocking him out of his chair.

"Now who's getting sappy? And 'I can't quit you'? What are we – a couple of gay cowboys? Christ, you're arrogant. Even if I was gay, you're not my type." Sawyer tossed his head back and eyed Dylan with cold triumph.

Dylan waved his hand in dismissal. "Bah. Whatever. I'm everybody's type. Be at my place at six." Dylan strode out the door conceitedly, but not before turning to face Sawyer with big, exaggerated eyes. "And find your balls because you're taking a turn at the bullwhip," he pointed his finger at Sawyer.

"Hell, if Isabel can do it, I can, too," he shook his head.

"I'll tell her you said that," Dylan warned, narrowing his eyes evilly just before exiting the room.

***

Both Sawyer and Dylan left work early to prepare for the evening of carousing. He was still having a difficult time wrapping his head around the idea of using a bullwhip for anything other than to inflict pain, but he reminded himself to keep an open mind. He had called Sarah on his way home and was happy to hear that she had the night off and could go, so before going home, he took a detour to pick her up.

Arriving at her small home on the outskirts of Denver in the suburb of Aurora, he scanned the area vigilantly. The home was nice but the neighborhood was iffy at best and he detested that she was not only putting herself in danger with her job, but in the area she lived. Perhaps he could remedy that.

He drove around her block several times before parking in her driveway. When he finally did, Sarah was waiting on her front porch with a bag slung over her shoulder. With such short notice, she hadn't had time to change before Sawyer's arrival and planned to get ready at his place. He met her, took the bag and opened the car door for her.

Climbing in, she smiled at him. "What were you doing?"

"Checking out your neighborhood."

"I know it's not the best, but the rent is unbeatable. After Master Doug died, I had to sell our home in Englewood. He didn't have a will and even though I got all his belongings, I couldn't afford the house payment on my own. Both of us being fairly young, we never considered that he might need one," Sarah commented.

"There seems to be a lot of that going around lately, but age has nothing to do with it. I just think people are never prepared for death and don't want to face the possibility of their own mortality and eventual demise. Hell, Isabel's father didn't have a will and he was much older than you."

"I remember reading about that whole mess. She and Dylan have been through a lot."

"Yes, they have," he agreed.

"You, too. Seeing as you're so close to them, I'm sure the events affected you greatly as well."

He didn't want to start his relationship off with Sarah with lies, so instead of responding, he sat quietly without commenting any further. Sonya was still on his mind, and that, too, made him quieter than usual.

"Is everything okay? You seem reserved tonight." Sarah remarked, squeezing Sawyer's thigh.

He sighed, irritated with himself. "My apologies, I recently ended things with someone I cared for a great deal. She's still on my mind, but I assure you I'll be fully attentive to you tonight."

"I didn't realize you had a girlfriend," Sarah stated barely audible, running her hand over the leather seat beneath her and scanning the floorboard.

"I don't. I didn't. We were on a hiatus."

Sarah turned her face away from Sawyer, looking out the window. "I feel terrible."

"Why? It had nothing to do with you," Sawyer replied without inflection.

"That's not what I feel bad about. It's..."

"Go on," he gently urged, fingering her chin and forcing her to look at him.

Sarah's squeaky, soft voice was crystal clear. "I feel awful for being glad you're not committed to anyone. We hardly know each other and it's a selfish thing for me to feel. I'm sorry."

Touched with Sarah's budding feelings toward him, one side of Sawyer's mouth lifted, the corners of his soft brown eyes wrinkling when he did so. So Sarah was interested in him for more than business, too. "There's no need to be sorry. In all honesty, I knew things were over between Sonya and me a long time ago, I just couldn't bring myself to face it."

"Can I ask what happened?"

"We want different things in life, that's all."

Sarah nodded and said nothing more for the majority of the drive and he was grateful for the time she allowed him to think things over. He also appreciated that she never pushed him out of his comfort zone when discussing things, but he suspected that may not always be the case.

Coming to rest at a stoplight, Sawyer revved the engine loudly making Sarah's eyes widen and flash her pearl-white teeth.

"I love that sound." Sawyer lifted his eyebrows at her and punched the gas pedal quickly, the mufflers of his 1970 Shelby Mustang rattling the windows. "And the smell of exhaust, too. Hot tamales, this is a gorgeous car," she gushed.

"Thank you. Restoring her took my mind off my wife's death. It was a lot of work but it was well worth the effort. I guess I'm a sucker for a nice chassis," he commented suggestively, his eyes moving over her body seductively.

"So, it's a *her*?"

Tipping his head back, he peered at Sarah's face. "All cars are females, don't you know that?"

"Why? If I ever get an old classic like this, it's going to be of the male persuasion with a manly name like Torin which means Chief of Thunder."

He tossed his head back and laughed. "It doesn't work like that. Them's the rules, you silly little girl," he joked.

Sarah's smile widened and she gestured toward her body, "Little? I'm 5'8" and there's nothing little about me."

"You're a great deal smaller than me so I can call you that. And your five feet, eight inches of perfection as far as I'm concerned," he smiled playfully.

Her eyes lit up. "I bet you say that to all the girls."

Sawyer huffed, "I'm not a man who doles out compliments just for the sake of it. If I say you have a perfect chassis, it's because in my eyes, it's fucking perfect."

Turning her body to face Sawyer, the lust on Sarah's face was easily readable. "Thank you, Sir. I can honestly say no one has ever said that to me, and I'll never doubt your sincerity again." She gently shook her head as if clearing her thoughts. "So what's your car's name?"

"This hot little vixen doesn't have a name. She simply *is*."

"She who has no name? Boring," she tittered, drawing out her last word.

That sounded like a challenge and Sawyer grinned. "I'll show you boring."

He punched the gas again making his tires squeal loudly. The back end of his black muscle car slid around as they sped away from the light, leaving a trail of thick, black rubber and smoke in their wake.

Sarah yelped and screamed with delight, and he smiled naughtily, envisioning her screaming the same way as he was thrusting into her.

***

Once at Sawyer's condo, Sarah laid out several outfits on Sawyer's bed.

Sitting on the edge of the mattress, she pointed to the clothing. "What would you like me to wear?"

"Leaving a decision like that up to me is a dangerous thing, Snowflake," his eyes darkened.

Her eyes froze on his lips. "Why?"

"Because if left up to me, I'd prefer you wear nothing at all and we stay in all night." Sarah's mouth parted but she said nothing. Sawyer raised his eyebrows hopefully, "Is your birthday suit an option?"

"No, Sir, it's not. Not yet anyway," she laughed nervously but smiled.

Mildly disappointed but not surprised, he shrugged his shoulders. "Oh, well, you can't blame a man for trying."

He picked out a sexy knee-length, dainty pink chiffon dress with lace-top, thigh-high stockings and corset undergarment for Sarah before climbing into the shower. To his surprise, she followed shortly after. Peeking into the stall, her bright azure eyes scanned his wet body.

"May I join you, Sir?"

"If ever there was a harebrained question that was it. Get in here."

Sawyer threw the shower door open and pulled Sarah in brusquely before she had a chance to change her mind. Steam bellowed all around them and Sarah's high-pitched laughter filled the bathroom. Sawyer promptly began studying her body. She was absolutely gorgeous soaking wet. Her skin was the most striking shade of ivory and her long cocoa hair clung to all the right places. The way her large breasts hung and swayed, Sawyer had to concentrate on not becoming erect.

"You're beautiful, Snowflake, and even more perfect than I imagined," he told her, his voice low and smooth.

Sarah's lips parted in surprise. "You imagined me nude?"

"I'm a heterosexual man, Sarah, not a robot. Of course I imagined you nude." Her rose-colored tongue poked out to slick her lips, making the task of not becoming hard even more difficult. "You're making this difficult for me. Was that your intention by joining me in the shower? Some kind of test to see if I can resist you?" he asked, lifting a mischievous eyebrow at her as he gripped his semi-rigid shaft.

Her eyes moved downward and fixed on his dick. "No, Sir, it wasn't. I just believe in conserving water," she grinned up at him guiltily.

Sawyer stared at her a moment before breaking out into full blown laughter. Sarah grabbed a large sponge from the shower shelf and lathered it with soap.

"May I wash you?"

"Another ridiculous question," he laughed. Was Sarah really going to ask permission to do everything?

Sarah began on his front, rubbing large circles on his firm stomach and moving up to the defined muscles of his pecs. She stopped and touched the scar over his heart tenderly, skimming her fingertip over the long mark that extended to his ribcage. The hand that held the sponge dropped to her side as her eyes roamed over his torso and biceps, noting the abundance of scars, pockmarks and burns that varied in size from large-to-small.

"You're very well formed, Mr. Morrison, but..." she touched each of the blemishes and her brows knitted together. "You've been through so much. Who hurt you like this?" she whispered sorrowfully.

Sawyer tilted his head back and closed his eyes without answering, allowing the water to run down his face and body. Running his hand over his rugged face, he wiped his eyes and focused on Sarah's expression. He truly hated talking about his past. The last thing he wanted was sympathy and the thing he detested even more than that was pity. Sarah stood patiently waiting but the peaceful look on her face and quietness motivated him to tell her.

"A lot of different people; all of them bad..." he started out unflinchingly. Sarah's head tilted with confusion and he suddenly felt exposed. She must have sensed his impending withdrawal because she drew nearer to him, dropping the sponge and rubbing her hands over his upper arms and chest, gently coaxing him without pressuring him. Swallowing hard, he continued. "Some of it was work related."

Some, but not all. It had been a long damned time since he had thought about his childhood and the things he had endured at the hands of his abusive caretakers. Sawyer eyed the small, round burn marks on his upper arms and closed his eyes tightly.

How do you tell someone about the pain of being six years old and ripped from everything and everyone you knew and loved, and thrown in with a group of unfeeling strangers? How do you put into words about the horror of when you were nine years old and having your arm broken by your older pedophile foster brother because you wouldn't suck his cock? How the hell do you describe what it felt like being used as a punching bag and human ashtray by your foster mother's sadistic, druggy boyfriend? Or how you spent nearly a year in juvenile detention when you were fifteen for strangling to unconsciousness and knocking the front teeth out of a school bully who had relentlessly picked on you for years? How the fuck do you explain all of that without sounding pathetic?

"Sir..." Sarah's whisper was barely heard over the sound of the water.

His eyes opened, dreading what he would see looking back at him. He didn't want Sarah's pity and if she dared look at him in that dismal, pitiful way, he would lose all respect and desire for her. To his absolute relief, her expression was only that of concern.

"Tell me in your own time," she finished.

Forcing himself to smile, Sawyer tried to lighten the heavy mood. "By the way, you're very well formed, yourself."

Sarah immediately picked up where she left off, causing him to moan out when her teasing touches moved further down to the hair framing his cock. She swirled her fingers into the hair and gently glided her hand over the head of his dick.

Dropping her hand to her side, she looked away, her cheeks flushing with embarrassment. "Mr. Morrison... I..."

When Sarah's eyes met Sawyer's he could sense her hesitancy once again.

Sawyer smiled kindly. "Do only what you feel comfortable with, Snowflake. Or don't do anything at all. Just having you in here with me is pleasure enough."

Sarah's look of anxiety melted away and one hand gripped his dick firmly while the other cradled his balls. She began to slowly stroke him, her eyes never leaving his gaze. They stared at one another as she began to jack him off. The way her hands were moving and her eyes watching his mouth, Sawyer's instinctive response was powerful. He grabbed her face and moved towards her slowly until their lips brushed each other's. He wanted to plunge his tongue into her mouth but withheld the urge and held her head steady.

"I want your kiss, Sir," Sarah whined.

Sawyer's eyes darkened with desire. "Say it again," he ordered.

Her blazing eyes flicked from his mouth to his eyes, her brows pinching together. "I want that kiss, Sawyer. It belongs to me. Please, please...."

Sawyer tingled when Sarah said his name and he quirked an eyebrow at her. "You're mistaken, my pretty little sub. *Your* kiss belongs to *me*, and tonight, so does this mouth," he breathed out just before he thrust his tongue into her imploring mouth. He kissed her ravenously, nibbling and biting her lips. His mouth covered hers briefly only to leave her panting and begging for more.

"I haven't been kissed like this in so long, Sir. Please... don't stop," she whimpered, her eyes remaining tightly closed.

Sawyer crushed his mouth to hers again, stifling her pleadings. He slowed his movements to gently kiss each of her eyelids, cheeks, then mouth, all the while, Sarah's hands moving up and down his hardness and kneading his tender sac.

Sarah's nearness was overwhelming and the electricity of her skilled touch pushed him closer to the edge as his end neared.

"Make me cum," he demanded.

"Yes, Sir," Sarah mewled.

Feeling all-powerful, Sawyer leaned his head back, allowing the water to run over his face once again as he grunted and came. Her strokes slowed, extracting every drop of cum out of him.

Prying his eyes open, he was greeted to Sarah's bashful smile and reddened cheeks.

"You're such a good girl, Snowflake. Has anyone ever told you that?"

Her watchful eyes traveled over his face and searched his mahogany eyes before answering. "Not in a long time, Sir. Thank you for allowing me to give you pleasure."

***

After dressing himself, Sawyer found Sarah in his bedroom waiting for him. Conscious of the drool that was quickly pooling in the corners of his mouth from the fantastic sight in front of him, he wiped his mouth.

His eyes started at her feet and moved upward, slowly taking in every inch of her body. She had perfectly shaped ankles that were made decadent by her three inch rhinestone studded heels. The exquisite geometry of her calves was enhanced by the soft curve of her thighs and her body was second to no other form he had ever laid his eyes on. When his gaze reached her waist, he could no longer resist reaching a hand out to glide his fingertips over the lace-top stockings, up and over her waist and along the curvature of her double D breasts that flowed over the top of the silk and bone under-breast corset.

"Good God, Sarah..." Sawyer's husky voice trailed off, his tonguing poking out to lick the bit of drool that had pooled in the corner of his mouth again. "You're truly stunning beyond words." Sawyer smiled devilishly. He had chosen his sex kitten's attire well.

"Help me with my dress, please?" Sarah asked, reaching over and handing him the pink frock.

"It would be my absolute pleasure."

***

Sawyer kept his eyes fixed on Sarah during dinner, his eyes rarely straying from hers. When his focus was taken from her, he would redirect it and shoot her a conspiratorial half-smile. Sarah simply smiled in return and averted her eyes downward in acquiescence.

Isabel was in a particularly chatty mood and Luke was proving to be very knowledgeable. His French accent took some getting used to but once Sawyer figured out what the hell he was saying, it made the conversation more palatable. Another submissive named Claire had been invited as entertainment for Luke and she seemed quite taken with the foreigner. The room seemed to crackle with sexual electricity as they all spoke of things to come.

When dinner drew to an end, they all made their way to the Youngs' dungeon. The last time Sawyer had seen it was when he helped Dylan design it as a surprise for Isabel. It was very much the same as it had been nearly two years before except for a few new additions. Proud of his playroom, Dylan showed everyone around while Isabel stood near the large four-poster wooden bed watching him lovingly. The room wasn't overly large and with all the equipment, it made for a close and personal setting.

Claire undressed down to her black, lace, crotchless panties and Luke pulled her medium-length hair up into a pony while whispering lusty secrets into her ear. Finally, he shackled her wrists to an overhead suspension bar and Isabel assisted by fastening the dark-skinned beauty's ankles to a spreader bar. In the meantime, Dylan began picking out music.

"This is exciting, isn't it?" Sarah whispered to Sawyer. "I've only seen a bullwhip used a few times and that was years ago."

"I've only seen videos," he admitted.

"Are you really going to try it?" she asked, her eyes gleaming like glassy volcanic rock.

"That's what I've been told." Sawyer's stomach clenched tight just thinking about it and he was becoming more uncomfortable by the minute when he saw Luke unfurl the long whip and circle it around on the floor.

Sarah seemed to sense Sawyer's tension and she pressed her body flush against his for reassurance. "You'll be fine, Sir. Luke seems to know his stuff."

"It's not me I'm worried about; it's whoever is on the receiving end of the whip."

"Me?" Sarah asked hopefully.

He faced Sarah and a probing query came into his eyes. "Would you like it to be you?"

She looked at him optimistically. "If you'll allow me."

He shook his head. Experimenting on his sweet Snowflake was out of the question. "I don't want to hurt you."

Sarah dropped her lashes to hide her disappointment. "I wanted to be the first to scene with you but work prevented that, and now is my opportunity to be the first at the end of your whip. Please don't deny me, Sir. Please use my body to learn what pleases you."

Becoming Sir

The heartfelt and beseeching look on Sarah's face almost prevented Sawyer from saying no, but he couldn't risk harming her. His forehead creased with seriousness and he smoothed a wayward strand of her hair. "We'll share many firsts, Sarah, but not this. My decision is final. Trust me when I say this is what's best."

She studied him thoughtfully for a moment before tiptoeing up to kiss his cheek. "Thank you, Sir, and I do trust you."

Luke looked to Sawyer. "I've brought a shorter-than-normal whip for this demonstration and lesson. Shall we begin?"

A knot rose in his throat but he moved without delay. The leather was long and he couldn't imagine that it was a shorter version. Luke swung the whip and snapped his wrist sharply, the air hissing around it loudly. All three women in the room jumped simultaneously to the sound in turn causing all three men to burst out into laughter.

The mood in the room seemed to lighten and Sawyer was able to relax as Luke went to work on Claire's body. Sawyer watched and listened closely to everything Luke was telling and showing him. On occasion he would look to Sarah who seemed to be mesmerized by the Frenchman's skill. Claire's entire body showed the damage of a masochist, but every one of the marks was like a finely etched tattoo, and each one told its own story. On her silky, dark mocha skin, they were nothing less than splendid.

Luke's movements were swift and calculated, but never harsh, and Sawyer was surprised at the finesse he demonstrated with the intimidating implement.

After nearly half an hour of setting Claire's body ablaze, Luke finished her off by slowly fucking her from behind as he held her out and away from his body as to not injure her freshly whipped back. Claire pushed her ass out to accept Luke's lengthy shaft as he thrust into her unhurriedly, penetrating her depths over and over while softly speaking his praises to her.

Sawyer looked away as the pair's orgasms neared and caught Sarah's eyes on him. There was an air of meekness about her that captivated him and something in her calm manner that soothed him. They locked eyes while Claire and Luke grunted and came together, and a hot ache grew in Sawyer's throat as Sarah's eyes implored him for something unknown.

Luke pulled out of Claire and rid himself of his condom, then unshackled her quickly and swept her up into his sinewy arms. Carrying her to the bed, he laid her out while both he and Isabel eased her wounds with a medicinal-scented herbal salve. Luke cooed sweet French words into Claire's ear while Isabel kissed her forehead and cradled her. Watching Isabel care so tenderly for Claire, Sawyer knew she would make a wonderful mother someday.

Luke began to suck at Claire's nipples while Isabel watched ardently and assisted by holding Claire's breast up for Luke. Claire wrapped an arm around Isabel's neck, raised her head and kissed the tender spot below her chin as she ran her fingers through Isabel's yellow curls. Isabel tilted her head downward and the two pressed their lips together, their tongues twisting together slowly.

The dazzling contrast in the two women's skin color reminded Sawyer of hot cocoa swirling around in warm milk. It was sensual and arousing to watch the two women engage in light petting, and Sawyer wondered how Dylan felt about Isabel being so affectionate and sexual with another female. Looking over, it was clear to see that Dylan was just as turned on as he was by Isabel's intimate gestures toward Claire as he stood at the foot of the bed, his hand gliding over the erection that was pressed into his pants.

Isabel's eyes fluttered open and without disengaging from Claire's mouth, her eyes shifted upward and locked into Dylan's heated gaze.

"That's it, Love, just like that," Dylan gave his authorization.

Moving behind Sarah, Sawyer wrapped his arms around her thick waist and buried his nose in her hair, inhaling her floral scent along with the sex still lingering in the air. He ground his erection into the small of her back and she responded by pushing back into him and accepting his touch as they looked on.

"They're gorgeous," Sarah stated softly.

"So are you, Snowflake. I would love to see you join them."

Sarah turned her head to the side, her eyes expectant. "May I, Sir?"

"Go."

Sarah turned her body to Sawyer and lifted her arms, allowing him to slip her dress up and off of her. Kneeling in front of her, Sawyer removed her pumps, and rolled each of her stockings down slowly, skimming his fingertips along the back of her legs. Just before standing, he planted a soft kiss on her panty covered mound and grinned up at her.

Wearing only her panties and corset, Sarah tiptoed to the bed and stood near, waiting for an invitation. Claire offered her hand first, then Isabel. Luke crawled to the foot of the bed and sprawled out, resting on one elbow like a lion watching his pride of lionesses play as the three women began to touch and massage each other, all the while whispering feminine nothings in each other's ears.

Sawyer would've given anything to know the words being spoken, but he was only left to his dirty imagination. His cock throbbed intensely and he was so excited, he felt as if he would implode from the sheer heat his body was putting off. Caught up in the vision of Sarah caressing Claire's mound and slipping her fingers in, he forgot about the other men in the room until he felt Dylan's hand on his shoulder.

"It's a beautiful sight, isn't it?"

"Fuck, yes," he growled.

Claire's body rose, allowing Isabel to spread out on the bed, and she and Sarah helped her to undress. The women moved leisurely, enjoying the show they were putting on for the three men, their movements slow and purposefully teasing. Isabel lifted her hips so that Sarah could slide her thong down her smooth thighs, while Claire pulled her pale-blue, satin top over her head and removed her corset. When Isabel was fantastically naked, she looked to Dylan for consent.

"My naughty places are in need of attention, Master," Isabel stated in a silky voice that was more of a request than a declaration.

Dylan smiled wickedly and nodded his head, his deep, thick voice filling the room when he spoke. "Let them feast on your sweet cunt, my little wench."

Isabel's eyes flickered keenly and she smiled as she lay back and spread her short legs wide. Claire dove in first, fingering and licking at Isabel while Sarah massaged and kissed her large breasts. Claire raised her head briefly to kiss Sarah, their tongues dancing in each other's mouths and sharing Isabel's taste before returning to the buffet laid out before her. After several minutes, Isabel's breathing quickened and her moans became louder. With her eyes tightly closed, she gently pushed Claire away.

Her eyes met Dylan's. "All my orgasms belong to you, Master. Finish me?"

Dylan moved to the bed and kneeled on it, holding his hand out to Isabel. "That's my good girl," he smiled. She met the smile and the hand which was offered to her, and stood.

"In due time, love, but first, I have an appointment with my Mistress," he grinned crookedly at her before leading her to the suspension rig. Handing her the whip, he bowed his head benevolently, "You're up."

Isabel's eyes dilated as she pushed her shoulders back and rubbed her hand over Dylan's rigid cock. She looked ethereal and dreamlike in the dim lighting, but fierce.

"So are you, my sweet lover."

***

Still mildly stunned by having watched Dylan submit to Isabel, Sawyer drove with Sarah to the Dark Asylum deep in thought. He was quiet the entire drive thinking about everything he had learned in the previous two hours and with the still lingering images of the three women fondling each other.

Thinking about the upcoming scene, he hoped he would give everyone a good show at the club and more importantly, not make a fool of himself or hurt Isabel. She had volunteered to be his first 'victim' and he wasn't sure if that was a good thing or a bad thing.

Sarah, too, remained silent and seemed to withdraw after having watched Dylan and Isabel's scene.

"Did seeing Isabel in control upset you?" Sawyer asked, reaching over and taking Sarah's hand.

"No, it was beautiful to see and I'm honored they shared that with me," she came back with.

Sawyer nodded, feeling the same way, but still wondering why Sarah was so distant.

"You looked amazing tonight with Isabel and Claire. Did you enjoy yourself?"

"Yes, Sir. Did you enjoy watching?"

Sawyer let out a short burst of laughter. "Three gorgeous women play-fucking... what do you think?"

"I think if your dick had gotten any harder, it could have doubled as a steel girder," Sarah quipped nonchalantly.

His eyes widened to her hilariously bawdy remark. "How uncouth!" he teased and she promptly blushed.

"I'm sorry, Sir," she stammered, her cheeks glowing bright red.

"Don't be. I quite like lewd Snowflake."

She chortled and squeezed his arm, but then quieted back down and stared out the window.

At the club, a small crowd had already gathered in anticipation of Luke's showing. A visitor from a far off land wielding a whip masterfully seemed like something everyone was keen on seeing. Luke would warm Isabel up for Sawyer and then hand over the reins, so to speak. Before having left the Youngs' house, Sawyer had tested out the menacing whip and swung it at least a hundred times if not more, getting a feel for how the whip felt in his hands. But testing it out on the back wall would be nothing compared to wielding it against flesh.

Sarah stood with the group while Isabel stripped down to her white satin and velvet corset and lace thong. Dylan whispered things in her ear and caressed her cheeks while Sawyer restrained her arms above her to a spreader bar that was hanging from the ceiling in a large room. He was still getting accustomed to using leather cuffs and he fumbled slightly. Feeling out of his element, he began to worry everyone around him would sense his inexperience, but was relieved that no one seemed to notice.

Next, he moved to her ankles. Placing a steel pipe with soldered metal cuffs at each end in front of her feet, Isabel adjusted her legs to a wide stance as he cuffed her ankles into place. Still kneeling, his eyes moved up Isabel's petite form, pausing briefly on the dark-blonde hair just visible through her sheer panties, her curved hips and overabundant, uptilted breasts oozing out the top of her corset. When their eyes met, Isabel was smiling down at him.

"You have a gentle yet firm and reassuring touch, Sawyer, and you're well on your way to making a wonderful Dom. I'm honored that you've allowed me to help you learn." Isabel's voice was fragile and shaking; her eyes half-closed and clouded.

Sawyer straightened himself with dignity, impressed with the obvious confidence he inspired in Isabel. He had always found Isabel charming in submissive mode, but to see her being docile for him, he felt a twinge of something unfamiliar for her; a combination of arousal and deep caring not unlike love. Normally those feelings would be accompanied with guilt, but Sawyer knew it was because of the setting and nothing more and that Dylan and Isabel wouldn't be insulted by his emotions.

Sawyer touched Isabel's cheek tenderly and skimmed his fingers down over her diamond and leather collar. Her seductive young body and scent were calling to him and she purred with appreciation as she leaned into his touch.

"When it's my turn, be very still, Cookie. I don't want to hurt you."

Isabel's eyes fluttered open. "But I want you to hurt me, Sir."

Oh, Isabel - always the masochist. Sawyer smiled and then grew serious. Only inches away from her face, he took her head into his large hands and held it securely. "That's my decision alone to make. Understood?" Sawyer growled, low and deep.

Isabel's eyes widened and she wet her lips. "Yes, Sir."

"That's a good girl. No more speaking unless it's to cry out in pleasure in which case, scream all you want."

Isabel nodded, her observant tawny eyes scanning his face.

Sawyer moved behind Isabel, loosening the strings of her corset slowly, teasing her with each of his movements and being mindful of where his fingertips touched her skin. When the fabric sagged revealing her pale back, he firmly pressed his fingers against her spine. He had always wondered what she tasted like so he licked her shoulder blade. Isabel's body shuddered and the chains overhead jangled loudly.

Sawyer backed away reluctantly, wanting to taste more of her salty, perfumed skin. Luke moved into Sawyer's spot. He was holding a much larger whip than the one they had practiced with and Sawyer's queasiness returned.

"Are you ready, Little Dove?" Luke asked.

When Isabel nodded, he began stroking her back with the whip at a steady pace, reddening her apricot and milky white skin. The mass that had congregated gasped when Luke's movements became more concentrated on the backs of her thighs and exposed ass. Several times, Sawyer had to focus on something other than the torture that Isabel was enduring. He would never understand how someone could delight in causing pain to something so fragile and delicate. He watched Dylan closely, waiting for the moment he would jump in and kick Luke's teeth in for handling his wife in such a manner, but no such thing happened. Dylan did, however, watch Isabel very closely, never taking his eyes away from her as his eyes inspected her for signs of impending danger.

After several minutes, Luke motioned for Dylan to bring the smaller whip over to Sawyer, but he stayed close, ready to assist and guide his hand. Sawyer felt immediate relief seeing the smaller leather tool. Feeling restricted, Sawyer kicked off his shoes and stripped down to only his slacks and tank top. Before he began, he looked to Dylan for reassurance who nodded his approval.

Sawyer put distance between Isabel's body and himself, and brought the whip up. She halted all movement and held her breath as the leather sliced across her back causing her to shriek out. He had angled his wrist too sharply creating more damage than he had intended.

"Fucking hell." he grumbled under his breath and froze. He looked to Dylan who had a pained look on his face and Sawyer feared it would be his teeth kicked in for mishandling his wife rather than Luke's.

"The error was in your wrist, my friend. Smooth movements only for now," Luke stated calmly, placing his hand on Sawyer's back in a placating gesture. "Become one with the whip; make it an extension of who you are."

Sawyer had already heard as much from Dylan. He moved in front of Isabel to see tears streaming down her cheeks and a wave of nausea washed over him. Wanting to soothe her, he dropped the whip and gripped her face, kissing her ravenously and smothering her sobs. She gasped for breath as his tongue probed her mouth. When he stepped back, Isabel's honey-colored eyes were wide and glassy with shock from his zealousness, but she was no longer crying. His plan had clearly worked in taking her mind off the pain he had inflicted, and he couldn't resist smiling at the surprise on her face as he swept the tears from her cheeks.

"Feeling better?" he asked without letting on to the displeasure of his mistake.

Isabel nodded, her eyes flicking rapidly from his eyes to his mouth.

"Besides bright pink – what's your color?"

Isabel sniffed and smiled sheepishly. "Green, Sir."

He let out a deep sigh then dabbed the corners of her eyes with his thumbs before picking the whip back up. Looking over his shoulder at Dylan, he waited for another nod of approval to continue. When Dylan gave it, Sawyer looked back to Isabel. He had to hear from her own mouth that she was okay with everything that was taking place.

"Do you want me?" he asked, holding the end of the whip in one hand and the handle in the other as he wrapped it around her waist to pull her close. Isabel's eyes darted toward Dylan and Sawyer adjusted his stance, blocking her view.

"I want whatever my Master tells me to want," she whispered.

"I understand and you're a good girl for wanting that. But I have to know right now Isabel that this is what *you* want."

Sawyer tugged the leather, making Isabel gasp out as their mouths brushed against one another. Her fluttering breaths panted out rapidly, the warm moistness touching Sawyer's mouth, the scent a combination of mint, fear and arousal. Her eyebrows pinched together as if she was fighting her own inner battle, her almond-shaped eyes roaming over his face and pleading for something. Stiffly, she nodded.

"I need to hear you say it, Cookie," his voice was deep, calm, his penetrating gaze unwavering.

Suppressing a groan, Isabel's eyes concentrated on his mouth. "Yes, Sawyer, *Sir*, I want this." Softer and more fragile than before, she answered, "I want you," her cheeks blushing from the guilt of her admission. After she spoke the words, her eyes averted to the floor.

Sawyer looked over his shoulder and motioned for Dylan to come over and reassure her.

Moving next to Sawyer, both he and Dylan ran their hands along her body; Dylan's on her face, running his index finger down her cheek and across her full, pouted lips and then her chin, guiding her to look at him. Sawyer released the whip from one hand, the leather falling to the floor with a soft thud, and skimmed his finger over the tops of Isabel's breasts and down to her waist.

"I want Sawyer to pleasure me, Master. I'm so sorry," Isabel whimpered, her eyes welling up with tears.

Dylan caressed her cheek and gave her his best sympathetic comforting and reassuring smile. "I want you to want him. Right now, at this moment, you belong to Sawyer and are at his mercy. But you'll always belong to me and only me. You know that. You're mine, Love... forever."

Isabel's mouth curved upward in a sexy smile as her reluctance pooled at her feet, freeing her from her guilt and setting Sawyer free to satisfy both he and Isabel.

Dylan redirected his heated and possessive stare to Sawyer. He dug his fingers harshly into Sawyer's shoulder while his eyes clung to him. "We owe you our lives, Morrison, and for that reason I will share with you, and *only you,* my most cherished possession – my wife and the love of my life. Make her soar, Sawyer, and hold nothing back."

Sawyer was crushed by Dylan and Isabel's surrendering words, and he suddenly felt light-headed and dizzy with excitement as the blood from his head rushed to his cock. He took a deep breath and held it to steady himself while Dylan gave his final instructions to Isabel as he kissed her.

"Fly, Baby Girl."

Dylan moved away, standing on the sidelines with Luke and leaving Sawyer to exert his power over Isabel. Closing his eyes, Sawyer rolled his neck, loosening his tense muscles and letting his apprehension go. He had Dylan's permission after all and Isabel was consenting.

He vowed to himself that he would try the whip only once more on Isabel's supple flesh, and if he made the same mistake as before, he would just have to move onto something more his skill level. Sawyer snapped the whip in the air loudly several times, re-acclimating himself with the instrument. When he faced Isabel, her eyes were dreamy and her body writhed with need.

Leaning into Isabel's ear, his long fingers clamped over her hip before easing their way down and past her panties, pushing them into her damp folds and pinching her clit. Her muscles tensed under his fingertips and she mewled in delight. Sawyer bit Isabel's lobe gently and breathed into her ear, "I know exactly what you need, my Sweetness, and it isn't at all what you think you want..." then slipped his tongue into the shell of her ear, circling it around. "It's to do what pleases me." He skimmed his tongue down her jawline to her parted lips, dipping it into her mouth, tasting her once again, "when and how I tell you to do it." He bit gently into her bottom lip before trailing his mouth down to her neck. "Any questions?" he asked with his words muffled as he buried his face against her throat, the pounding of her rapid pulse throbbing in her jugular vein felt on his lips.

Isabel moaned and nodded her head. "Good. We'll start with something simple to see how well you can follow my orders." Isabel's eyes flickered open and she waited for his command. "Fuck my tongue with your mouth," he ordered, his words cool and clear like ice water.

He stood, tilted his head and opened his mouth, his thick, rigid tongue sticking out just far enough for Isabel to get a hold of it. Eagerly complying, she pushed her head forward and latched onto his tongue, sucking at it greedily as if it were his hard cock and bobbing her head forward and back. He thrust his fingers deeper into her pussy, making her moan out and her limbs tremble.

Drawing away from Isabel abruptly, he left her hanging in mid air, needy and whining for his touch. She opened her mouth to speak, but Sawyer placed his index finger to her mouth, silencing her.

"Only screams of pleasure, remember?" he reminded her, poking his wet finger into her mouth, allowing her to taste herself. "How do you taste, Isabel?"

She closed her eyes and swirled her tongue over his index finger, then answered, "Salty and..."

"Tell me," Sawyer demanded.

"Aroused."

Pulling his finger out of Isabel's mouth, he dipped it back into her pussy, soaking his finger again and bringing it to his mouth to confirm her assessment. He licked and sucked his fingers and agreed wholeheartedly. "Yes, Cookie, you do taste aroused. But you left something out."Cocking her head to the side, Isabel's brows knitted together. "Delectable."

* * *

Sawyer's left shoulder ached from all the whipping and sensual torture he had inflicted on Isabel, and he rubbed it with his right hand while he and Sarah drove away from the club. The scene was still playing in his mind as he thought about how he could've made it better for Isabel and himself. He had left her begging to be fucked and though he suspected Dylan would've allowed it, he just couldn't cross that line out of respect for the two of them. Having remembered Isabel's statement that all her orgasms belonged to her husband, he handed her off to Dylan to finish her off completely. The scent of Isabel's pussy was still lingering on his clothing, making him smirk wickedly. He could completely understand why Dylan was so enamored with her; she was quite a tasty little sub. He hoped by assisting Dylan in making Isabel cum, he had made up for his egregious mistake with the whip.

Perhaps Snowflake would be up to allowing him to try his hand at the whip again on her the next time. Sawyer inwardly laughed, surprised that he was even considering doing it again. He couldn't wait to get the thick beauty back to his condo.

105

"I'd like if it you stayed the night with me, Snowflake."

She stared at her hands before answering. "I can't, but thank you for the offer," she said softly.

"You're very quiet. Tell me what you're fighting with." Sarah swallowed hard to Sawyer's statement and slumped into the leather seat. "Please sit up and look at me," he stated decisively. There was nothing more frustrating than seeing a beautiful woman lose her confidence.

She squared her shoulders and faced him. "I can't put it into words right at the moment, but I assure you it wasn't anything you did or did not do. It's actually been a very pleasurable night for me."

Sawyer nodded and let it go sensing that Sarah was clearly struggling with her own demons. He had wanted to spend the night exploring her curves, but resigned himself to the fact he may just have to jerk himself off for release.

Arriving at her home, he walked her to the porch. Sarah unlocked her door slowly and turned to face Sawyer. With the moon shining in her glassy eyes and glinting off her hair, Sawyer leaned forward. She opened her mouth to say goodnight and he wrapped the fingers of one hand around the back of her neck and pressed his open lips to hers. She tried to pull away but Sawyer refused her denial. He was a patient man, but he wouldn't be denied her kiss. Realizing her feeble attempts were useless, Sarah gave in to the forceful domination of his lips. Dusting his fingers up her smooth thigh, his hand moved under her dress to skim her hip and squeeze her waist. Sawyer continued to kiss her with a hunger that belied his outward calm, lingering and savoring every bit of her that she was allowing him to explore. He moved his mouth to her earlobe, grazing it with his teeth before ending their dreamy moment. The kiss obviously left Sarah weak and confused as she wobbled on her feet and held onto his biceps for stability.

"I wish I had this effect on all women," Sawyer smiled down at her, proud of his effect on her.

With half-closed eyes, Sarah answered unequivocally, "You do, Sir, and don't you ever doubt that."

Chapter 9

The following day at work was busy and it wasn't until mid-afternoon that Sawyer was finally able to speak with Dylan. When he entered Dylan's office, he was greeted with a slightly raised eyebrow and a crooked accusing half-grin.

"Did you rub one off thinking about my wife last night, Morrison?" he asked.

Sawyer shook his head and laughed. "It wasn't Isabel I was thinking about."

"Good. I know how hard it can be not finishing at the end of a scene. *Hard.* See what I did there? How *hard* it can be?" he chuckled at himself. "You left before I had a chance to commend you on how well you handled yourself last night. And my wife, too, but don't get used to it. As much as I enjoyed seeing you tease and nearly fuck her, I'd like to be the only one who satisfies her. She's still available for 'educational' purposes, of course," he smiled.

"Thanks. I honestly don't think anyone else could satisfy Isabel."

Dylan's lifted his eyebrows. "Do you think she was holding back?"

"A little."

Dylan shook his head and huffed. "I'll have to have a talk with her about that. Perhaps a spanking is in order."

"No, please don't do that. All-in-all, the scene was very enjoyable. Anyway, I don't think she was holding back per se. I think she just would've preferred pain interspersed with my teasing."

Dylan's stern looked softened. "Well, that's my little masochist for you. And admit it: it was more than just 'enjoyable'."

Unable to hide his wayward thoughts, Sawyer nodded. "Yes, fine. I admit it." Seating himself across from Dylan's desk, he got back down to business. "I'm going to be paying a little visit to a certain Mr. Christopherson."

Dylan rocked his chair back and gave Sawyer a sharp, assessing look. "You have everything in order?"

"Absolutely. It turns out Emilio's business partner has been a very naughty boy. I'm sure his wife would love to know about his years of promiscuity and drug use. And if that doesn't persuade him, then perhaps Uncle Sam would like to know about his under the table dealings with a local contractor."

"Jesus, you are thorough, aren't you?" Dylan sneered. "Emilio was surrounded by nothing but shit. First, Simons and now this Christopherson guy? I can only imagine what it was like for Isabel growing up around such scumbags."

"Anyway, I just need the go ahead to get things rolling. Also, if I'm not able to verbally persuade him, how far do you want me to take matters?"

Swinging his chair around, Dylan looked out the window while he thought things over. Sawyer knew what needed to be done for a satisfactory resolution, but with everything that had happened he didn't want to bring anymore negative attention to the Youngs' lives.

"Let's not do anything rash. If Christopherson doesn't agree to back off, we'll follow through with our threats and expose him. Maybe that will be enough that the judge in charge of Emilio's case will dismiss the appeal and relinquish all funds to Isabel. If not, then we'll just let things play out," he finally answered.

"Good plan."

***

Several hours later, Sawyer was surprised by a courier dropping off an envelope addressed to him. The flourished feminine handwriting wasn't one he recognized and he quickly tore into it.

"Mr. Morrison, let me start by saying this letter is not only to apologize for my distance last night, but an admission of guilt. I was not myself. I was nervous and

I could feel myself drifting away with each passing minute. Let me be clear – it was not because of you, but rather my own fears. I felt so unsure of myself next to you, but you made me feel something I haven't felt in a very long time – needed. Being back at the club during our first introduction felt like home, but it was like an empty home without my Sir.

Last night, however, was different and I'm having a difficult time with that. I find you very attractive and while I watched you with Isabel, all I kept thinking about was that I wanted you to push my limits the way my Sir had done. Our shower together was amazing and giving you pleasure set me on fire, but I'm afraid of what I'm feeling because of shame. My mind knows I am not betraying my Master, but my heart tells me that I am, and my body says something altogether different. It says: take me, Mr. Morrison. So you see I have many emotions to contend with. Which part of me do I listen to?

I realize that we've only met and I am not trying to force anything, but I am a strong believer in full disclosure and communication so I am merely being up front with you about how you make me feel. You will be in contact with many submissives over the next several weeks and months, but I sincerely hope you find your way back to me and know that whatever your decision is, I will remain at your service until you feel comfortable as a Dominant.

As someone who will have a direct hand in your training as a Dom, from here forward, this is my promise to you: I will be nothing less than courteous and helpful to you at all times. I will be open and share my experiences with you, along with the knowledge that I have acquired during my years in the BDSM community.

Sincerely, Sarah.

P.S. Thank you for taking a chance on a still grieving and confused submissive.

P.S.S. That kiss was amazing."

Sawyer was touched at Sarah's honesty and he quickly put pen to paper to respond.

"My sweet Snowflake, you're much too hard on yourself. You really have no idea how amazing you are do you? Fear is not always a bad thing. Living your life the way you want and taking risks is terrifying. But fear of losing someone is a far greater thing to be afraid of. This is what you truly fear, isn't it? A great many things scare me, too – most especially loss. Since you're disclosing fully, let me do the same: I am not afraid of your attraction to me nor am I afraid of your honesty. It's refreshing and nothing less than alluring.

I do not take promises, written or spoken, lightly and I fully intend to hold you to the promises you have made to me in the letter you sent. In turn, I will make you a promise: I will be responsive to all that you have to offer me and take full advantage of your knowledge and experiences. Difficult as it may be, I will not hide what my mind and body are feeling so that I might learn the responsibilities as a forthcoming, conscientious and trustworthy Dominant. Above all else, I will wear the title of Dominant with honor and never give reason or cause for others to think negatively of the roles of Dominant and submissive.

Only time will tell if our destinies are meant to be. Until then, I look forward to our time together. Thank YOU for taking a chance on me, despite knowing nothing of my past offenses.

Sawyer

P.S. Yes, the kiss was amazing. So was watching you. You elicit the hardest of steel girders, Snowflake."

When Sawyer put the pen down, he felt inexplicably liberated. He found it so much easier to write what he was feeling rather than to speak it aloud. Having alluded to his murderous past was a big step for him, knowing he would eventually have to reveal everything to whomever it was he chose to be his submissive. *If* he found someone to be his submissive.

Sawyer sealed the letter in an envelope, addressed it to Sarah, and had it sent out immediately. He picked up his phone and considered texting her, but decided to wait instead until after the letter had been delivered to her.

**

Two days had passed and Sawyer kept himself occupied with work and prepared for the meeting with Jameson Christopherson. Fighting the overwhelming urge to contact Sarah, he kept his evenings full by filling his brain with as much BDSM information on slave relationships as it would hold. He felt as if he was a master craftsman in the making, trying his best to hone his skills to a degree and level of competency that he wanted to far exceed the average Dom. He took his work and research seriously, and came to the realization that it would take years to complete his training and that in reality he would probably never be done learning everything there was.

Lying in bed with his iPad in hand, he was alerted to a message from Sarah.

SarahH: 9:53 PM: Thank u for your kind response in writing to my letter. I've always cherished the written word and it was a treat to receive.

S.M.: 9:55 PM: I'm glad to hear from you.

SarahH: I've spoken with the Young's and they've suggested we write out a temporary contract of sorts between us so that u can get the feel for what's involved in creating one.

SarahH: 9:56 PM: I would've contacted u sooner but I've been hard at work putting it together. I'll send it now. We'll talk once you've gone over it and made revisions. Can I expect your response in 2 days' time?

S.M.: 10:01 PM: I may need until after the weekend as I'll be busy at Kerian's home. The beginning of next week I'll also be dealing with a work issue, but I promise I'll be going over it every spare moment that I get. I look forward to reading what you've sent.

SarahH: 10:14 PM: That sounds acceptable. I'll speak with u soon.

At that moment, Sarah's email came through. Sawyer retrieved his laptop and downloaded the document.

"Sir, here is my mock-up of our proposed temporary contract. I found the sample document online at http://houseslut.tumblr.com *and have amended it to suit our needs. It does not include all of the fine details that a normal contract would have, but I've tried to make it fit within the confines of your training. In your next communication to me, please provide me with daily tasks and chores to keep us grounded and connected even when we're not in contact."*

EXPECTATIONS

I, Sarah Henderson, hereinafter referred to as submissive, does of my own free mind and open heart, offer myself in consensual submission to Sawyer Morrison, hereinafter referred to as Sir, during his training period so that we may both grow, and I may assist him during his transition into the BDSM lifestyle, beginning immediately and ending when his training is completed as deemed by his trainers, the BDSM community, and myself.

OBJECTIVE

The objective of this temporary contract is to make clear the expectations of both Sir and submissive and the consequences for failure to abide by this agreement. This written treaty shall serve as the basis for teaching how to live a healthy and happy BDSM lifestyle, while improving both lives in the spirit of a loving and consensual Dominance and submission relationship. It is the intention of this trainer, i.e. submissive, to help further Sawyer Morrison's knowledge by guiding and assisting in his self-awareness and exploration.

Submissive desires that trust and open communication be a significant and vital part of this relationship on the part of both parties, in addition to obedience by the submissive.

The terms and conditions set forth in this agreement are a formal way of defining the rules by which both enter into this safe, sane and consensual relationship.

By accepting and signing this temporary contract, both Sir and submissive agree that these terms and conditions cannot be altered in any way except by shared approval. These terms and conditions may be negotiated; meaning Sir will hear any arguments or suggestions that are presented in a clear, concise and calm manner.

Note: No part of this temporary pact can interfere with the professional life of the submissive or Dominant. It is meant to guide them and cannot be harm their ability to get their jobs done.

SUBMISSIVE RESPONSIBILITIES (suggestions, please revise and/or add as you see fit)

1. It is the responsibility of submissive to be pleasing in all ways – intellectually, visually, sexually and domestically.

2. Submissive is required to obey all commands given by Sir within reasonable and fair limits.

3. Submissive agrees to show an attitude of respect and reverence to Sir at all times.

4. Submissive must be calm, clear and to the point when relaying opinions any time she disagrees with Sir, but accepts that Sir has final say in all matters.

5. Rash or disrespectful behavior of any kind is a punishable offense.

6. Submissive shall address Sawyer as "Sir" as frequently as possible in private, and as often as opportunity allows in public.

7. Sir and submissive will have daily discussions in regards to all activities that have transpired and progression of Dominant training.

8. Submissive will use the power granted to her in her role as a trainer in assisting Sir to strengthen his character, integrity and Dominance.

DOMINANT RESPONSIBILITIES

1. Sir is responsible for being courteous and respectful to submissive at all times.

2. Sir will be patient with submissive as she learns his needs and preferences.

3. Sir will maintain an honest and communicative relationship with submissive.

4. Sir will use the power and authority within his role in assisting submissive to grow in character, strength, and confidence.

5. Sir will respect the use of safe word as designated by submissive (see below).

6. Sir cannot dominate while inebriated, and drug use and excessive alcohol use is grounds for termination of contract and training.

SAFE WORD

1. Submissive is permitted use of a safe word in all activities, and will never be denied the use of it.

2. If a situation arises where a safeword is necessitated, Sir will immediately terminate the current course of action and re-evaluate the situation with submissive.

3. Following the use of a safeword, a candid and straightforward discussion is to be had in a calm manner to explain why the safeword was used. Sir and submissive will then develop a clear and concise plan of attack to avoid any further miscommunication (if any) and use of safeword.

4. The safewords of choice will be: Orion (for red) and Andromeda (for yellow)

PUNISHMENT (please specify your choice of punishment)

1. No meditation for one day = _____

2. Failure to comply to a direct order in private/*public = _____

3. Backtalk/disrespectfulness = _____

*Penalties earned in public will be dispensed in private at the first available opportunity.

HARD LIMITS

At no time will the following be forced upon submissive:

1. Other male sexual partners (unless discussed prior to scene)

2. Mental, physical or verbal abuse.

3. Breaking laws

4. Threatening of life, verbally or physically

5. Any activity that will cause irreparable bodily damage and/or harm.

6. Edge play (unless discussed prior to scene and done under direct supervision of an experienced edge player - see stipulation #5)

7. Scat play.

I, submissive Sarah Henderson, offer my submission on loan to Sir Sawyer Morrison under the terms stated above on this the _____ day of _____ in the year 2013.

Signature of submissive (to be signed in presence of Sir)

_____

I, Sir Sawyer Morrison, offer my acceptance of Sarah's temporary submission while training to be a Dominant under the terms stated above on this the _____ day of _____ in the year 2013.

Signature of Dominant (to be signed in presence of submissive) _____

Chapter 10

Sawyer had dreamt of Sarah after reading the contract. Having lacked structure in his childhood, it was something that he craved and insisted on as he grew into an adult, and BDSM was giving him exactly that. Of course, sexual power and control was a significant part of the equation and charm that appealed to him, but he had come to the conclusion that sex wasn't *everything* about BDSM that attracted him to it. There was so much more to it than he had ever anticipated.

The evening promised to be informative and he was going to be introduced to a new submissive – one who was experienced in living as a slave. Sawyer had jotted down all the questions he could think of before meeting her, wondering why and how someone would want to live in such a controlled environment and with having no say in making their own decisions.

Before he could write anything else down, he needed to focus on the task at hand.

He contacted the company pilot and scheduled a flight to Atlanta the following Monday to have either a come to Jesus or go to hell meeting with Jameson Christopherson. He had made a promise not only to himself, but to Dylan and Isabel to see things through to the end and hopefully, this would be the end of all things relating to Emilio Ibanez. Sawyer didn't notify Dylan of his trip because the last thing he needed was a tag along, but instead he invited Murphy, a fellow employee and close confidant. They had been through some rough shit, but Murphy had stayed loyal despite everything that went down the previous year. It was Murphy that Simon's gun had been pointed at when Sawyer had stepped in, taking the bullet for his friend, and he knew if Murphy found out he was planning on going alone, the shit would hit the fan and he would most likely end up with a size 11 foot up his ass.

***

Evening came faster than Sawyer had wanted. He felt ill-prepared despite having done his homework and written out his thoughts ahead of time. Neither Isabel nor Dylan would be accompanying him to the private gathering that was being held by Kerian. It was going to be held in the personal Master's Quarters of his home, and it was a great honor that Sawyer had been invited. One of Kerian's slaves was on a weekend loan to Sawyer to command as he wished, and it was daunting to think about. Sawyer would be staying the weekend at Kerian's estate so he could be coached extensively on Master/slave etiquette. Having Kerian in close proximity and on hand for personal instruction put his mind at ease. Somewhat.

Setting aside a few minutes for Sarah before he left for Kerian's, he texted her some of his thoughts on the contract and some of his wishes.

S.M.: 5:22 PM: I've been thinking about you today and wondering what you do with your time when you're not with me. It got me thinking about tasks/chores that can keep us connected.

SarahH: 5:24 PM: I've been thinking of u, too, Sir. I'm super excited for your upcoming weekend and what it holds for u.

SarahH: 5:25 PM: It's a great opportunity to really study Ciara and, of course, take advantage of her knowledge ;) What did u have in mind for my tasks/chores?

S.M. 5:28 PM: Dinner is scheduled every evening for 6:45. I would like for you to eat at the same time so in spirit we will be together sharing a meal. For you, I would like you to save me the last bite of every meal you eat, regardless of whether we are together for me to actually eat it.

S.M.: 5:29 PM: Only one other thing (for now): set a reminder for 1and 9 pm. I expect you to find somewhere private, remove your panties and finger yourself to near orgasm while you think of me. BUT, do not cum. Am I clear? I will set my watch to the same times and be imagining how glorious you look.

SarahH: 5:33 PM: I love it, Sir. I will set my reminder right this instance. Do we start tonight?

S.M.: 5:34 PM: Absolutely. Even though I will be very busy the next few days, I will still be thinking of you and the contract. Also, I haven't decided what form of punishment will be delivered when (if) you fail to follow my rules, but I'm thinking simple swats on the bottom will suffice or even a time out. The number of swats will be dependent on how severe the offense is.

SarahH: 5:35 PM: SIMPLE swats? Is there such a thing?

S.M.: 5:36 PM: I suppose there isn't, but don't let the word confuse you. Even though I'm not fond of delivering punishment in any form to someone as beautiful as yourself or any female for that matter, it doesn't mean I won't follow through. Like I said before, promises mean a lot to me, so if one has been broken, I WON'T be lenient.

Sarah: 5:37 PM: I have to admit to feeling a little giddy at the moment from your authoritative words and even though I don't like punishment, I look forward to your first 'swat':D

Sawyer laughed as if sincerely amused. He was actually looking forward to delivering his first swat to Snowflake, too, though he hoped it was merely for pleasure.

S.M.: 5:38 PM: I'll be envisioning your sweet body tense with the need to cum at 9 pm. We'll be in contact soon and I'll let you know how things are going with Ciara. Sweet dreams, my precious Snowflake.

*SarahH: 5:40 PM: *sigh* Have fun this weekend, Domly One. Ciara is one lucky slave girl to have u all to herself for an entire weekend.*

***

Twenty-five minutes later Sawyer pulled into Kerian's expansive drive way. His estate was enormous and resembled an old castle with its old stone construction, gothic architecture and gilded wrought-iron fencing. The only thing missing were the gargoyle statues in the front yard. Sawyer grabbed his bag and walked around the property. The sun had already set so he dug out a flashlight from his bag and scanned the perimeter for any breaches in security while making note of all the points of entry and exits. As he stood in the backyard studying the tall fence for any breaks, he heard a gentle laugh ripple in the air from behind him and felt a hand on his shoulder.

"Damn, Sawyer, you're always on the job, aren't you?"

Sawyer shrugged his shoulders in mock resignation and swung his head around to face Kerian. "It's in my blood. You have an amazing place."

"Thank you, it's been my pet project for around ten years and it's nearly cost me my entire kinky fortune from the Dark Asylum to fix it up. It was in pretty bad disarray when I bought it, but I think I've made some nice progress. Come inside and see for yourself. Ciara is anxious to meet the Dom in training everyone is talking about." Kerian's tall figure turned and headed toward the mansion, leaving Sawyer to follow behind and ponder what everyone was discussing about him.

When Kerian and Sawyer entered the large foyer that was decorated with several of Isabel's risqué artwork hanging on the walls, they were greeted by two women who looked almost identical in body shape and hair color, kneeling by the door. Their wrists and necks were ornamented with thick, black leather cuffs, their arms outstretched in front of them with their heads down in a praising position. Each had raven black hair pulled into a high pony-tail and donned only red ruffled panties and a matching lace tank top. Their olive skin looked magnificent under the yellow-hue of the overhead chandelier.

"This delicious piece of fuck-cake is Ciara," Kerian stated, bending down and touching the top of the head of the woman furthest from Sawyer. "Say hello Precious."

Without raising her head, Ciara spoke softly. "Hello Master Morrison."

"I'm not a Master, yet, Ciara."

"Soon, Sawyer. From what I've been told, you're training is coming along well. Your scenes have been the talk of the club and the feedback from the other patrons has been good with only a few pointers and suggestions mentioned. I'll pass those along to you in writing before you leave. So tell me: do you have an interest in obtaining and caring for a slave?"

Sawyer rubbed his chin as he eyed the two stunning women. "I don't know yet. I've never considered it. From what I've read, it seems like a lot of work."

Kerian laughed jovially, his eyes smoldering as he tugged the pony on Ciara's head, forcing her head up off the floor and gazed down into her deep brown eyes. "Yes, they're most definitely a lot of work and require the utmost attention. But it's the kind of work that brings nothing but pure enjoyment. Perhaps after this weekend you'll have a taste for collaring your own slave. It's like nothing else, Sawyer. Julia is my most prized asset and I can't imagine my life without her. I would give all my material belongings for her, including this house, if I were forced to choose only one thing on this Earth to keep."

Sawyer stood staring at Kerian, astounded and wordless at the sheer love he was exuding while talking about his slave. Kerian caressed Ciara's cheek causing a soft gasp to escape her lips. Ciara's beautiful Asian eyes were dark and unfathomable, and the look shared between the two was compelling and magnetic.

"Ciara makes the most amazing love, Sawyer. Not to say my Julia doesn't either. And their obedience is unsurpassed," Kerian stated, gliding his fingertips down Julia's spine. "Ciara's training is nearly complete and she'll make someone a very lucky Master someday. I'm a very blessed man to have found such devotion and sexual prowess in not only one, but two women. I'll be sad to see Ciara go, but such is the fate of training - to learn to satisfy, be gratified, and then set free to journey the path of BDSM and enjoy all the wonders held within this lifestyle."

Sawyer wondered when his time would come to be set free and what things awaited him. Would he find *'the one'* submissive that was right for him? Perhaps even a slave? He had no idea.

Kerian's deep green eyes met Sawyer's and a devious smile touched his lips. "It's worth mentioning that these two beauties fit well together; like two puzzle pieces," he waggled his eyebrows. "It would be their pleasure to give us all a show later. Isn't that right, my dirty little whores?"

Sawyer winced at what Kerian had called the pair, but both women nodded obediently and without so much as a hint of offense.

Kerian moved toward a large room that looked to be a library of sorts. "Everyone else will be here shortly. Venire," he spoke firmly causing the two women to jump to his command.

"I didn't know you spoke Italian," Sawyer commented.

"Yes, my mother was Italian, my father American. All commands for my slaves are in my mother's native language. I've written them down for you."

"I speak Italian, as well, so that won't be necessary."

Kerian's brows rose in surprise. "Very well. How many languages do you speak?"

"A great many; my work with the CIA necessitated it. Now, let's get down to business shall we?" Sawyer stated resolutely, moving the subject along.

Kerian guided Ciara over to Sawyer by her shoulders as Sawyer's eyes roamed over her 5'6" frame, small breasts, slightly protruding, soft belly and firm thighs.

"I am loaning you my slave in training until Sunday evening, 5:00 p.m. with strict instructions on her treatment. She is in no way to be harmed physically or mentally. Even though she is merely one of my trainees, she is a cherished belonging and I do not loan out my slaves frivolously. I believe experiencing the hand of another Master is essential to her training, even if the Master is still in training himself. It will be a learning and growing experience for the both of you. She demands great care and attention and I expect nothing less from you as her temporary Master. Am I clear?" Kerian pushed his shoulders back squarely and puffed his chest out as he spoke fiercely and protectively, and his masterful and unambiguous statement resonated and echoed, filling the large room with the deep timbre of his voice.

Holding a tight grip on Ciara's shoulders, he waited for Sawyer's acknowledgement of what was expected of him.

"Of course, Kerian. I'm honored that you and Ciara have allowed me to enjoy her company so that we may learn together what these complex roles entail. I would never harm this exquisite specimen in any way or take advantage of the gift you have both given me, even if it is only for a short while."

Sawyer took note of Ciara's full bee-stung lips curving upward ever so slightly.

Kerian smiled broadly, flashing his crooked teeth. "Well said, Sawyer, but before I hand over the reins to this stunning slave, I should disclose an important bit of information: the effects of a woman's willing surrender can be mind altering and life changing. I guarantee you'll never look at another woman in the same light after you've been given complete control over such a docile being. You'll also never view yourself the same after being granted such a privileged opportunity. Now, shall we make our way to the dining room to prepare for dinner and discuss what kind of sexual activity is permitted with her?"

***

Dinner had been enjoyable and Sawyer's brain was still buzzing from the heated conversations about sex, politics and everything BDSM. He and Ciara retired to a large suite on the third level with a picturesque view of the distant Denver cityscape and the large tract of land that Kerian's home sat on. He stood staring out at the fall colors barely visible in the darkened sky. With the silence that enveloped him, he momentarily forgot he wasn't alone. When he turned, Ciara was standing near the door with her eyes downcast.

"Are you chilled, Angel?" Sawyer asked, grabbing a light blanket off the massive king-sized, mahogany canopy bed.

Ciara tipped her head back to peek at Sawyer and smiled. "A bit, Master Morrison. How did you know?"

Sawyer was baffled by Ciara's question. "What are you referring to?"

She turned her back to Sawyer, revealing large, beautifully detailed, black angel's wings tattooed on her shoulder blades. She had never turned her back the whole evening, and followed several feet behind Sawyer up the passageway to the suite and he hadn't seen them until that very moment. Sawyer dropped the blanket and rose from the bed, moving stealthily toward Ciara. The wings were glorious on her flawless skin. She was a true angel if he had ever seen one and the wings only proved his assumption. He rubbed his fingers over both blades to reassure himself they were ink and not real. When his fingers swept over her back, her skin prickled and she inhaled sharply.

"What heinous act did you commit to be cast out from the heavens above, Angel?" Sawyer spoke with desire, deep and animalistic.

"It was man that I desired to be owned and commanded by, not God," Ciara answered without hesitation.

"I can smell your sexuality on you, Ciara, and it's intoxicating. Do you have this effect on all men or just me...?" Sawyer broke off midsentence and gripped her upper arms firmly before gently biting into the nape of her neck causing her to mewl loudly and shiver.

He reached behind and retrieved the blanket, and spun Ciara around to wrap it around her bare shoulders. Holding her close, he let her sap the heat from his body. Ciara buried her face in his neck, accepting his primal touch.

As they stood silently bonding, Sawyer thought back to dinner. He was still reveling in the thoughts of how Ciara had served and cut his food, and fed him. The first few bites felt awkward but everything seemed to fall into place once he saw

Kerian, and the other guests being treated in the same royal manner. There were two other slaves present for dinner, along with their Masters and one submissive and her Dominant. One of the slaves was a male which Sawyer found enthralling to watch. The dinner party was small and intimate, and he looked forward to the upcoming fucktivities and scene play in Kerian's legendary dungeon.

"May I dress you for the evening, Master Morrison?"

Sawyer chuckled. "I can dress myself, but thank you for the offer."

Disappointment flashed in Ciara's eyes. "Of course, Master. I didn't mean to insinuate that you couldn't do the job yourself, but merely that it is not only my duty to do it for you, but it would be my absolute pleasure."

Standing immobile, Sawyer watched Ciara pensively. "Exactly what is your role as a slave, Ciara?" She suddenly looked frightened as if she was being put on the spot or called out because of inadequacy. "Angel..." Sawyer spoke softly, "I'm only asking because I'm not precisely clear about the role of a Master/slave; nothing more."

Ciara sighed and visibly relaxed. "Thank you for clarifying. My role as a slave is to make your life easier and to bring you joy in all things. To dress you, feed you, bathe you, sexually gratify you, and whatever else you want me to do."

Sawyer chewed his bottom lip and seated himself on the edge of the bed. "But what about your needs?"

Ciara smiled and her cheeks brightened. "My needs are met by being the best slave I've been trained to be and by being pleasing in all ways. I guess what I'm trying to say is, I need to be used. I know that sounds degrading, but I've made that choice of my own free will and I give myself to only those who are worthy of my complete submission and slavery. If you don't allow me to do the things that I've been trained to do, the things that I *want* to do for you, then what good am I? If all you want from me is to stand in the corner and look pretty, I can do that, but I'd much rather be useful somehow."

"Where's the challenge, though, Ciara? I mean, if you do everything I ask without question, where's the excitement in that?"

Ciara blinked rapidly and scanned the floor. "May I speak freely?"

"From here forward when I ask you a question, I want your words to come nothing less than freely. Pronunziare," Sawyer gave the order to speak.

"The excitement is all in the limits, Master Morrison, and pushing them. Yes, I will do whatever you ask, but it doesn't mean that I'm mindless and without opinion or that I will like or enjoy everything I'm ordered to do. It's your pleasure that I seek; your desires that I long to fulfill, and it's your duty as my Master to coax consent out of me. To seduce me and make me want to do the things that I would otherwise not want to do. Just because I'm a slave doesn't mean that I can't walk away at any time if I feel like my submission is being abused or my needs aren't being met. Does that make sense?" Ciara asked earnestly, tugging the blanket around her shoulders tighter.

Sawyer beamed. Ciara was not only gorgeous and subservient, but intelligent. "You're quite an interesting woman, Angel. Thank you for sharing with me. Your honesty and openness means everything to me, and I look forward to seducing consent out of you. Now, what was that about dressing me?"

Ciara's eyes widened with joy. "Yes, Master Morrison, I would love to dress you. May I choose your attire as well?"

Sawyer waved his hand toward his bag lying on the floor. "Please do, but I didn't bring anything formal."

"I believe Master K has something that will fit you."

While Ciara dug around in a large armoire to find appropriate apparel for Sawyer, his watched beeped, signaling 9:00 p.m.

"Excuse me. Right at this moment the sub who is training me is pleasuring herself and I need to focus on her image."

Sawyer moved directly in front of the window again and closed his eyes, thinking about Sarah's hypnotic blue eyes, pink lips and fantastic curves. He fantasized about her undressing and slipping off her panties. He tried to imagine the look on her face as her fingers teased her clit and penetrated her pussy, all the while thinking about him. Sawyer's cock hardened under the strain of his slacks and he adjusted himself before facing Ciara.

In the time that Sawyer had focused on Sarah, Ciara had picked out a costume that any grand Master would be proud to wear. She had found a charcoal gray, double breasted suit amongst Kerian's clothing and laid it out for him. Kerian was about the same size as Sawyer, just over six feet tall and 190 lean pounds.

Sawyer eyed it and smiled. "You have fantastic taste in attire. So does Kerian. What next?"

Ciara smiled and began to undress Sawyer slowly. Her movements were smooth and fluid and it was apparent she was proficient at undressing the male form. When he was down to his briefs, Ciara's eyes scanned his numerous scars but she said nothing and asked no questions. Her hands then roamed over his muscular form – first over his biceps and down his abs. She lowered herself to her knees and rubbed her palm over his still partially erect dick and tugged at his underwear, revealing the soft hair that framed his shaft. The head of his cock poked out from the top of his briefs and Ciara grinned up at Sawyer before releasing his manhood from its fabric prison.

"You have a fine-looking cock, Master Morrison; long and thick, and the perfect size to bring pleasure without causing pain. I would be grateful if you allowed me to pleasure you."

How could Sawyer say no to an offer like that? "I'd like that very much."

"What's your flavor for this evening? Maybe there's something you've been wanting to try but been unable to?"

"Mmm, yes. I've never tried anal and it sounds fucking incredible."

Ciara's eyes lit up and a lop-sided smile graced her face. "Oh, Master Morrison, I would be so honored to be your first. Please, if Master K allows, may I be your first?" The eagerness and enthusiasm in Ciara's voice was like that of a child on Christmas day as she rose and bounced on her toes, and Sawyer tossed his head back and laughed.

"Yes, you can be my first..."

A knock on the door interrupted their discussion.

"It's Julia. Playtime will be starting in exactly twenty minutes," she stated muffled through the door.

"Twenty minutes isn't nearly enough to enjoy your body. Perhaps later, Angel?"

Ciara bowed politely, "Yes, Master Morrison."

"Will you be dressed for the evening or are you going like that?"

"That's your decision to make, Master, but please keep in mind I will be undressed shortly for the festivities that Master K has planned."

"I see. Well, I would still like to see you dress for me. Is there something in here that you can model for me?"

"Yes, Master K has every guest room outfitted with clothing. I respectfully remind you that it's your duty to choose something for me."

Ciara pointed to another larger armoire. Sawyer sifted through the expensive satin and velvet gowns and lace lingerie, and found something he liked the looks of. He motioned for Ciara to stand front and center and started by letting her long flowing hair down. It touched her lower back and he ran his fingers through before braiding it and pulling around her shoulder.

"Christ, you truly are an Angel."

Sawyer's heartbeat began to throb in his ears when her body responded to his touch and words. His hands continued to glide over her body, seeking out her pleasure points. Palming her small breast, he tweaked her nipple, making her close her eyes and moan out. Sawyer seated himself in a white leather duchess chair. Feeling a little more comfortable with his role, he instructed his slave-on-loan what to do.

"Dress for me. Give me a good show, and keep your eyes on me at all times," he said with staid calmness while looking her over seductively.

Her eyes remained steadily focused on Sawyer's chestnut irises while she put on a see-through, black strapless piece of lingerie that fell mid-thigh. The areola of her breasts could be seen and her puckered nipples strained through the fabric. Ribbon ties needed to be cinched at the back and she knelt between Sawyer's feet, keeping her head turned to the side so that her eyes remained on him. Sawyer pulled the strings of the frock tight, taking Ciara's breath away. Wrapping his fingers around her swan-like neck, he guided her head back and placed a kiss on her mouth, then trailed his lips down the curve of her collar-bone.

"I hope I'm allowed the pleasure of being buried in your ass, my obedient little slave. Are you looking forward to teaching me the finer points of anal sex?"

"I can't imagine there's anything you don't know, Master Morrison, or that I can teach you," she stroked his ego.

"We'll soon find out, won't we?"

***

Ciara and Sawyer made their way down the stone spiral stairs to the dark basement. The smell of sex, incense and leather got stronger as they neared the dungeon. When they entered the expansive room that was brightly lit by several crystal chandeliers, they were treated to a scene already in progress.

Kerian moved quietly over to them and whispered, "Some of the participants were eager to get started a little early. I like to keep my private scenes more relaxed than those at the club, and the rules and regulations that we adhere to there, for the most part, don't apply here. Of course, it goes without saying that everything here is always safe, sane and consensual. With that being said, feel free to join in at any point." Kerian must have seen the apprehension on Sawyer's face because he laughed softly and squeezed his shoulder. "Or just sit back and watch if you're more comfortable with that."

Sawyer nodded, glad to hear nothing was expected of him.

Ciara's eyes brightened and she bowed before Kerian. "Master K, Master Morrison has voiced a wanting to experience anal sex with me this evening. If permitted, this will be his first encounter of that type. I respectfully ask your consent to be allowed to pleasure him in that way."

Kerian's eyes widened with surprise. He stepped back and eyed Sawyer head-to-toe, then huffed, "A man of your intelligence and unique, good looks has never experienced the pleasure of a tight ass? Damn the vanilla world to hell for keeping such enjoyment from you. I generally save my slave's ass for my use only, but seeing as this is a special occasion, I will share it with you. In fact, I'm thrilled it's my slave that will be your first and that it will be in my home. Take her, fuck her hard and may the experience be memorable for the both of you." His eyes then narrowed and focused on Ciara. "Make me proud, my delicious little piece of fuck-cake. Give in to him in all ways as if he were your true Master."

Ciara dutifully kept her eyes and head lowered, "Of course, Master K. I would never let you down."

"Very well. Find yourselves a spot and get to it." He directed his next remark to Sawyer. "Precious will show you where all the necessities are. She'll clean everything up when you two are finished. I hope you enjoy my slave's ass; it's one of the tightest around," he winked.

Sawyer felt the blood rise to his cheeks. He doubted he would ever get used to people being so sexually liberated and speaking so openly about such private things.

Seeing Sawyer's color-stained cheeks, Kerian stifled a laugh as to not interrupt the intense flogging that was taking place only twenty feet away on a large metropolitan table. "Why the sudden shyness?"

Sawyer shrugged, unable to put his thoughts into a logical explanation.

"Would you prefer some privacy or are the rest of us free to watch?" Kerian asked.

Sawyer rubbed his chin mulling over the question. He would be more comfortable if things were done privately considering it was his first time. But then again, he would be apt to fuck more admirably if people were watching and judging his performance. "I'd prefer privacy for now. Maybe later this evening I'd be more comfortable performing in front of everyone."

"Later?" Kerian chuckled. "Do you think you have the stamina for more than one encounter this evening?"

Sawyer felt mildly offended but scoffed, "Of course, I do."

"Enjoy it while you're still young!" Kerian slapped Sawyer's back and walked away, his black and silver hair swinging around his neck.

"Shall we, Angel?" Sawyer took a hold of Ciara's hand.

"This way, Master Morrison. The lubricant, condoms and towels are over here. Where would you like me?"

Sawyer looked around the huge room and spotted a large Trousdale four-poster bed. Lascivious thoughts filled his mind at the different possibilities and positions he could take Ciara on such a large area. He pointed to the bed and seated himself on the edge when he approached it. While Ciara readied things, Sawyer took in the remainder of the room.

The brick walls were painted a deep blood-red and the floors were covered in hand-woven tapestries like those he had seen on his travels to India and other exotic locations. The equipment within the room rivaled that of things he had only read about in gothic times, from large intimidating St. Andrew's crosses, of which there were two, three queen-sized beds like the one he was on, three spanking horses of various sizes and in different locations, two large golden cages, one massive suspension rig, and mirrors on every wall and above every bed, reflecting the lights and leaving no corner darkened.

One particularly unusual looking bed caught his eye. It was made of old, distressed wood and had shackling points on every corner like all the other beds, but this one also had a large hole on the footboard that looked to be just big enough to fit a head through.

On one wall, there was an array of belts, whips, floggers and sharp, prickly sexual tools that would make the vanilla world's skin crawl and send them running for high ground or the nearest confessional. Sawyer shook his head and inwardly laughed thinking about how Sonya, a devout Catholic, would've reacted had she seen the room. She would've ended up in therapy, no doubt.

At the far end of the room and near the entrance, there was a seating area that featured two long demilune sofas made of silk mohair and silk cord trim, along with four matching club chairs. Just to the side of the seating was an elegant Lafayette Bar that featured gold marble tops on front and back bars, with gold and silver leaf finish, and illuminated shelves and a mirrored back. The room when taken in small bite sizes was lovely, but when viewing it as a whole, was staggering. The room easily contained enough equipment and furnishings that cost one year of Sawyer's earnings, even with his pay raise.

"It's a beautiful room, no?" Ciara asked as she brought over a tall, six panel privacy partition and set it up, blocking their view from the rest of the players.

Sawyer chuckled with casual amusement and shook his head. "Beautiful is an understatement; it's more like magnificent and a bit frightening."

"The same could be said about you, Master Morrison," Ciara whispered, undressing and letting her gown pool at her feet.

Sawyer's eyes lowered as did his voice when she crawled between his legs on all fours. "How am I frightening?"

She responded in a voice that was like velvet – soft and thick. "The power that you exude is fear-provoking. I'm not sure if you're even aware of it, but you give off the most spellbinding dominant vibes I've ever been faced with. Perhaps it's because it's natural and not forced. Whatever the case may be, it's alarming to think about what I would allow you to do to my body and mind if I were to give in to you."

Ciara looked shocked when Sawyer's eyes suddenly filled with fierce sparkling. He moved swiftly before she had a chance to process what was happening. Grabbing her around the waist with one hand and behind the neck with the other, he laid her body out beneath him and pinned her down on her back.

Pure, raw and unadulterated desire blazed in his eyes. "What do you mean *if* you were to give in to me?"

She was too surprised to do anything more than gasp out from the sudden submission that was being forced on her and she froze. She swallowed loudly, her eyes rapidly darting from Sawyer's mouth to his eyes, and back.

"Master Morrison..." she exhaled almost inaudibly, her voice shaky. "I didn't mean..."

Pressing his body harder against her, the air left her lungs and cut her statement short. Sawyer's hand moved from her neck down and underneath her as he explored the hollows of her back "Are you not giving in to me now? Were you not giving in to me when I sunk my teeth into your soft, delicious flesh? Tell me, Ciara." Sawyer's roving hand stilled and locked against her spine. "Is this all of you? Because I fucking want *all* of you. Now tell me, are you my slave to do with what I want or not?" Sawyer spoke calmly but with an intensity that belied his furious passion.

Ciara began to pant uncontrollably and twist in his arms on the bed beneath Sawyer. When she tried to resist him, his heart thundered in his chest and his grip tightened. There was no way he was releasing her without sampling her first.

Sawyer's attitude became lethal and suddenly his dark eyes grew wild. "Don't you dare try and resist me, Angel. You've given me a taste of Mastery and I want more. Now tell me what I want to hear," he spoke louder, his voice echoing his longing.

Ciara settled back, her body becoming limp in his arms as her eyes grew large and liquid. Sawyer's eyes in return caught hers and held her gaze steady. When the muscles of his forearm hardened beneath her, she nearly sobbed out her response.

"Yes, you are my Master, and I am giving in to you. Completely. Fuck me, Master Morrison. *Please,* take all of me."

"I will and I'll start with your ass." Eager to have the piece of Ciara that she and Kerian had offered up so kindly, it took everything Sawyer had to temper his enthusiasm. "Are you ready for me?" he asked, gliding the hand that rested on the small of her back down to her ass cheek.

A meek, barely noticeable smile curved the corners of her lips upward and she nodded. With her eyes focused on his, it was hard to miss the gleam of excitement shining in her deep-brown irises. Squeezing a cheek, he leaned down and nipped at her lace covered, hardened nipples. He rose and lifted the fabric of her lingerie over her head, exposing her body to him. Sitting up on one elbow, he took in the vision of her splendid, lightly tanned body and curves, and doing as Sarah had suggested – burned the image into his memory for future enjoyment.

As his eyes roamed over her physique, the throb of his heartbeat could be felt in his cock. Just thinking about what was about to happen made his body ache with an intense urge. Grunting sounds from just beyond the paneled partition reminded him that they weren't alone and everything around him - the setting, the smell of sex and incense, and the sight of Ciara impatiently anticipating his next move, all seemed surreal. He reached over and pinched his arm just to make sure he hadn't been roofied or was the victim of some vivid hallucination.

Becoming Sir

"Just making sure…" he waggled his eyebrows at Ciara who let out a short burst of laughter.

Gripping her waist, he gently flipped her over, bringing her pretty, small, round ass front and center. Ciara tucked her hands under her, resting them on the tops of her thighs and raised her bottom up high. Sawyer may have been an anal virgin, but he was no novice when it came to sex and a woman's needs, and though no words were spoken as she peeked over her shoulder inviting him to take her, the message her body and eyes were sending left no room for doubt – she was his to do with what he wanted.

He reached for the lube and condom that Ciara had laid out on the bedside table for him to prepare for her taking. As much as he wanted to rip his own clothes off and lunge on her like a ferral animal, he paced his movements in order to prolong his and Ciara's anticipation. He started by casually sliding his slacks off and then slowly removing his shirt. When he was down to his briefs, he rubbed his palm over his rigid shaft, delighting in the quickening of her breath and the flare of her pupils. She wanted him just as much as he wanted her and he could feel her longing radiating off of her like a blue-hot flame being stoked by desire. Finally, he removed the last piece of his clothing and when he did, Ciara graced him with the kind of smile he would happily kill for again. Reaching for the condom, he ripped open the foil packet, pinched the tip of the wet skin and slid it over himself.

Next he held the tube of lubricant in his right hand while he straddled Ciara and showered her tattooed shoulder blades and spine with kisses. When just enough time had passed to warm the lube, he squeezed a liberal amount on his middle finger and rubbed it into her ass crack. Soft whimpers came from above and her ass rose in the air further as he teased her puckered entrance and slowly inserted his finger, pushing it in as her muscles constricted and relaxed with each of his movements.

She pulled her hands out from underneath of her, grabbed a pillow and pushed it under her pelvis, bringing her rear-end higher yet. Reaching behind her, she spread her cheeks for him. The sexy, skilled casualness of her actions was almost too much to take and Sawyer feared he would shoot his load before he had even gotten to the ultimate prize. She looked over her shoulder once again and smiled as if she had read his thoughts and all he could do was return the smile she had given him.

Lifting an eyebrow, he asked, "Am I doing okay?"

A soft breathy giggle slipped past her lips as she flashed her teeth and licked her lips. "Oh, Master, you're doing more than okay. I'm ready whenever you are."

And with that, he rested the head of his cock on her opening and gently eased into her, inch by slow inch. The tightness caught him completely by surprise and he unexpectedly grunted when her ass contracted down onto him.

"I love that sound," Ciara moaned out as she ground herself into Sawyer, taking all of him deeply. "Mmmmmaster..." she continued to groan lustily.

"And I love that sound," he countered as he grabbed a hold of her waist and plunged balls deep into her tight canal.

It was the sound of wicked bliss, the likes of which he would never get tired of hearing. God, how he loved being the reason for that sound. And her ass... sweet Almighty, how he loved being inside that forbidden place. Why had he been deprived of something so breathtakingly decadent? Why had he been denied the sweet indulgence of a woman's ass when it was so clearly meant to be fucked? Watching Ciara's pink hole clutch his cock as he slid in and out of her, Sawyer knew her ass would be his unraveling.

"Oh, hell, Angel..." he gritted his teeth as he continued to thrust in and out, knowing that he wouldn't last much longer.

He tried to redirect his attention to a swirled pattern in the woodwork of the bed frame to prolong the deliciousness of Ciara's perfectly fuckable rear-end, but it was no use. The sensation of release was building hot and fast. Ciara must have sensed his impending climax because she disengaged from him and quickly pulled the pillow out from beneath her. Repositioning herself on her back, she tipped her pelvis upward, opening herself up to him once again.

"Just a little longer, Master... please..." she begged as she held her knees firmly against her chest.

Sawyer closed his eyes tightly and swallowed hard, trying to suppress the urge to come, but he knew his efforts were for naught. He just hoped that his Angel would come soon because there was no way come hell or high water he would last any longer than a few minutes, no matter how he much he tried. It felt too damned good and oh, so right.

Once back inside Ciara, he began to thumb her clit vigorously while he pumped into her over and over. She began to squirm and pant uncontrollably and as her orgasm descended on her, the muscles of her anus began to constrict almost painfully around him. His hand stilled against her pussy and without warning, his come pulsed out of him causing him to hiss through his teeth and throw his head back. A long line of grunted and mumbled obscenities followed before he collapsed onto the bed next to Ciara. Turning his head, he found her watching him and smiling bashfully while shaking her head.

"Well done, Master Morrison. I suspected there wasn't anything I could teach you."

***

Dressed and still dazed from the passionate fucking he had just engaged in, Sawyer stumbled to the bar area and retrieved the largest bottle of water that was available while Ciara cleaned up. He gulped it down, droplets of water dribbling down his chin.

"A little sex drunk, are you?" Kerian laughed from behind.

"Uh-huh" he mumbled, chugging down the last bit of water before cracking opening another bottle.

"Well, then, Precious has made me proud. I hope you found her ass sufficiently tight for your needs."

Coughing and sputtering, Sawyer wiped his mouth and laughed. "Damn, Kerian. Yes, it was tight enough."

Just then Ciara made her way over and it was hard to miss the healthy glow on her gorgeous face.

"You've made me proud, Precious," Kerian stated, pulling his fingers through her hair. Sawyer couldn't help but feel a stab of jealousy at the loving gesture that was being displayed toward his Angel. It wasn't only anal sex he had gotten from his encounter, but an intense bonding experience. Ciara had given herself over to him completely and Kerian was right, he would never feel the same about such a woman again, or look at himself in the same way.

Looking away from Kerian, her starry eyes focused on Sawyer.

"Master Morrison," she smiled and promptly redirected her eyes to the floor.

It had only been moments since their anal-fest, but Sawyer's cock hardened thinking about her svelte body and the feeling of her snug ass around his cock. He had never felt such exquisiteness as the feeling of her puckered hole clutching at his dick. He wanted to experience all of her, and that included her mouth.

"Are you ready for more, Angel?" he asked.

Kerian's eyebrows shot up in surprise. "My, my, Mr. Morrison. I guess you weren't lying when you said you go more than once. I'd be lying if I said I wasn't a bit envious of your stamina. I have the stage set if you're feeling up to scening."

"As a matter of fact, I am feeling *up* to it. I saw a few things lying around in your kinky trove that I'd like to try out if you're feeling *up* to sharing your expertise and guiding my hand."

"You know how to stroke a man's ego, Mr. Morrison! I'd be delighted!" Kerian perked up.

Becoming Sir

Gripping Ciara's elbow, Sawyer guided her to a long table that looked like something from medieval times that could have doubled as a sacrificial alter. During the very short walk, he whispered in her ear, "I want to see you squirm, Angel; like you had me squirming just moments ago. This body of yours was built for sin and decadent pleasures, and I'm thankful you were cast out from the heavens to please me." Her body shivered and a small moan slipped past her lips. "Are my words making you wet?" he asked, nipping the lobe of her ear as they paused at the side of the table.

"Yes, Master Morrison... so very wet."

"If you're a very good girl, I might taste you. Now, lie down on your back and spread those beautiful legs wide for your Masters."

Moving quickly but with the grace of a dancer, Ciara climbed atop the table and did as she was told. Music was cued overhead to the tune of Carmina Baruna, O Fortuna. He had never been fond of classical music. It reminded him too much of the kind of upper-class pricks he would rather shove his foot up their asses than to be in their company, but the song spoke to him. Maybe it was the setting or the sight of Ciara's willing, sweat-glistened body and everyone's eyes on him. He couldn't be sure exactly what it was, just that the feeling of excitement started in his toes, worked its way up to his hardened cock and settled in his brain.

He set aside several items to play with and pointed out a few others to Kerian before moving to Ciara. Leaning down, he placed his palm flat against her soft belly.

"I'm enamored with all your curves and edges, and perfect imperfections, Angel," he quoted one of his favorite songs.

A distinct quivering was felt emanating from her core and Sawyer smiled at the way her body answered to him. He had never felt so physically attracted to any one woman in his life, ever. Not his wife, not Sonya, not even his dear Snowflake. His draw to her was entirely physical and instinctual, and came from a place of pure masculinity. It made no sense – he hardly knew her, but her submissiveness had triggered something in his brain and he couldn't turn it off. It wasn't only his cock doing his thinking for him but his ego, and he was well aware of it, but he wasn't going to deny those feelings or his desires.

A low growl started in his throat and made its way past his lips when Ciara licked her lips.

"Are you ready, Mr. Morrison?" Kerian's voice broke through his aroused trance.

Sawyer hesitantly looked away from Ciara and nodded yes. He grabbed the electro double Warternburg pinwheel that looked much like a regular double pinwheel but with an electroeroticism twist. Sawyer clicked the button and touched the prickly end of it to his index finger. He felt a jolt of electricity surge through his hand when he rolled it over the pad of his finger, causing his wrist muscles to stiffen. Yes, it would work well for his needs. He smiled down at Ciara whose eyes were glassy with anticipation.

"I'm not going to bind you because I want to see you writhing with need. Don't disappointment me and make me resort to bondage. Can I count on you to keep your arms beside you, palms flat against the table?"

"I'll do my very best for you, Master," she answered with a pensive twinkle in the shadow of her eyes.

"I don't want your best; I want your everything. Now tell me that you won't disappointment me and don't make me ask again," he came back with more sternly.

Ciara cringed at the tone of his voice. "Yes, Master, I won't disappoint you."

Sawyer looked to Kerian. "Would you mind giving me a hand?"

"Of course. I'm always keen on helping a fellow Master engage in wicked play," he smiled evilly.

"The Magic Wand, will you stimulate her gently while I try this out?" he gripped the pinwheel.

Kerian nodded, retrieved the Wand, and began his sweet torture of her clit.

Sawyer set the wheel on the lowest setting and glided it over her arms in short bursts before making his way up to her puckered and erect nipples. He bent down and bit into one, redirecting her focus while he turned up the power. When his mouth left her breast, he ran the barbed device over her pebbled areola. The wetness of his saliva in combination with the electricity caused Ciara to arch her back and mewl out loudly, in turn stirring Sawyer's inner Dom. When she did so, Kerian began circling the Wand around.

Looking to Kerian, Sawyer asked, "Is she wet?"

"Deliciously so, Master Morrison," his eyes twinkled playfully.

Focusing once again on Ciara, Sawyer spoke definitively, "Don't you dare cum without my permission. Am I clear?"

"Yes, Master," she moaned.

"That's a good little slave."

Next, he reached for the Violet Ray. It was a deceptively unassuming-looking piece of equipment. After having watched Liz and John's demonstration, he had Googled all sorts of ways for sensual torture and this was one of the things he most wanted to try out. He looked to Kerian who was diligently working Ciara's pussy with a fervent and concentrated look on his face.

"Teach me, Kerian."

Kerian smiled and powered the vibrator off. Moving to the head of the table, he placed a glass tube on the end of the Violet Ray and turned it on. The loud crackling surprised Sawyer and his eyes widened with enthusiasm when a beautiful purple spark lit up the tip like that looked exactly like a mini lightning bolt. Kerian skimmed it along Sawyer's forearm so he could feel its effects. To his relief, it wasn't painful. Instead, it jolt of electricity emitted elicited a hot, tingling sensation.

"Try it for yourself, Sawyer, but be mindful of where you place it. It might sound thrilling to place it on very delicate areas, like the nipples and clitoris, but it may cause oversensitivity and even pain. Unless of course that's what you're going for."

No, pain wasn't his turn-on and he was grateful for the advice. Beginning on the larger surface areas of Ciara's body, he tested out the Ray while Kerian went back to work on her clit. He was getting a wonderful response and wondered what else could be done with the magical Tesla wand. He tried another attachment that resembled a glass comb. Cranking up the voltage, he raked the comb over her scalp, then over her hip and thighs. Ciara screamed out when he briefly touched her nipples. He liked the sound of her whimpering so much, he lowered the voltage to deliver more zaps to her breasts.

When he was finished, he massaged and kissed every part of her body that he had electrified. The experiment had only gone on for fifteen minutes or was it forever? He had no idea. Time had ground to a halt and everything around him seemed to slow down and come into crisp focus, even the music which had momentarily been drowned out by the sound of the Ray. The deep female voices rose and fell as did Ciara's with each of Kerian's manipulations of the vibrator. With his head cloudy with desire, he decided it was time to taste his Angel.

"Trade me places, Kerian, and fill her mouth while I taste her arousal."

"It would be her pleasure to be taken by two Masters. Wouldn't it, Precious?" Kerian asked Ciara, putting the vibrator aside.

"Yes... yes... my honor and pleasure," she whined.

Sawyer moved in between her legs. Her pussy was bright pink, her labia swollen and her clit rigid from all the stimulation. Spreading her moist lips, he blew up and down slowly. His eyes darted upward to see Kerian grip his Angel underneath her armpits and drag her to the end of the table so that her head was hanging off. He unbuckled his pants, slid his cock out and stroked himself, preparing to fuck her mouth.

Sawyer readjusted himself and lay on his belly, ready to partake of the buffet laid out before him. When he heard the wet sounds of Ciara's mouth being taken, he dove into her pussy ferociously, biting and sucking at her labia and inflamed pearl. He held her thighs firmly apart and circled his tongue around before slipping it into her. Loud gagging momentarily broke his concentration and he looked up to see the most glorious deep-throating ever taking place. He could see the bulge of Ciara's neck as Kerian penetrated the tight-depths of her throat and precum wet the front of his pants. He slipped two fingers into her and pumped them in and out vigorously until she nearly came undone. Slipping his hands under her ass, he tipped her pelvis upward and licked from her clit to her ass crack, his mouth resting over the hole he had fucked. He sucked at it too and poked his tongue in. It was a dirty thing to do, but he didn't give a fuck. He was in a room full of people who were not judging him so why should he care? He let go of all his feelings of shame and went with what his instincts told him, and what they were telling him to do was everything he had always been denied. It was cathartic and energizing and some unfathomable feeling of power surged through him.

He stood, kicked off his slacks and grabbed a nearby condom that Kerian had been kind enough to lay out for him. He spit into the palm of his hand, lubing his dick for another go at her ass. He guided the head of his dick to her anus and pushed gently until he felt her body relax. Slowly, he began pumping into her tight hole. Over and over, he slid his cock all the way out only to thrust into her again.

Doing his best to stay focused was difficult with the delicious sounds from above. Shaking his head, he glanced upward again. He couldn't take anymore. He had to have her mouth, too. Kerian read his thoughts, disengaged from Ciara and stepped aside for him to take over. Like a well-choreographed dance, they traded positions again, only this time Kerian began to fuck Ciara while Sawyer plundered her mouth.

After snapping the rubber off, he guided his shaft past her drool-soaked lips, he held her shoulders down, pinning her to the tabletop. He pushed past her tonsils slowly, feeling the tightening of her throat around him. Other than her ass, it was the most fantastic thing he had ever felt. She didn't flinch once and opened her throat to him unwaveringly. He propelled deeper into her throat with each thrust, pulling out on occasion to allow her to breathe and look into her eyes. Every time he did, they shared an intense physical awareness of each other, the web of attraction building with every wet, intimate, debauched moment they shared. The sweetly intoxicating musk of their bodies, sweat and sex began to overwhelm Sawyer. His heart beat wildly in his chest and his cock began to pulse in time with the music as his finish neared. His eyes darted to Kerian who was thrusting at a frenzied pace and thumbing her clit causing Ciara to squirm uncontrollably. With everything that she was being submitted to, he was amazed that still, her hands remained palms down.

"Are you ready to cum for your Masters?" Sawyer grunted.

Unable to respond verbally, Ciara lifted her hand and slapped the table.

He pulled out long enough to hear her cries of passion and gave his order. "Cum, and say my name, Angel – loud and clear. Say it like I'm the only one in this room."

"Sawyer!" she cried loudly without an ounce of hesitation.

He promptly pushed back into her, feeling his shaft hit the back of her tonsils. Two long, slow pumps later, Sawyer's seed pulsed out and down her throat. He stumbled backward and only a few short moments later heard the loud grunt of Kerian. Wanting nothing more than to throw himself onto a bed and crawl into the fetal position and sleep for hours, he found the strength to gather Ciara into his arms and carry her to the bed with him.

"I'll clean up…" she whispered weakly with cum dripping down around her mouth.

"No, you've done enough this evening, my dark Angel. Rest."

Chapter 11

Having carried a sleeping and nude Ciara to their suite, Sawyer cleaned her up before crashing next to her and slept as if he had been knocked over the head by a kinky cupid. He woke early in the morning on Saturday to Ciara's shimmering eyes concentrated on his face.

"Good morning, Master Morrison."

"I thought you'd be showered by now, Angel," he yawned.

"I need your permission to leave this bed first," she smiled, reminding him that she was no regular submissive, but a slave.

"Yes, how silly of me. By all means, make yourself pretty and clean for me. I'll join you in a few minutes."

Sawyer found his phone and quickly texted his activities to Sarah, excited to share his three-some with her.

S.M.: 8:08 AM: Your Domly One has been a very naughty boy, Snowflake.

SarahH: 8:12 AM: Good morning, Sir! I can hardly wait to hear the details. Is Ciara treating you well?

S.M.: 8:15 AM: More than well. I'm being treated like royalty. A man could get used to this kind of pampering. Last night was AMAZING. Hint: three bodies, one table. ;)

SarahH: 8:16 AM: 0.0 Two vajays and one peen or two noodles and one hoo-haw?

Sawyer threw his head back and laughed joyously.

S.M.: 8:17 AM: No noodles involved – only solid MASSIVE cocks!

He was feeling particularly happy and he could only guess it was because of Ciara.

SarahH: 8:18: AM: Lucky slave girl alert! Did you experiment with anything new?

S.M.: 8:20 AM: The Violet Ray and the electrified double pinwheel. Good stuff. I have a slave who needs attention, but I

*just wanted to say I was thinking of you. Don't forget about 1
& 9. Have a good day.*

SarahH: 8:20 AM: You, too, Domly One. :*

Sawyer jogged to the shower, eager to feel Ciara's hands
on his body.

Twenty five minutes later, he was being given a full body
massage while he sat in the duchess chair, nude. His cock was
semi-erect from all the blood flow being caused by Ciara's
skilled hands. She had just finished with his feet and was
working his shoulders as his thoughts wandered. He wanted
to know everything about the beautiful woman who had
awoken his deepest dominant tendencies in a mere few hours
of knowing her.

Grasping her wrist, he brought her around and seated her
in his lap as he stretched his long legs out leisurely.

Holding her face between his hands, he bore his gaze into
her. "What are your wants, Angel?"

"To be pleasing in all ways; to do without hesitation
those things which my Master asks," she answered quickly.

Shaking his head, he swept his thumb over her bottom
lip. "You've already made that abundantly clear, and you do a
fine job at accomplishing that, but this isn't an exam, Ciara.
Tell me what you *really* want."

With her thick dark hair hanging over her shoulders and
shrouding her breasts, her pupils roamed over his face
endlessly, her liquid eyes imploring him for some
indecipherable thing. "I want to be needed; wanted; and most
of all, cherished and loved," she whispered.

A hot ache grew in Sawyer's throat and he felt the blood
surge from his fingertips to his groin. "You want the very thing
we all seek, Angel. Yet..." he paused, his heart thumping
erratically, and his hands moving to her shoulders, "you've
chosen this path as a slave. Why not just be a submissive?"

Ciara's hands moved over Sawyer's chest, her warm
touch inviting him to caress her. He moved his hands down
the center of her breasts and around her waist, his fingers
snaking up her back and skimming the tattoos on her shoulder

blades. He tugged her to him, pulling her close to not only hear her response, but to feel it against his mouth.

With her eyes resting on his lips, she whispered her answer into his parted mouth. "Because for me, it's not enough to just be obedient. I *need* to be owned - body, mind and soul; to be guided and told what to do on every level and controlled utterly. I *need* to be overtaken. I always have. I'm not even sure where it comes from..." she paused as if pondering her response before continuing. "It starts here..." her fingertips touched the center of her belly and moved upward over her heart, "I feel it here..." then up to her temple, "and that need speaks to me here. It's who I am, Sawyer. I no longer question and deny that yearning like I used to. I've struggled my entire adult life and young adulthood with what I felt and what everyone was telling me I should and should not be. I was shunned from my family for my perceived wayward wants, but I hold out hope that someday they will accept me for who I truly am, like I have accepted who they are. I am a slave, Master Morrison; a slave to man; a slave to love and ownership, and I do not regret the choices that I have made in seeking a life that can give me my true desires."

He took her mouth with such savage intensity, Ciara's body softened in his arms and a gasp left her mouth. Forcing her lips open with the thrusting of his tongue and smothering her lips with his demanding mastery, his tongue caressed the inside of her mouth, devouring her unique taste. If being overtaken is what she needed and yearned for, then by God, he would give it to her.

Gently pulling away, Ciara smiled and answered, "Oh, and I also want to have my own book store someday; a small out of the way place that caters to the romantic and naughty-at-heart. With maybe some sex toys thrown in just for fun."

Sawyer smiled and kissed her chin. "Kerian was right: someday you're going to make some man a very happy Master, Angel."

"Some man?" she asked, her eyes hopeful, even optimistic.

He gave her a secret smile, leaving her suggestive question unanswered but commented, "A weekend with you doesn't seem like near enough time to get to know all your finer points, does it?"

"No, Master, it doesn't, nor enough time to get to know your wants."

"Perhaps Master K will be amenable to a time extension."

"We can hope, Master."

***

Saturday and Sunday had gone by in a flash and before Sawyer knew it, his time with Ciara was over, and the realization that he wanted more time with her was glaringly apparent. The afternoons had been spent talking of their losses and achievements. Sawyer even divulged a bit of the neglect he had endured growing up. Ciara had hung on his every word, but never once forced any more information out of him. He had learned of how her overzealously religious parents had disowned her when they found out about her involvement in the BDSM community. He felt her hurt and wished he could protect her from the harsh world. Wanting to defend her, he briefly considered calling them up to plead her case and to tell them to pull their heads out of their asses so they could enjoy the wonderful person that Ciara was, but decided against it.

Even with his every minute being accounted for with Ciara, he didn't miss his appointments with Sarah at 1:00 and 9:00. He had requested she send a snapshot of herself so that he could carry her to bed each night, even if it was only her image on his phone.

When Sunday evening approached, he had begun to feel torn between his burgeoning feelings towards the twenty-eight year old slave who had crept into his heart, and the flame that was still burning steadily for Sarah. Except for their desires to want to be submissive, they were completely different. But still, they both seemed to be exactly what he needed and wanted in a woman. He quickly banished the thought of having to choose one over the other. After all, he hadn't even told either of them about his murderous and corrupt past. If they knew, he dreaded what the outcome would be, and he reminded himself to just enjoy the allotted time he was allowed with each of them and to learn everything he could from their knowledge.

With his bag in hand and at the door, he was met by Kerian, Ciara and Julia. Seeing the girls standing next to each other, visions of the evening before seeped into his mind. He had watched them perform their magic on each other and they had given him and Kerian quite a show. They did, indeed, fit together like two puzzle pieces. With her eyes to the floor, Sawyer reached over and fingered her chin.

"Look at me before I leave, Angel." She stared back with longing at him and an undeniable glimmer of sadness flashed across her face. He blinked long and hard wanting to soothe her ache before mustering up the courage to ask Kerian what had been on his mind since Saturday morning. Facing Kerian, he asked, "May I speak with you in private?"

In the study, Sawyer paced near the window like a caged animal.

"What is it, Mr. Morrison. You're beginning to make me nervous," Kerian glared.

Sawyer chewed on his bottom lip and stole a look over his shoulder at Kerian. Bravely, he faced him and pushed his shoulders back. "I respectfully request more time with Angel... Ciara. Respectfully."

A cheesy grin spread across Kerian's squared and slightly wrinkled face. "Is that what you're so tense about? Hell, Morrison, I was going to suggest the same thing myself!"

Kerian laughed obnoxiously, causing Sawyer to bristle and wince at his own juvenile anxiousness. It reminded him of having to ask a father for his permission to take his daughter on a date. "Is that a *yes*?"

"Well, I'm not sure. I rather like seeing Sawyer Morrison, otherwise known as the Domly One, a little fretful. Say it just once more in that deep and concerned voice… RESPECTFULLY," Kerian mocked.

"Shit, you're just as bad as Young. And who the hell told you about Domly One?" Sawyer glowered.

"I overheard Isabel and Sarah," he continued to laugh.

Crossing his arms, Sawyer waited impatiently for Kerian's laughter to die down. When it finally did, seriousness crossed his face.

"Yes, Sawyer, I can grant you more time with Ciara, on the condition that a task be completed. This is for her sake as her training is near its completion. I had planned on doing this final test of willing and openness with her myself, but seeing as she has 'respectfully' requested to spend more time with you as well, this will be a good chance for the both of you to once again learn from each other."

Sawyer's mouth twitched into a small smile. "She asked to spend more time with me?"

Kerian rolled his eyes and waved in dismissal. "Yes, she asked and I agreed. You two are like a couple of teenagers, I swear. Next thing you know I'll be passing notes between the two of you. Now for that homework assignment - it's not going to be easy… for either of you. But, if this thing between the two of you is going where I think it is, it's going to be an excellent way to gauge if you're truly compatible."

Sawyer's body stiffened. Where exactly did Kerian think this thing was going? He had simply asked to spend more time with his Angel, Ciara, not for her hand in marriage. His breath caught in his throat and his heart began pounding as he struggled with the probability that had been alluded to.

Kerian moved to a large locked cabinet, withdrew a key from his pocket and retrieved a file. "This is the contract that was signed upon the commencement of Precious' training. It contains a detailed questionnaire, profile, and history. It's with great discretion that I loan this to you for your perusal. It also contains her hard limits. Keep in mind that these limits were set six months ago when her training began."

Sawyer listened with bewilderment and curiosity. Six months of training? He had no idea slave training was so exhaustive and time intensive.

"We have stringently stuck by these limits. However, it's time for her to grow and let go of all those old fears. I am a firm believer that yesterday's boundaries are to be crossed on tomorrow's horizon."

Some sixth sense brought Sawyer fully awake and uncertainty crept onto his expression. He didn't like where the conversation was going. Was Kerian really going to ask for Sawyer to disregard her hard limits?

"Kerian, I won't..." Sawyer barked more loudly than he intended.

Raising his hand, Kerian cut him short, his eyes clinging to him and his voice remaining calm. "Let me finish. I know this sounds unorthodox, but this is a time-honored method for training slaves and has proven good results. I assure you no one has ever been hurt; at least not on my watch or anyone who has trained that I know. I will give you a week to go over her limits. Choose only one that you can work with, and find a way to seduce consent out of her as creatively as you can. I want you to break her walls down, as well as letting go of your own fears to achieve that. This is a great opportunity for you to push both your limits and deal with your fears. I truly believe this is necessary in order to fully accept the roles which the two of you are seeking to fulfill or I wouldn't ask it. You are NOT to tell her what your end goal is, but let her see it for herself. I want her to learn that boundaries and limits are soul crushing and, well, limiting. As your knowledge of BDSM expands, so does your mind and ability to accept the things that once seemed unthinkable, allowing for a deeper connection of who you really are. Tell me you understand."

Sawyer turned away, wearied by indecision. Yes, he understood, but he still didn't know if he could go through with it. Suppressing the bile rising in his throat at the thought of not spending more time with his Angel and doing the things that Kerian was asking, he silently nodded and took the file from Kerian's hand.

"Very well. I wish you the best of luck. When coming up with a plan, I encourage you to consult me and other experienced Doms for ideas and instruction, and have someone in close proximity as a safety measure. One last stipulation: I would like the experience to be filmed so that I can critique it at a later time with Ciara."

Sawyer's face creased into a deep frown. There was no way in hell he was putting down his sexual escapades on film, most especially not one where he would be pushing the limits of some unknowing innocent whose only goal in life is to be pleasing. He knew the kinds of things that could happen if a video like that got into the wrong hands. Kerian's eyes seemed to shine with awareness of his unspoken reluctance.

"After everything that has happened with the Young's, I understand your hesitation, Sawyer. The video will never leave your hands and you will be present when I view it so that it can be destroyed immediately afterwards if you so choose. This is a necessary step. Viewing yourself after the fact gives you a fresh, emotion-free perspective on the scene. I would even go as far as inviting your other trainers to watch it and give their opinions. As an experienced sub, Sarah is an excellent resource and her thoughts would be helpful, too, so utilize her knowledge as best you can. I want this to be a memorable event for both you and Precious."

Oh, it would be unforgettable, all right. He just hoped the memories it evoked would be fond and not horrific, and that Ciara wouldn't end up hating him after everything was said and done.

Chapter 12

An hour later, Sawyer was unpacked and at home. The following morning would be spent dealing with Jameson Christopherson and he needed to get in to his dark headspace. With all the stress of the upcoming week fraying his nerves, a shot or three of Jack D. sounded good right about then. He went into his closet and pulled down a box that was hidden away in a dark corner on a back shelf and pried open the lid. Gliding his fingers over the cool, clear glass and black label, he could almost taste the liquor and feel the smooth burn down his throat. It was difficult to remain coherent when the alcohol was so close to him and he gripped the neck as his tongue slicked over his top lip. Just one drink, that's all he needed to see things more clearly. Who the hell was he kidding? The booze never made things clearer; it only blurred the lines of reason and logic.

Squeezing tightly, his knuckles blanched and his skin squeaked over the glass as his eyes roamed over the bottle, watching the brown liquid slosh around inside. The sound of his own deep breathing and his mouth smacking anxiously filled the small closet. Suddenly his phone chirped in the other room, bringing him back to reality. He quickly lidded the box and pushed it back to its hiding place and let out a loud sigh.

He found his phone and smiled to see a message from Sarah.

SarahH: 6:47 PM: Sir! I have wonderful news! I have been accepted into the Denver Community College RN program for next spring!

Sawyer immediately dialed her number. He wanted to hear the joy in her voice and take his mind off of his worries. And the Jack Daniels.

"Oh, Sawyer, isn't it great?" she answered enthusiastically after only one ring.

"It's fantastic news. I had no idea you wanted to be a nurse. What other secret desires have you been keeping from me?"

Sarah's smile could be heard, "Just a few others. I would've told you, but we really haven't spent any time together other than at the club and via phone." She was right and it was completely unacceptable. She was one of his trainers after all. "I'm not complaining, Domly One. You've been very busy learning and I'm working extra hours anyway to try and save for school so it's worked out okay," she quickly added.

"No, it's not okay. We need to spend time together, in person. There are going to be no more excuses. I have something important to deal with at work tomorrow afternoon, but I suspect I'll need some company afterwards if you're feeling up to it."

"I'll do my best to trade my shift and be available. Do you have something in mind or can I plan on cooking a nice dinner for you?" her voice resonated with zeal.

"I'll let you plan to your heart's content. We can eat here."

"I look forward to it. So have you had a chance to think about the contract anymore?"

"Honestly, I haven't. My Angel has kept me busy this weekend. She's an amazing woman."

Sarah's voice lowered only slightly, but noticeably compared to the excitement she had exuded only moments before. "I'm glad you enjoyed yourself. Will you be seeing her again?"

A knot rose in Sawyer's throat. "Yes, this coming weekend. I've been tasked with a monumental undertaking at Kerian's request."

Sarah immediately brimmed with curiosity. "Oh? A test for her training?"

Chuckling nervously, Sawyer shook his head. "How did you know?"

"I know her training is almost over, and it was just a lucky guess. How exciting to be involved with something so important. I would love to help out any way I can. I mean..." she stammered. "... I don't mean to be pushy. I just mean if you need an extra hand or advice or anything."

"Absolutely. Your opinion is crucial to me and especially with what's been asked of me, I need all the help and support I can get."

She let out a long audible breath and the volume of her voice dropped, "Thank you, Sir. It feels good to be needed again."

The slow burn in his chest for Sarah warmed his insides. Her sincerity and honesty was crushing. How could he choose? He swallowed hard and decided to share a bit of his dark past with her.

"Sarah... Snowflake... there's something I want to tell you..." he started out apprehensively.

"Mr. Morrison, I didn't mean to insinuate anything or try to make you feel something that isn't there. I was told by others that your weekend with Ciara was promising and that things look to be going in a possible committal direction. Please disregard my letter from previously. It was wrong of me to say such things so early on. I want only what's best for you and if that person is Ciara, your Angel, then I... I really am honored just to be involved in some small way to make that happen."

Sawyer sat dumbfounded. Perhaps he didn't need to choose – Sarah was making the decision for him. And maybe that was a good thing considering how wishy-washy he was being regarding the two women. He chewed the corner of his lip tensely. Sarah spoke determinedly, but the tone of her voice alluded to something else, or was he just imagining things? Caught up in Sarah's words, he forgot what he had started out saying.

"Thank you, Sarah," he stated softly yet firmly. "But that letter meant a great deal to me and the last thing I intend on doing is disregarding it. I haven't made any decisions about anything and that includes Ciara. My course is still unknown."

"Of course it is, Mr. Morrison," she responded without inflection. "Is dinner still planned for tomorrow?"

"Why wouldn't it be?" he sniped, put off by Sarah's withdrawal from him.

There was a long silence before Sarah finally responded in a husky whisper. "I'll let you know if I'm unable to trade my shift, otherwise, just text me when you get done with work. I'll keep my appointment for nine this evening and be thinking of you. Good night, Mr. Morrison."

***

Fourteen hours later, he and Murphy were pulling into the parking lot of an upscale office complex. It was go time. The flight to Atlanta had been just long enough to give him time to think about Ciara. He had spent the remainder of his evening the night before going over her history and profile. She was truly a remarkable specimen. She was well-educated with a Master's degree in English Literature and had even been bestowed the honored MAGS Distinguished Masters Thesis Award. He would be lucky if she considered him as a candidate for her Owner. Beauty, intelligence, and a kind and serving soul - what more could one man ask for?

He had avoided going over her hard limits and decided he would save that for another night. Perhaps tomorrow. Or the next. No, he couldn't put it off if he was to plan out his seduction of consent diligently. Sarah's input was vital and he decided at that moment to discuss it with her that evening during dinner.

"You okay over there?" Murphy cut in.

"Yes. Let's do this. You wait here."

"I'll survey the area. How much time should I give you before I come busting balls?" he asked.

"No busting balls today, Murphy; just a little persuasive discussion."

Murphy's craggy, aged face contorted into a sarcastic, sour grin. "I remember the last time we went to have a 'discussion' with someone," he tapped on Sawyer's chest, directly over the now-healed gunshot wound.

"That was a fluke. This is going to go smoothly. I can feel it in my bones."

"If you say so, but you have exactly twenty-five minutes until I'm hauling ass in your direction to end the 'discussion'," he turned on his heel and strode off in the opposite direction.

Sawyer smiled as he watched Murphy disappear. He had a soft spot in his heart for that old man. At the receptionist's desk, he watched as someone asked for Jameson and was promptly denied access. He seated himself away from the secretaries' view and waited. Fifteen minutes later he texted Murphy that it may take a little longer than twenty-five minutes when the scumbag finally made his appearance and headed for the restroom. Sawyer moved swiftly, giving Jameson a light shove before locking the door behind him and pushing the man down into a long bench.

"What the hell is this? I ain't into men, you faggot!" Jameson bellowed.

"So in addition to being a lying, cheating waste of space, you're a foul-mouthed bigot?" Sawyer growled, crossing his arms over his chest and glaring down at the man. He fought the urge to knock his teeth through the back of his head for even suggesting that his worthless ass would be his type. "Now shut your mouth, you pudgy, out of shape, used-up bastard," his deep voice boomed and echoed against the tiled walls.

Jameson's black eyes widened and then narrowed just as quickly. "Who the fuck are you?"

Easing his stance and widening his step, Sawyer answered coolly. "That depends on how you respond. If you do exactly as I tell you, then I'll simply be a ship passing in the night. I'm a man you don't want to piss off and if you decide to do anything other than what I've told you to do, I'll be your worst fucking nightmare and the person who will bring the world as you know it crashing down around you." Sawyer stood wordless waiting for some kind of reaction. When Jameson huffed and attempted to stand, he poked four fingers into his sternum harshly and pushed him back down. "You haven't heard what I want from you yet."

"I don't need to hear anything. Now back off before I wreck that pretty face of yours," he scoffed.

Sawyer's eyebrows went up and he smirked. "I thought you weren't into men." Just as quickly as his smile appeared, it was gone. "Lose interest in Emilio Ibanez's estate. It's not a request. "

Jameson pulled back and glared up at Sawyer incredulously. "So that's what this is about?"

Sawyer was quickly losing his patience and his heart rate spiked. To hell with doing things the old school way. Staring into the pompous jackass' eyes, slicing his throat from ear-to-ear and watching him bleed out slowly suddenly seemed like a viable and enjoyable option. Lucky for the man, Sawyer didn't have a knife handy or else it would've happened.

"Shut up and let me finish. I won't repeat myself. If you don't back away from contesting the will, everything about your life will be exposed. *Everything.*" The man waved his hand and looked away as if he had nothing to be ashamed of. Leaning down into the man's face, Sawyer gritted his teeth and hissed acidly, "Let me rephrase, Mr. Christopherson: everything about your *other* life; the one where you snort coke on a regular basis and free-base with hookers; the one where you deal in cash under the table, avoiding your financial and legal responsibilities as a US Citizen; the one that your wife, adult children and the law would be less than forgiving of. Am I making myself perfectly clear? I hope so because I'm a man who keeps my word in all things and when I say that I will fuck your life up so badly a gun to your head will sound better, take heed the warning."

The man's breath hitched and his face paled under the fluorescent lighting. His portentous stare turned into something pathetic, and his shoulders slumped when he realized the seriousness of Sawyer's threat.

"One hour is the time frame you have to get it done, starting..." he glanced at his watch, "Now. Drop what you're doing, make the call and End. Your. Involvement," he ground out with finality.

Jameson sat frozen, causing Sawyer to lunge abruptly at him, grabbing his lapels and forcing him against the wall.

"Speak!" he barked.

"Y... yes," Jameson stuttered.

"That's yes, *Sir*."

***

"How did the meeting go?" Dylan asked impatiently.

"As well as can expected. Have you received any news yet?"

Dylan sighed, the agitation in his voice spilling over. "No."

"Well, give it a few minutes. Jameson still has sixteen minutes left until I deliver these files to the intended recipients."

"Wait... there's an incoming call..."

Waiting, Sawyer flipped through the files nonchalantly, his mind wandering back to Ciara. And Sarah. Had he misread her feelings toward him? No, he doubted that. He was adept at reading body language. And the feelings evoked by the kiss they shared were undeniable. It was magical. Sawyer rolled his eyes at the cheesy thought.

Dylan clicked back over. "Well done in thoroughly scaring the shit out of Jameson. He's backed off and no blood was shed in the process. I'm proud of you, Morrison."

Sawyer rolled his eyes, "Let me just say it was a difficult task for me not to kill that SOB."

Task. The word reminded him of his upcoming homework assignment.

After his flight back to Denver, Sawyer decided to take an early day and go over not only Ciara's hard limits, but the temporary contract between he and Sarah. Sarah had done a thorough job with the contract and he only needed to fill in the blanks where necessary.

161

Making himself a snack, he settled in to finally look over the hard limits which were not listed out, but written in. Kerian had stated to choose one, but coincidentally there was only one hard limit to choose from.

"I'm deeply afraid of being unable to breathe. My last boyfriend was a mean drunk. He knew I was mildly asthmatic and would hold me down and try to strangle me as some sort of cruel joke. The idea of a hand near my throat or any sort of breath play is an unbreakable hard limit for me."

Sawyer's heart sank and his stomach cramped at the thought of breath play. He had read about it briefly and knew that it carried serious risks, including death. It was ironic how just hours before he was considering violently murdering someone, yet again, but doing something like sexual asphyxiation under a controlled setting was completely out of the question.

He picked up his phone and dialed Dylan and who had no sooner answered when Sawyer started talking.

"Do you have experience with breath play?"

"Yes, but it's been a long time since I've seriously done it, years actually; before Isa. Why? You interested in that?"

"No, but I've been asked to push Ciara's hard limits. Damn Kerian," he said in a dull and troubled voice.

"That's a tough one. Well, I can speak with Isa and see if she's up for a demonstration. We've only played around with it very mildly, but for you, I'm sure we can work something out."

"Thanks, Young. I hate to ask..."

"Why? You know you can ask for anything. It's good for us to venture out into new things, too, so this is a good chance for us as well. I'll call her right now. When did you want start practicing?"

"I have to scene with Ciara this weekend so as soon as possible. I have a dinner date with Sarah tonight but how about tomorrow?"

"Sounds good. I'll see you at work tomorrow and we can go over things."

Right after his conversation he texted Sarah and sent the company driver to pick her up while he made his condo presentable for female company. Just as he was unloading the dishwasher, she arrived. Opening the door, he was flooded with the same feelings he had felt the night he kissed her. He had missed her eyes. Inhaling deeply, he savored her scent. He had missed that, too.

"Snowflake," he whispered seductively, his cock hardening to nearly full-staff. What was it about her that evoked such intense emotions? He had no idea and he didn't care either. Clutching her upper arm, he pulled her into the doorway and wrapped a hand behind her neck, bringing her so close he could feel her breath on his mouth.

"Mr. Morrison," Sarah stated softly, her brows knitting together.

"What happened to *Sir*?"

"Okay. Sir. I have everything I need to make you dinner right here," she looked down at the bags in her hands. "I hope you like seafood alfredo. It's one my specialties," she moved past him, pulling out of his grip.

Inside, she laughed a little. "Actually, it's my only specialty. I wish I made it more often but seafood can be pricey as you know."

"I hope this didn't set you back too much. In fact, let me reimburse you the cost," Sawyer replied.

Sarah's eyes flashed embarrassment. "I didn't mean to suggest I wanted you to pay me back. I've been working plenty of overtime and I can afford this."

"Of course. Thank you, Snowflake," he quickly let the subject go, but made a mental note to never assume such things again. Sarah worked hard and he didn't want her spending her money on him. "Do you need my help with anything?"

Sarah visibly relaxed and began to set everything out. "No. Just point me in the direction of your cookware and I'll get everything ready."

After putting on some music, he settled into his oversized leather chair, turning it to face the small kitchen so he could watch Sarah at work. On occasion, she would glance up at him and smile. He was deep in thought about his upcoming scene with Ciara when she chimed in.

"That chair fits you, Domly One. It's like a king's throne," she giggled.

"Yes, I guess it sort of is. Why don't you hurry up and come join me. There's enough room in this thing for two," he grinned waywardly.

"The King's throne isn't meant to be shared," she commented without any emotion. "And neither is the King. Not that you care," she stated more softly, turning away to wash her hands.

Sawyer stood and walked over to Sarah quietly, taking her by surprise when he whirled her body around. "Would you care to elaborate on that last statement?"

Sarah brusquely pulled out of his clutches and pushed past him, "No, I wouldn't. Take it however you want."

Reeling from Sarah's coldness, irritation quickly set in. Was this jealousy on her part? If it was, then why the hell wouldn't she just state her feelings. She was the one who was pushing the issue of open and honest communication, after all.

They were under contract and her actions were unacceptable. No, actually they weren't under contract – yet. He walked into his office and retrieved the contract. A few minutes later, he found Sarah setting the timer on the pasta.

"Shall we sign it?" he asked, handing her a pen.

Without saying anything, she grabbed the pen and scrawled her name, and again turned away from Sawyer. He penned his name and without any further hesitation, he grabbed a hold of her wrist and swung her around.

"Now that it's official, I can act on it. Being my submissive you agreed to show an attitude of respect and reverence to me at all times, and refusing to answer my question after you made an ambiguous remark, in my eyes, is not only disrespectful, but rude. I'm not a mind reader so if you have something to say about how you feel, then say it. Also, I don't like you pulling away from me and turning your back on me. How many swats do those actions deserve, Sarah? One? Two? Is that enough?" he asked crisp and clear, his heated stare burning into her.

Sarah's bottom lip trembled but she shook her head in response. "No, Sir, that isn't enough."

"You're the experienced one here, so how many is appropriate?"

Her eyebrows pinched together and she glared at the floor, "Ten, Sir. Ten sounds fair," she sniffed.

Jesus. Ten? He wasn't sure that sounded reasonable either. No, five would have to do. Okay, six just to make it an even number. Oh, hell. There was no going back now. She had written the damned agreement and now they would both have to abide by it.

"Six will suffice. Let's do this."

Sawyer seated himself in the chair and motioned for Sarah. Standing directly in front of him, she removed her panties and lifted her skirt over her hips. She then leaned over his knee, tucking her feet under one of his legs and hiding her face against her arms that were folded neatly over the arm of the chair. Damn, her ass was a fine sight. Having her splayed out on his lap was an exhilarating thing. It wasn't only empowering but arousing, despite the reason for her being there.

He caressed her bottom and almost waivered. He'd rather fuck her ass than punish it. Why did she have to be so disrespectful to him? Counting down from ten slowly, he slowed his heart rate, and steadied his breathing. He swept her long hair over her shoulder and out of the way and brought his hand up.

Peeking over her shoulder, Sarah's bright, tear-filled eyes met his. "Shall I count them out, Sir?"

"Yes, that's fine," he whispered, not giving a shit one way or the other. He held his hand in midair for what felt like an eternity. He didn't want to harm his Snowflake, but knew it had to be done. She had broken her word and consequences had to be faced.

"Do it, Sir. The soft, fleshy part or the crease is where it's most effective without causing damage," she stated confidently, the tone of her sweet voice motivating him onward.

Finally, he brought his hand down, the sting on his palm and the sharp skin-on-skin sound making him wince and Sarah gasp out.

"One," she sputtered out when she caught her breath.

When he pulled his hand back to see the damage he had done, the red imprint on Sarah's ass simultaneously tore at his heart and invigorated him. But still, he knew there was no way in hell he could've delivered ten swats. He would be lucky if he could go through with the six he had proposed. Pushing forward, he smacked her five more times, alternating each time where he swatted her and each time, Sarah dutifully counting them out.

When it was all over, he yanked her up and into his arms and buried his face in her neck, surprised and even dismayed that he had been able to go through with what he had just done.

"Don't ever make me do that to you again. Promise me you'll follow the rules…" His voice was stern but caring. When she didn't answer him quickly enough, he pulled back and held her head between his large hands. "I won't tolerate breaking the rules, Snowflake. Now tell me," he said more firmly.

Sarah's kind gaze bore into him as tears trembled on her eyelashes. "You're a true Dom, Sawyer Morrison; kind yet stern, and a man of his word. I fear there is nothing I can teach you."

A pain squeezed his heart and he tried to swallow the lump that had formed in his throat, "Don't say that. I have so much more to learn. I need you to teach me."

"Don't be angry, but what I just did was to test your ability to follow through. I would never truly disrespect you the way I did and it wounded me to have to go through with it, but..."

Sawyer sat back, his mouth twisting into a frown. "You did that on purpose to try and get me to punish you?"

A look of sincere sorrow passed over her features and shimmered in her eyes. "It was a trial, Sawyer. Please don't be angry with me."

Taking in a sharp breath, Sawyer blew it out slowly. He hated to admit it, but it was a necessary evil in his training. He had proven not only to his trainer but to himself that despite what he thought about his own abilities, he could go through with punishment if push came to shove and if his dominance was questioned. Her actions also proved to him that she wasn't jealous like he had initially thought and he couldn't help but feel more than a little let down.

"I should give you the remainder of those swats just for putting me through that," he finally spoke, shaking his head.

Sarah stood, placed her hands on her thighs and pushed her ass out to him. "It would be my pleasure to accept them, Domly One," she managed a tremulous smile.

Faced with her plump and supple ass, he was unable to resist and flicked his wrist as he spanked Sarah two more times on each cheek. Still watching him, a loving curve touched her mouth and a small excited moan slipped past her lips. Instinctively, his hands lightly traced a path over her exposed skin and down her ass crack, the tip of his index finger resting over her anus.

Becoming Sir

"I was introduced to anal sex this weekend, Snowflake. I've taken quite a liking to it," he leaned forward, his tongue skimming where he finger had just been. Sarah's thighs squeezed together and she attempted to straighten up, but his hands found the soft lines of her waist and hips, and rigidly held her in place.

"No worries, I would never take that which isn't offered to me. Now, spread your legs and stay just like this, Sarah, and let me enjoy the vision of this glorious ass in front of me while I examine you thoroughly."

"Yes, Sir," she wet her lips timidly, watching his every movement.

Sawyer ran his thumb deliciously up and down her ass crack to her clit, pausing briefly to dip it into her pussy. He then spread her ass cheeks and leaned in to slip his tongue into her pussy from behind.

"Oh, God, Sawyer..." she groaned when his tongue explored her depths.

"You taste pure and clean – like freshly fallen snow," he smirked at his own comparison to her nickname.

His lips traced a sensuous path of ecstasy over to her hips where he delivered several small, gentle bites. Abruptly, he stood her up and spun her around. Staring up into her eyes, he nibbled her smooth, hairless labia, the tip of his tongue slipping in and tickling her clit. Just then, the timer dinged loudly, startling them both and making them laugh.

Sarah promptly redressed and went to the food to finish preparing it. Completely hard, Sawyer excused himself to try and get his erection under control. When he returned, the food was decoratively plated at his small bistro table.

"Do you have anything stronger to drink than tea?" she asked, peering into the refrigerator.

He rubbed the back of his neck then ran his palm over his face. Should he tell her about the whiskey in the closet? If he told her then he would have to explain why it was there and about his alcoholism.

"Yes, there's some J.D. in the closet."

Sarah gave him a half-smile. "The closet?"

"Yes, it's that way. Top shelf, far back corner," he waved in the direction of his bedroom.

She laughed and disappeared. Upon her return she was not only holding the bottle of liquor, but the old guitar that had been stored on the same shelf.

Sawyer smiled at the sight of it. He hadn't laid eyes on it since Serena's passing.

Sarah cracked the seal on the alcohol and the smell immediately hit him, making his mouth salivate.

"So what's the story on the guitar?" she asked as she began to pour a glass of whiskey.

"My wife gave it to me as a wedding gift, along with guitar lessons. She always wanted to marry a rockstar," he laughed. "I hated the damned thing..." he stopped, looking down at his fingers and rubbing his thumb over the pads. The calluses were long gone but he remembered the pain of earning them well. "I grew to love it, though. Serena loved it, too. I used to play it for her when she was going through chemo."

When he looked up, Sarah was standing immobile and watching him thoughtfully with two half-full glasses of Jack in her hands. Her deep-set eyes were large and wet, and she cleared her throat before finally lifting her arm to hand him his drink.

"I can't, Sarah; I'm a recovering alcoholic. But if you want to drink, feel free. I just can't join you."

She dropped her hand to her side again. "Don't be silly. If you're not drinking, then neither am I," she stated resolutely, walking over and emptying the glasses into the sink.

Sawyer cringed at seeing the Jack go to waste but was touched at the gesture. Sonya consistently drank alcohol in front of him despite his addiction, and never once gave a second thought to how difficult it was at seeing her do it.

Facing him, confusion flashed in her eyes. "Why do you have whiskey in your house?"

He shrugged guiltily and seated himself at the table. "It's a good reminder of where I don't ever want to end up again."

Placing her hands on her hips, she raised her brows suspiciously. "That's not the only reason, though, is it?"

Picking up the fork, Sawyer poked at his pasta, not wanting to answer the question. He felt exposed once again. Sarah seemed to have that effect on him. Glancing up, he moved his shoulders in a half-assed shrug and puckered his mouth.

"Okay. Then we'll just have to get rid of it. Do you want to do the honors or should I?" she asked, grabbing the bottle and moving to the sink.

Sighing loudly, he moved next to her. He knew it had to be done. Hell, he should've done it himself eons ago.

"I'll do it," he replied, taking the bottle from her hands and quickly pouring the remainder of the liquid down the sink.

Sarah's eyebrows went up in shock at how swiftly he moved and Sawyer huffed, "What?"

"Nothing. I just thought..." she shook her head.

"Well don't think. Just because I'm an alcoholic doesn't mean I don't have the balls to do what needs to be done," he sniped defensively.

"A *recovering* alcoholic," she politely corrected.

"Whatever; same fucking difference," he grumbled.

"No, it's not, Sawyer, and you know it," her accusing voice stabbed the air.

"Are you done lecturing me, Sarah?" his tone was inflamed and thunderous.

Her eyes darted around the room nervously before resting on the floor. "I didn't mean to lecture."

Sawyer suddenly felt like a complete shit. "Fuck..." he breathed out. "I'm sorry. I just hate talking about my issues. You're right; it isn't the same."

"You don't ever have to apologize to me, Sir. Simply acknowledging that you were mistaken is enough. I'm sorry for pushing you," she countered timorously.

His hand lightly touched her chin. "Trust me when I say I need to be pushed."

In one forward motion Sarah pressed against his chest, wrapping her arms around his waist and hiding her face in the fabric of his linen shirt.

***

Post dinner discussions began and Sawyer was eager to get Sarah's take on his upcoming scene with Ciara. He read to her Ciara's one and only hard limit and she gave him a probing stare with something flickering far back in her luminous eyes.

"I have experience with breath play, Sir," she stated matter-of-factly, her voice carefully colored in neutral shades.

His lips thinned and his eyes narrowed. "What are you suggesting?"

"I'm not suggesting; I'm stating a fact. If you want to learn from me, then use me. We're both sane and consenting adults, Sawyer. If you want to wait for Dylan and Isabel, that's fine, but I'm sitting here in front of you, willing and ready to begin your lesson," she regarded him with intense analysis.

"But…" he tried to come up with an excuse, but could think of none. "How much experience do you have?" he was finally able to ask.

"Compared to whom? To you? An immense amount. It was one of Master Doug's fetishes."

He hadn't been prepared for her response and fear, cold and stark, washed over him. What if he hurt her? Or worse… killed her? Sawyer closed his eyes and leaned his head back, his mind congested with doubts and worries. What if he couldn't stop himself in time? What if his dark headspace overtook him?

"You won't hurt me, if that's what you're afraid of. I know my limits. You need to learn to trust, Sawyer; not just me, but yourself. Just hours ago you didn't think it possible to punish me. Oh, Sir, don't you know that on the edge of fear is where trust grows?"

He was momentarily speechless in his wonderment of Sarah's confidence in him. But it was false confidence as far as he was concerned if she didn't know his past and why he was fearful of experimenting with something so dangerous.

He drew in a deep breath and forced himself to respond. "I need to tell you something first before we go forward. You can decide if you still want to go through with this only after you know everything about me."

Chapter 13

Sarah became instantly interested and moved closer to Sawyer. He turned his face away and physically withdrew from her. She might retract her statement of him being sane once she knew all the facts. After a long pause during which he struggled for the words to say, he gave in to the inevitable and confessed in three simple yet tortured, quiet words.

"I'm a murderer."

He glanced at Sarah to see intense astonishment on her face as she stared at him, tongue-tied. After another protracted and painfully quiet moment, he forced himself to face her, wondering why the hell she wasn't hauling ass in the opposite direction.

"Say something," he demanded.

Her mouth dropped open. "I'm not sure what to say without you first explaining what that statement means."

He clenched his mouth tight, the muscle in his jaw quivering from agitation at the whole situation. "A statement like that doesn't need further explanation, does it?"

Blinking rapidly, she gave his face and body a raking once over. "Of course it does. You say 'murderer' as in present tense. Are you a serial killer or vigilante?"

Rolling his eyes, Sawyer chuckled. "No, I'm not that kind of murderer."

"Then what kind are you?"

"The kind who's murdered a lot. On the orders of others. When I worked for the The Agency. Even a few after," he answered in clipped sentences as the thoughts came to him, hoping that his admission wouldn't send Sarah running to the police. Of course the CIA would deny his employment so it's not like anything would ever come of it if she did.

"So you *were* a murderer; not you *are* a murderer," she plunged on, obviously not as shocked by his statement as he had expected her to be.

"Semantics, my dear," Sawyer answered, his vexation with her response clearly evident.

"Since we're coming clean, I should tell you something about myself, as well. I'm a cheater and a liar," she fidgeted with the ruffled hem of her shirt, her voice dropping in volume to barely a whisper.

Sawyer bristled and shifted in his seat. "What do you mean?"

"Before I married Master Doug, when we were still dating, things had gotten bad between us. I was so unhappy. We hardly spoke or had meaningful physical contact. I'm sure he was miserable, too, but he never let on. Or maybe he did and I just didn't see the signs..." she stared off into the distance. "I cheated on him. Worse than that, I had an affair. When Doug found out, he... he..." her eyes welled up and she swallowed hard, "...he forgave me. He said it was both our faults for not being honest with our desires and wants. It's what got him interested in BDSM. He forgave me, Sawyer. Can you believe that? I still can't." She dabbed the corner of her eyes with the back of her hand. "I didn't deserve his forgiveness. I cheated and lied, but he loved me anyway..." she smiled and tucked her hair behind her ear, "and we learned about BDSM together and exonerated each other of the hurts that we caused one other, and he never held it against me. And that wonderful man eventually married me. Me, Sawyer, a cheater and a liar. He married a cheater and a liar..."

"Stop calling yourself that," he cut in, responding in a critical tone, his dark eyes searching her gloomy face.

"Why? Isn't that what I am?"

"No. You made a mistake, that's all. You're human."

"So are you. Don't you get it? I'm not a cheater, I *was* a cheater. I was a different person then just like you are now. So you see? You're not a murderer, you *were* a murderer. Or is it still just semantics, dear?" she responded with light sarcasm in her tone.

He smiled and lifted his eyebrows at her. "Is that sarcasm I detect, Ms. Henderson? Because I believe that's grounds for punishment."

She turned away embarrassed and shook her head, but the seriousness of the situation was still lingering in the air. "I appreciate your opinion, but you're wrong. First of all, you're comparing apples and oranges. Second, I'm still the same man I was then with the same feelings; I'm just a little less quick to pull the trigger than I was before. And though I'm not proud of my actions, I'm not ashamed of them. And I'm sure as hell not sorry for the lives I've taken."

He paused, momentarily confounded by the sparkling passion in her eyes. He had just admitted he would kill again if he had to, but she showed no fear. Reaching out, Sarah touched the top of his hand, the warmth of her skin sending tingling sensations over his entire upper body. No. He couldn't accept her touch and pulled his hand away. Maybe if he clarified things a little more she would take his admission more seriously.

"I've done atrocious things, Snowflake. Ghastly, brutal things; bloodied and buried men without compassion or conscience; seen and done vile things you can't even fathom; covered my tracks; and lied to the only person who meant anything to me to hide it all. Trust me when I tell you my dark headspace isn't somewhere you want to be. Doesn't that bother you in the least?"

Taking in a quick breath, she let it out slowly and dropped her eyes to the floor. His heart sank. It was the same look Sonya had given him not so long ago right before things ended between them.

"Yes and no. Do I like what you've done? No, but those things are in your past and it's not my place to judge the decisions you've made. I was under the impression you were seeking to change your life. Was that a lie?"

Raising her eyes, Sawyer scanned them for some kind of revelation into what she was thinking and feeling, but once again they were like the ocean - deep and unfathomable. "No. I do want to change my life."

"So then you're not the same man, are you?"

Sarah's dogged stubbornness was exasperating and all he could do was shake his head and sigh. He was the same man. Why couldn't she just accept that?

"Why are you telling me all of this? Do you want me to run the other way? Are you looking for an out? Is that it?"

Sarah's question stunned him and the surprise was hard to hide in his voice. "Of course not. Do you think I wanted to tell you about this side of me? No. I had to. I simply don't like bringing up my past because of the scrutiny and unwarranted fear it causes in people," he commented with heavy irony.

"You just said it yourself: *unwarranted* fear. And why is it unwarranted?"

Sawyer thought long and hard when realization hit him, "Because I don't want to harm everyone, just those who truly deserve it and those who have harmed the ones I love."

"And that just goes to prove that you're valiant at heart. Does knowing all of this change how I feel about you? In all honesty, yes, but not so negatively that I can't get past it. It takes a brave person to be truthful. Do I still trust you? Yes, undoubtedly. If you wanted to hurt me, you could've done it at any point tonight. You also could've harmed Isabel and even Ciara, but you didn't. It's been a very revealing night, Sir, and it's a lot to take in, but my decision remains the same and my offer still stands. I'm here for you to learn from, take this opportunity or leave it."

Sawyer shook his head once more. He had never considered himself valiant at heart, much less brave. But who was he to dispel Sarah's image of who she thought he was? She was eager to teach and please him, and he was more than willing to learn from her and accept her pleasure. No, not just willing – craving and longing for what she could do for him.

***

Preparing to test his mental limits and learn from Sarah's vast experience, Sawyer dressed down in loose-fitting running pants, socks and a tank top while she unclothed herself down to her bra and panties, and spread out on his bed.

"It's times like these I wish I had my own dungeon," he commented.

She giggled, raised her arms above her head and grinned. "Dungeons are over-rated. A good quality, under-mattress tie-down set and waterproof sheets are all you really need to get the job done."

"I'll have to look into that," he laughed as he picked out a slow intense song for the occasion.

"I have one that I'd be happy to donate toward your educational endeavors if you're interested. It might as well get put to good use, and since there's no Master in my foreseeable future, it's all yours."

So Sarah had made the choice for him. Standing at the foot of the bed, Sawyer watched her closely, slightly put off by her statement. He had never misjudged a situation so badly in his life. After everything they had shared, it shouldn't have surprised him that she didn't want a future with him.

Lifting her head, Sarah gave him a puzzled look. "Is something wrong?"

"I just thought…" he gritted his teeth. "Are you sure about this?" he changed the subject.

"Yes. Since I won't be able to speak, I'll touch your chest or forearm as a signal to stop action. Come closer and straddle me," she instructed.

He reached for his phone and cued *Love Songs, Drug Songs* and *Inconsolable* by X Ambassadors.

He needed the music to calm him. The song began and he let the sexy words wash over him before climbing onto the bed. He did as he was told, placing his legs on either side of Sarah's chest as she lay splayed out on his queen-sized bed. Taking his hand, she guided it to her throat as he wrapped his long fingers around her neck.

"I'll keep my hand on yours for starters. Master Doug used to say it was all in my eyes, so keep a close watch on them. Gently, squeeze, like this..." she applied pressure over his hand, her breath hitching slightly and her eyes rolling back. He was mesmerized by what he was seeing - his hand wrapped seductively around the delicate neck of a beautiful, willing participant. Who would've ever thought something so disturbing could be so erotic and exciting.

"Yes, like that," she squeaked out lustily, her body twisting beneath him. Only a few seconds later, she released his hand. When his grip loosened, she took in a slow deep breath.

"God, that feels so good, Sawyer," she panted out. "Again, a little harder and longer this time. Wait for my sign."

Sawyer's cock hardened when Sarah once again guided his hand to her neck and applied pressure to her carotid artery. He thought taking Ciara the way he had felt powerful, but it didn't compare to what he was feeling at this moment. How could he be aroused by something so unsettling? Conflicted by his feelings of shame and arousal, he did his best to brush them off like he had with Ciara. It was time to awaken his true sexual desires and give Sarah what she was undeniably turned on by.

Slowly, his grip intensified and Sarah's gaze drifted to some other place. The color of her eyes reminded him of the sea, shimmering like pools of deep blue, still water. His eyes darted back and forth between each of her eyes, seeking out the sign that he was delivering too much pressure, but he saw nothing and began to worry maybe he had missed it. He attempted to loosen his hold, but Sarah mouthed the word 'more.' Her eyes widened infinitesimally and her pupils flared. In a flash she released his hand and touched his forearm. Immediately, he let her go and she inhaled sharply.

"Oh, Sir," she began to cry.

Dismayed, he pulled her up by the shoulders and held her against his chest.

"Are you okay?" he whispered.

"It's been so long since I've felt this good; too long. You're strong hands feel so amazing around my throat. I'm so close to coming, please do it again, this time on your own."

Sawyer laid her back down, his eyes scanning her face, then body. Again, he had misinterpreted the situation.

"You're an ever changing mystery," he beamed down at her.

"I'm no mystery; I'm just a simple woman with complex fantasies and fetishes," she batted her tear-covered lashes at him.

"I thought this was Master Doug's fetish?" he lifted one side of his mouth in a wry smirk.

"What my Master loved, I learned to appreciate and even love. Please, Sir, again?" she begged.

"You look nothing less than stunning when you beg, Sarah," he growled, snaking his hand up to her throat intentionally slow and teasing. After he repositioned his hard body over hers, his other hand slid between them and into her panties, seeking out her clit. "There it is…" he licked his lips, pressing his thumb against it firmly.

Wrapping his long fingers around her neck one final time, he slowly began to clamp around her throat, his eyes piercing into her, watching closely. Sarah's breathing halted the harder he squeezed, her lashes fluttering wildly and her body writhing beneath him, eager for his touch. An unknown potent emotion surged through him when he felt Sarah's heartbeat against his fingertips in a way that alternately thrilled and frightened him.

Sawyer didn't think it was possible for Sarah to look any more enticing than she had only moments before, but there it was – the look of complete surrender making his pulse skitter and his brain fuzzy with lusty intoxication.

As he searched her eyes, they exchanged a look, and suddenly he could feel the air in the room shift - like the way the atmosphere changes right before a fierce storm. He could feel the storm's power twist around his heart as his fingers clenched tighter yet, causing his cock to throb and his body to ache with an intense need to control her. He wanted to tie her down and fill her roughly and nothing less than her quivering release would satiate his hunger.

Circling his thumb over her wet nub, a tormented groan escaped her lips and her eyes rolled back for a split second before focusing on his mouth. Her body began to shiver and a barely visible flare of her pupils signaled for him to free her. He withdrew his hand and Sarah's chest heaved as she gasped for breath and screamed out, her orgasmic roar a heady invitation to give her more. And, God, how he wanted to give her more. He had entered his dark headspace, even if only for a brief moment, but this time there was one major difference – there was Sarah's whispered voice and loyal eyes beckoning him back into the light.

Rising up, Sawyer hauled Sarah into his cradling arms, tucking her curves neatly into his contours as she continued to pant and cry from her massive orgasm.

"You've given me my first true taste of ultimate power, Snowflake," his raspy, hushed voice whispered into her ear. "Stay with me tonight so that we can take the time to explore, arouse and give each other pleasure. Stay with me and teach me more."

"Yes, Domly One... yes... yes," she smiled up at him.

Chapter 14

While Sarah slept, Sawyer made a quick trip to a clothing store not far from his condo to pick out something for her to wear seeing as she hadn't been prepared for her overnight stay, as well as some fruit from a local market.

Once back at home and seated in his King's throne, he began writing ideas for Ciara's scene. Seduced consent, albeit sexy sounding, seemed a bit deceiving. Semantics, he laughed to himself.

Ciara had written that she had a mild history of asthma so he would have to be prepared with some kind of medication in case she was to have a flare up. Also, he needed to speak with Kerian about his past. He suspected when his past wrongdoings were made known, Kerian would change his mind about allowing him to perform something as risky as breath play with Ciara.

He had already spoken of his bloody past with Sarah, so the initial sting of having to speak about it was gone, but it was still distressing to think about having to do it again. Before he had a chance to rethink his decision, he dialed Kerian's number.

"Mr. Morrison!" he answered. "Working hard on your homework assignment?"

"Absolutely. You're a shit for making me do this. You know that, right?"

Kerian laughed loudly and spoke away from the phone. "Sawyer Morrison has called your Master a shit after I shared Precious' ass! Can you believe the gall?" He coughed and deepened his voice. "I have no idea why you would say such a wretched thing."

"Right. Anyway, there's something I need to speak to you about. I feel this information is something that should be disclosed in order for you to make an informed decision before allowing me to test Ciara's limits."

"You're always so somber, Sawyer, but, fine, speak up."

Taking a deep breath, he closed his eyes. "I was an assassin for the CIA for many years. I... If you want me to back away from Ciara... I..."

"I see. Well thank you for sharing this information with me..." Kerian cut in.

"Let me finish. I'll tell you the same thing I told Sarah: this isn't a case of 'I was a different person then.' I'm the same man now that I was then. I've also done heinous things post CIA. It's not something I'm proud of, but it was my duty and job, and other than the regret of having to lie about my actions to my wife and the ones I care about, I don't regret my actions. The men I killed deserved to die and if I had to do it all over again, I wouldn't change a thing. There. I said it. Now, if you want me to back away from Ciara, I'll respect your decision."

There was a short moment of silence and Sawyer wondered if he had been disconnected or hung up on. "Are you there?" he asked after checking his phone to make sure the call was still in progress.

"I'm here. Are you finished?" Kerian asked without emotion.

"Yes, I think so."

"Now it's my turn. First: thank you for sharing this information with me. Second: I already knew about your past, but the fact that you shared it with me on your own only proves what I and everyone you care about already knows - you're trustworthy and will make an excellent Dom or Master someday. Hell, you already are."

How the hell did Kerian know? Had Young revealed his secrets to him? No, he doubted that. Young was also trustworthy.

"How?"

"I'm a man with friends in high places, Mr. Morrison, and the Dark Asylum is my life's work. I don't allow just anyone through my doors and I insist on very thorough background checks being done on all patrons before accepting their membership applications. I never would've offered you

Precious, Sarah, or any woman for that matter, if I hadn't known everything about you. And I most certainly would never have asked that you to push a trainee's hard limits without delving into your background and knowing what kind of man you are. I'm a shrewd businessman and knowing everything about my members is not just good business but good manners, and the gentlemanly thing to do when given the honor and trust of a submissive or slave."

Sawyer couldn't resist a smile. Well, damn. Sarah hadn't balked and neither had Kerian, and he felt a little ridiculous for having made such a big deal about everything.

"Precious is very special, Sawyer, and I didn't come to the decision lightly when asking you to push her hard limits. Her training has been unusually drawn out and because of that, my cherished Julia and I have grown more attached to her than any other who has crossed our paths. She's gifted and intelligent, and unlike any other trainee I've ever had the pleasure of guiding. My two beloved slaves hold a special place in my heart..." he sighed as if pained thinking about relinquishing her to another man. "Anyway, I digress," he quickly pulled himself together. "Was there anything else you wanted to discuss about your upcoming scene?"

"Yes. Would you like to be present?"

He chuckled lightly. "Of course, but it would only hinder your abilities in breaking her walls down. When she begins to feel panicked, and she will, she'll look to me for help and I will be unable to provide it for her in order for her to overcome her fears, leaving her feeling betrayed. I wouldn't be able to live with myself seeing that look of hurt in her eyes, especially knowing how abandoned by her family she feels. Having another person present is a good idea though, just so she has some sort of reassurance."

Sawyer could think of only one person he wanted there. Sarah. Not only for Ciara's comfort, but for his own.

"Also, does she have medication for her asthma? I will need that handy in case she has an attack."

"Excellent idea. You've really been thorough, haven't you?"

"I'm doing my best, Kerian."

"And your best is all that I will accept and nothing less, Mr. Morrison. I'll send over some of my thoughts and ideas via email and speak with you at the end of the week. I'm going to insist that you spend the entire weekend with her again in order to gain her full trust, if that's possible, before scening with her on Sunday. Good night and, again, thank you for your honesty."

***

Nearing 11:00 p.m., Sawyer was finally finished with his homework and ready for some sensual playtime. He cut some fresh fruit, caramelized a bit of sugar, and filled a bowl with ice cubes. Next, he brought out his emergency candles and placed it all on a tray. He crept into his bedroom as quietly as possible and lit the candles and placed them on the nightstand. Tip-toeing to his closet, he brought out three of his best silk ties and a dark-brown, worn leather belt, laying them on the bed next to Sarah. His eyes wandered around his bedroom, searching out more play things. The flame of the candle glinted off a pair of platinum cufflinks that were lying on his night stand and wicked inspiration hit him. He touched the sharp edge of one to his fingertip noting that the prickly end would work well for the sensual sadism he had planned. He smiled and placed it next to the other items.

After undressing, he turned up the heat in his condo to a sweltering 90 degrees, wanting to see Sarah sweaty and uncomfortable while he teased and pleased her body. While he waited for the air around him to heat up, he found the perfect song to play, *Stay the Night* by Zedd and Hayley Williams.

Seated on the edge of the bed, he watched and waited, wondering what Sarah was dreaming about. Her eyelids flicked and she mumbled something unintelligible. Tracing his thumb over her bottom lip, he leaned down and kissed the corner of her mouth.

When the air became sultry, a fine layer of sweat beaded on her forehead and she kicked off the covers.

"Snowflake," he whispered while gliding his fingers down the center of her glistening double D's.

Sarah's eyes fluttered open and strained against the darkened room.

Ghosting his fingers down her arms, he gripped her wrists and pulled her arms above her head in one swift motion, the corners of his mouth ruffling into a sinful grin. "Want to play?"

Without saying a word she returned his smile and nodded compliantly, her eyes gleaming brightly and reflecting the glowing light that flickered nearby.

"Be a very good girl and lie still for me, okay?"

Again, she only nodded. Reaching for his favorite fandango pink, paisley printed tie, he slipped it around her eyes, tying it tightly and shielding all light from her vision. The next two ties were used to secure her ankles to the footboard, and the belt he used to bind her wrists together.

She breathed lightly through parted lips with each of Sawyer's movements, small moans occasionally slipping out. He pressed his mouth to her throat and flicked his tongue over the bend of her neck. With every lick of her sweat-covered skin, he tasted her acquiescence. It was delicious and entrancing, and his need for her grew more.

Hovering over her and staring down at her covered eyes, he asked, "How much do you want me, Sarah?"

Her bottom lip trembled, "More than I want to admit."

"Show me."

***

Sawyer woke hours later to the sound of out-of-tune guitar strings in the distance. Unsure if he was still dreaming, he reached an arm out only to feel an empty bed next to him. Rising, he followed the sound and found Sarah in the darkened living room sitting in his large chair with her feet tucked beneath her and awkwardly strumming the guitar. He watched her quietly for several minutes, fascinated by the fire that she stoked within his heart. The serenity that she evoked within him was the thing he longed for even more than her beauty and curves.

"Let's tune it," he commented, sitting next to her and taking hold of the instrument. When she attempted to stand, he pulled her down next to him, their bodies pressed tightly together. After tuning it by ear, he wrapped an arm around her shoulders. He placed the guitar between her arms again, guiding her hands and fingers into the D chord position. Sarah curled into the curve of his body, allowing his instruction. They sat wordless like that for several minutes as he continued to move her fingers into place through several mellow chords. Memories of Serena washed over him and his body stilled.

Looking up at Sawyer, Sarah's eyes glimmered with understanding and she touched his mouth. "I'm sorry for your loss," she whispered, the light that was filtering through the large window making her ethereal features glow. "If it's not too much to ask, can you play something for me?"

Unable to deny the heartfelt request, he gave her a tentative smile and took the guitar from her hands. "Only for you, Snowflake."

He played a few chords absent-mindedly and suddenly grinned widely. He knew just the song to play. Without further delay, he started plucking the strings to the upbeat tune *You're the Shit 2 Me* by Elvis Orbison. His deep, rich voice resonated through the small condo and Sarah's eyes widened with shock from the lyrics, but the joy on her face was purely genuine.

"You're the kind of girl that just might get me fired. You're so fucked up, but you're the shit to me..." he sang on, enjoying the stunned and cheerful look on her face as he serenaded her. "I know it sounds foolish, but I really get the feeling that we were meant to be..." he sang louder than before, losing himself in the moment and the look in her sparkling eyes.

Without warning, Sarah jumped up and began swinging her hips in time and dancing around in only her panties and bra, all the while smiling radiantly.

"You have the most delightful taste in music," she giggled wildly.

Sawyer paused briefly to join in laughing but finished the song in full, his mouth dry and parched when he was done. Sarah took the guitar from his hands and set it aside, then threw herself onto Sawyer and hugged his neck tightly while straddling him.

"Thank you, Sir. Thank you..."

He took her face in his hands and kissed her passionately. "No, thank you, Snowflake. I've haven't been this content in a very, very long time."

Chapter 15

Sawyer sped home from work, impatient to see his Snowflake. She had the day off and they were looking forward to a night at the Dark Asylum to demonstrate his newly found talent at breath play. With all the hands-on training Sarah had provided him, it wasn't even necessary for Dylan and Isabel to help. They had been practicing all week for his private scene with Ciara, but he was excited to try his hand in front of an audience to get their collective opinion.

During his drive, his thoughts drifted to the previous week and how it had been spent with Sarah at his condo. It hadn't taken much persuading to get her to stay and they had decided it would be a good exercise in learning his role as a Dominant while having his submissive on hand at all times. She had brought over work clothes and he was more than happy to chauffeur her around. It not only allowed him to be in control and know her whereabouts at all times, but being responsible for her safety gave him a sense of purpose.

With built up vacation time, Dylan had insisted he take a few days off to get as much practice as possible with breath play and he was grateful for it. It not only gave him more time with Sarah, but ample opportunity to get hands on training from her and a few others who had experience at the club.

He and Sarah had worked out the upcoming scene together and had even gone as far as rehearsing it in the privacy of his bedroom. Time-and-time again she had submitted to his every whim and never shied away when he wanted to try something new. They had put to good use her under bed restraint system and waterproof sheets, and Sarah had been correct: they didn't need a dungeon to make playtime memorable.

Always, she was a beacon of light and knowledge, and he soaked it up in full. She had taught him that there was no need for him to be rough, raise his voice or use force; that he could gently lead and dominate, and she would follow.

Ella Dominguez

They learned each other's darkest secrets, their sensual intimate yearnings shared by only the two of them as they talked about the fetishes he had always thought too taboo to mention. Perhaps someday when he had a submissive of his own, he would get the opportunity to try them.

Even though they hadn't engaged in sexual intercourse, they had tasted each other's sexuality and pleasured each other night-after-night. Of course Sawyer had wanted to be with Sarah in that way, but knew she wasn't ready for that step. It made no difference - their bond was greater than the mere act of sex.

The previous night Sarah had finally broken down and spoke of her husband's death. They had been trying to get pregnant just before Doug had been in a head-on collision. He lingered in a coma for nearly three weeks before finally succumbing to his massive head trauma. Sawyer's heart swelled after her revelation because he knew how tough it was to speak of such things, and he felt privileged that she had shared such pain with him. Sawyer could feel her anguish when she spoke of all the things she regretted and that which she wished she would've done before his passing. He knew all too well those exact feelings. If there was any way he could take away the pain she was still dealing with, he would.

In turn, he had talked about his loss. He had even told her of the hell he had gone through in Serena's last days. He had never spoken about that time in his life to anyone or about the devastation he had felt which watching her take her last breath and not being able to do anything for her except to whisper his undying love into her ear. He cringed when he thought about how the tears had come unbidden and how they had both wept and held each other. Still, it had been liberating to finally grieve his wife's loss in a way that wasn't destructive to him.

Feeling calmed in Sarah's arms, he had finally given in and revealed his childhood, and the neglect he had suffered. It was a difficult thing to do, but she held him and kissed each of the scars that covered his body, and never once showed him pity.

He couldn't believe everything that had happened in only five days with Sarah. It had felt like so much longer.

When he arrived at home, he found her waiting by the door on her knees. It was an act of capitulation he had grown to treasure in their short time together. He moved past her without saying anything, laying his briefcase down on the counter and removing his coat before he addressed her. Touching the top of her head, she responded by lifting her face.

"I've missed you, Sir," she smiled.

"Of course you did, Snowflake," he lifted one side of his mouth in a half-smile. "All good submissives miss their Dominants when they're away. Did you play with yourself at 1:00?"

"Yes, Sir, and I'm eager to cum for you."

He licked his lips and rubbed his hand over his dick. "And I'm ready to make that happen."

Unzipping his pants, he pulled his cock out and stroked it. "Play with yourself while I fuck your beautiful mouth."

Without another word, Sarah slipped her hand under her dress and past her panties while her full lips caressed his aching and rigid shaft. He pulled her hair back away from her face to get a better view of her lips wrapped around him and held her head as she bobbed up and down.

"That's it, take it all, Snowflake," he whispered, pushing her head down gently and holding her steady until she became breathless.

She looked up and they shared a moment of connection. Her eyes began to water when he hit the back of her throat but she never once gagged. After several minutes, her body stiffened.

"Cum for your Sir," he commanded, knowing well the look of elation on her face. Her hand moved frantically as she moaned out, closing her eyes tightly. When she was finished, she placed both hands on his thighs, concentrating all her efforts on his cock. Another several minutes later, her wet, greedy mouth had satisfied him and his hot load hit the top of her mouth without warning. She swallowed his gift and he sank to his knees, the wind temporarily knocked out of him.

"Thank you, Sir," she licked her lips.

***

Isabel and Sarah chatted the entire drive to the club. They were gushing over the gift Sawyer had given Isabel; a white-gold bracelet with an engraving with three simple yet meaningful words that he felt personified her: spirit, beauty, and imagination. He had bought it weeks earlier as a thank you for all the changes she had inspired in both he and Dylan, and also for introducing him to Sarah. The sexual tension was crackling all around them and his nerves were getting the best of him, but he was happier than he had been in years.

They were all laughing at a lame joke Dylan had just told as they made their way to the door of the establishment when Sawyer heard a familiar voice calling out to him. He turned and came face-to-face with Sonya. He had been holding onto Sarah's hand, but the surprise of seeing Sonya momentarily stunned him and he dropped it.

He smiled at her, hope filling his heart that perhaps she had changed her mind about BDSM, but those feelings were short-lived when she opened her mouth.

"It's time to end all this nonsense, Sawyer. I want you to come with me right now," she said unflinchingly, looking him dead in the eyes.

Sarah immediately hid behind him to avoid whatever fallout was about to happen.

Taken aback by Sonya's off-putting remark, he met her gaze boldly. "Excuse me?"

"You heard me. We're here to take you home," she pushed her chin out, her hands clenched stiffly at her sides.

Sawyer was confused and becoming quickly irritated with her demeanor. Who the hell was she referring to anyway?

"We?" She motioned to a tall, thin, attractive man who looked the same age as himself standing several feet away and within earshot. "What do you think you're doing?" he asked, agitated by the man's presence and her comments.

"Intervening," she replied in seriousness.

He almost laughed at the absurdity of her remark. His eyes darted to the man again and he looked him over closely. "Who is that?" he gestured with his head.

"A friend," she answered frigidly.

Crossing his arms over his chest, he gave her a pointed stare and responded just as coldly. "I see you've found your next whipping boy."

"What's that supposed to mean?" she asked, affronted, resting her hands on her hips.

"Don't play coy. You know exactly what it means. It means you've found someone who will jump when you say jump and follow your orders without question. Why the hell else would he be here when he knows nothing about me?"

The man moved forward defensively and Sawyer shot him a murderous look. "Don't come any closer," he growled, pointing his finger at the stranger's face.

Sonya dramatically flung her hands onto his shoulders and got in his face, "Sawyer, please. You need help getting out of this situation. That's all we're here for."

The ridiculousness of her statement made him unable to hold back his ironic laughter anymore and he let out a breathy chuckle. "What is it that you think I need help getting away from? BDSM? Where do you plan on taking me, Sonya? Bondage lover's anonymous?"

At that moment, a cold gust of wind moved past them causing Sonya to shiver. Despite being irritated with her, his protective instincts kicked in, and he took his coat off and wrapped it around her shoulders to warm her. When he did, her features softened.

"Can't you see how wrong all of this is?" she asked glumly.

Isabel moved forward to place a kind hand on Sonya's shoulder, obviously touched and saddened by the look of misery on her face, but Sonya promptly jerked away.

"Are you happy?" she snapped. "Do you see what you and your husband have done?" Isabel winced and shrank away. "You and your filthy paintings!" she continued shouting.

Dylan moved in, ready to fiercely protect his submissive. "My wife's 'filthy paintings' have brought your art gallery a windfall. Who the fuck do you think you are talking to her like that?" he ground out between gritted teeth.

Sawyer put a hand up and without taking his eyes off of Sonya, he spoke, low and deep.

"I've got this."

He clutched the lapels of the jacket wrapped around Sonya and pulled her close, forcing her to focus her attention back onto him. He had heard enough. Outraged at her hurtful words towards his friends, his heart beat erratically and his breathing came out harsh and ragged. Glaring down into Sonya's heated gray eyes, he ripped into her, his smooth baritone voice belying the fury he was fighting to contain.

"Have I ever disrespected you, Sonya? Have I ever spoken to you negatively or said or done anything unkind to you?" She stood frozen, her eyes wide and her mouth parted. "Answer me," he barked. She shook her head. "Has Isabel or Dylan ever hurt you in any way?" Again, she shook her head. "Then what gives you the right to say such cruel things to them or me?" Sonya stood motionless and unblinking, her eyes nearly popping out of her head. "Do I look like I'm being forced to do something I don't want? Does it look like my arm is being twisted into being here?" Once more, she stiffly shook her head and the edge to his voice lessened. "I'm here because I want my life to change for the better. I wanted you to be a part of that and to share my past with you, but instead you chose to bury your head in the sand and to judge that which you know nothing about."

Her bottom lip trembled and her eyes shined with tears. As cross as he was, he couldn't stay angry with her and he eased his grip. She cared enough to show up and even though it was for the wrong reason, he knew she had acted irrationally because she was concerned for him.

"Jesus, Sonya, I don't need a fucking intervention. Can't *you* see how right this is for me?" he asked, his voice a husky whisper. Pushing her brown and silver, wind-blown hair away from her eyes, he skimmed his thumb down her cheek. "Sometimes our balance has to be upset and our course reset in order to help us navigate to our final destination. This is my final destination and where I was meant to be. I've never wanted anything more and No. One. Is making my decisions for me." Sonya started to shake her head again in disbelief, but he gripped her chin and held her steady. "You of all people should know that my mind is my own. I'm never going to be the man who follows your orders or be your whipping boy."

She cast her eyes down and buried her face in his chest, a sniveling sigh heard muffled against him. "I never meant for you to be that. I only want what's best for you."

"It's not up to you to decide what's best for me and it's time for you to accept that," he stated decisively.

Still pressed into him, she let out one last pitiful sob before straightening herself up. She handed him back his coat and let out the deep breath that she had been holding in.

Fingering her chin, he narrowed his eyes and gave his final order. "Now you're going to apologize to Isabel and Dylan for what you said. Then you're going to say sorry to my date for having frightened her."

The appalled and dazed expression on Sonya's face almost made Sawyer laugh out loud again, but he suppressed the urge. "I'm not letting you leave here until you do," he finished.

Knowing Sonya's stubbornness would keep her from acting on his order, he firmly pushed her body toward the Youngs. Isabel was tucked into Dylan's arm and peering out timidly while he was glaring angrily down at Sonya.

Sonya picked at her fake nails nervously and tried to back away, but Sawyer halted her escape with firm hands on her shoulders. Standing behind her and out of her view, he winked to Dylan and Isabel and an ornery smile briefly flashed across his face.

"Do it, Sonya, or else I'll drag your ass into that club and make you watch a flogging scene." Peeking over her shoulder and raising fine, arched eyebrows, she huffed in protest. "Or perhaps I'll flog you myself seeing as you clearly need discipline and I've taken a liking to that sort of thing."

Sonya inhaled sharply, wrinkled her nose in horror and pulled out of his reach, but summarily apologized, albeit less than sincere. She then faced Sarah and made her amends, and quickly retreated to the man who had pussed out and was hiding in her car. Just as she opened her car door, Sawyer called out to her. Lifting her face to him, he gave her a sympathetic smile.

"Take care of yourself, Lady Sonya."
***

The night had been one of good conversation and shared knowledge, and he wondered why he had waited so long to go through with his training. The scene with Sarah, as always, had calmed his nerves after the drama with Sonya.

The highlight of the night had been the Youngs' announcement of Isabel's pregnancy. He couldn't believe he was going to be an uncle. Or something like that. A bruncle? He laughed quietly to himself.

Everything seemed to be falling into place and it was an exhilarating feeling, but as Sawyer walked Sarah to her front door, he felt as though something was ending and a shiver of sadness rippled through him. Standing on the porch while she unlocked the door, he stared at the full moon in the darkened night sky.

Snowflake. The name formed on his lips unconsciously. It wasn't so long ago that they had shared their first kiss in that very spot. He felt her arm slip into his and glanced in her direction.

She was staring at the moon as well and had a pensive, heartrending look on her face.

"Speak," he touched her ruby lips.

"I can't help but feel sorry for Sonya. She let a good man slip through her fingers and she knows what she lost. She looked so sad..." she sighed gloomily.

"You're so kind, Sarah," he leaned down, leaving small kisses all along her lips and jawline. "I guess we should say goodnight," he said quietly, knowing he had to be up early and at Kerian's first thing in the morning.

"Should we?" she asked, tilting her head back and peering at his face.

The beginning of a shy smile tipped the corners of her mouth. Her pull was magnetic and his arms encircled her, one hand on the small of her back.

She put her arms around his neck and breathed out, "Please, Sir, stay one last night with me before you give yourself to Ciara."

His emotions whirled and skidded, and his senses reeled as if they had been short-circuited. He had never said he was giving himself to Ciara, or anyone for that matter. Why then would she assume such a thing? He let out a deep sigh, but drew his face near to hers.

"Yes, one last night," he answered just before his lips captured hers.

His mind relived the velvet warmth of their first kiss and every one after that. Backing her into her home and into her small bedroom, Sawyer eased her down onto the bed. The outline of her form could be seen only faintly in the darkened room. Gently he lifted her dress and yanked the lacy cup of her bra down and traced the circle of her breast with a fingertip. His eyes traveled over her body and his hands slid across her silken belly.

As he removed his tie, Sarah moved instinctively, raising her hands above her head and crossing her wrists in anticipation of his wants.

"You know your Sir well..." he smiled, dipping his head down and skimming her sensitive, marbled nipples with his teeth. "...but right now I want to feel your hands on me. All of me."

His tongue made a path down her ribs to her stomach while one hand slid down her waist to the swell of her hips. Passion pounded the blood through his heart, chest and head when Sarah spread her legs for him.

Nipping at her panty-covered mound, he held her gaze and breathed against her pussy, "I should probably apologize in advance for the ungentlemanly and filthy things I plan on doing to you. Like ripping the clothes off your perfect form, tying you down to within an inch of your life, and fucking that intelligent brain of yours out. But I'm not going to because I would be lying if I said I was sorry for doing it. And sorry, I am not nor ever will be."

"It's been too long since I've been with a man. Take me, Sir, and make me forgot just how long it's been."

Oh, he would make her forget. He was a man of his word and did exactly as he said he would by ripping her panties from her body roughly, the fabric disintegrating under his strong hands. Next, he pulled her dress off in one fluid motion above her head and tore at her bra, leaving all her clothing in a crumpled heap at the side of the bed.

Sarah clawed at him frantically, tearing at his clothing and panting like a wild animal. When they were finally naked, he reached over and flicked the lamp on so he could see every part of her physique in vivid clarity. He took in all the beautiful details of her body as if he were photographing her with his eyes. Her heated and languid eyes burned into him in silent expectation, and he couldn't hold out any longer. He positioned himself between her legs and sank into her with one purposeful thrust, causing Sarah to moan out and thrash her head. The wet skin-to-skin contact and the sound of her voice was more intoxicating than any alcoholic beverage or drug, and Sawyer knew at that moment, with Sarah beneath him, submitting to his will, he would never need another drink again.

He lowered himself and buried his face in her tits, his grunts and moans smothered in her soft flesh as he pumped into her. Sarah's hands found his hair and her nails grazed his scalp sending shivers down his spine.

"Sawyer... my Sir," she breathed out.

Her hands then cascaded down the length of his back to his ass where she squeezed and dug her nails into him. The thrilling pain surged through his thighs and he ravaged her mouth, their tongues twisting together in rhythm like lovers on a dance floor. All of the sensations assaulting him were pure otherworldly bliss and electrifying.

Grabbing her around her waist, he flipped onto his back and hoisted her on top of him. She straddled him and planted her feet on the bed on either side of his thighs and lowered herself back onto him. She lifted herself slowly to the tip of his cock only to lower herself and engulf his dick completely, torturing him with her casual pace.

Sawyer watched her closely as she fucked him sweetly, her eyes fixed on his shaft as she impaled herself deeply over and over.

"What is that you're so focused on?" he asked as if he didn't know the answer.

Sarah gasped and looked up when he raised his pelvis and thrust up into her, breaking her concentration.

Her cheeks flushed the same color scarlet as her lips and she smiled, "I forgot how good my pussy looks being fucked."

"Such a dirty mouth, Snowflake," he smiled, pushing himself up on his elbows to get a better look. The shapely vision of her naked body taunted him and her words were crude, but she was absolutely right. "I concur, but not just your pussy, Sarah; every part of you looks good being fucked."

It had been too long since he had such a meaningful connection. He had fucked Ciara and Sonya, but it wasn't the same. It was powerful on both accounts, yes, and even more so with Ciara, but not this intense. His attraction to Ciara was undeniable and the pull he felt toward her irrefutable, but Sarah... his Snowflake... His bond with her was deeper, tangible, devastating... and something else... Something he didn't dare speak.

His hands seared a path over her breasts and up to her neck. When his fingers gently clamped around her throat, she cast her indigo eyes on him. A wicked smile touched her lips and her mouth soundlessly formed the word 'yes.'

Sarah's body was built to be taken by him. Like this. Deep and dirty. Wet and hard. Forbidden and filthy. Intimate and sensual. He would give her what she craved - total domination, and she would give him what he could no longer live without – utter submission.

Chapter 16

After having fallen victim to the numbed sleep of a satisfied and worn out lover, Sawyer woke early. He stretched and yawned loudly, the world around him spinning and careening on its axis from his night with Sarah. He dressed quietly and seated himself on the edge of the bed, watching her sleep. The thought of saying goodbye to her left his body feeling as if he were half ice and half flame, and his brain a mixed hodgepodge of confused feelings.

Sarah's eyes popped open and she sat straight up, panicked for a brief moment until she saw him. Letting out a loud relieved breath, she gripped her chest. "I thought you had left without saying goodbye, Master."

Sawyer's mouth dropped open. The term Master had been strictly reserved for Doug and he wondered if Sarah even realized what she had said. A floodtide of emotions washed over him and he cleared his throat nervously.

"I would never do such a despicable thing and I should paddle your backside for thinking so lowly of me," he half-kidded.

She smiled impishly and rolled onto her belly. Pushing her bare ass out at him, she glanced over her shoulder. "If it pleases you, Sir."

"Maybe just one," he laughed, bringing his palm down onto her bottom swiftly and catching her by surprise. She shrieked and flipped back over, rubbing her ass briskly and her eyes rounded as wide as saucers.

"You offered!" he bellowed.

"I didn't think you would really do it," she fake pouted.

The room grew silent and she stood and robed herself. A look of tired sadness flickered in her eyes, but she forced a smile.

"Ciara is waiting for you, Sir. Be gentle with her."

Sawyer gave her an ironic accusing smile. "Do you really think I would I be anything less?"

Her eyes brightened and her mouth upturned into a guilty smile. "I didn't mean..."

He placed a finger to her lips, "I know. I'll see you on Sunday. I'll be focusing all my attention on Ciara, so our normal scheduled activities will have to be put aside. Tell me you understand."

He hated having to miss their 1:00 and 9:00 appointments. They were part of a cherished routine they had fallen into and he did love his routines. But he knew it had to be done. Ciara was to be his only focus. Sarah lowered her eyes and nodded, but he knew he had wounded her and he suddenly felt cruel for insisting on it. He tipped her head back and kissed her forehead and trailed his fingers sensuously down her arm to try and comfort her.

"Forgive me?"

She offered him a merciful smile and wrapped her arms around his waist. "No, Sir, forgive me. My disappointment is selfish. I know you wouldn't have asked if you didn't feel it was important."

"You're always the picture of perfect submission, Snowflake. Thank you for understanding." His words made her visibly relax and she offered him a sudden arresting smile, throwing his balance off. He shook his head to clear his thoughts and got back to business. "Our scene is set for 3:00 p.m. I expect you to be there a little early to help me set up."

"Of course." She reached for a folded piece of paper on the nightstand and placed it into his pocket. "I've written you something and I ask that you not read it until tomorrow before your scene."

Sawyer reached into his pocket and touched it, wondering what kind of cryptic message it contained. Hopefully it held words of encouragement seeing as he would be needing them.

"When did you write it?"

"Last night after we made... after we had sex," she stammered, looking past him and avoiding eye contact.

Love. Yes, that's exactly what they had done but he wasn't about to say it either.

"I'll bring my camcorder as well," she kept moving right along.

"Ugh," he rolled his eyes.

"It'll be fine. I promise you won't see your fine naked body on YouPorn," she giggled.

"Thanks for the reassurance," he leaned down and pecked her lips. He pulled her close and so tight he squeezed the air from her lungs. Pressing his forehead to hers, he closed his eyes to try and relay what he was feeling. "Last night was..." he couldn't find the words. All the most amazing descriptive words he could think of didn't seem like nearly enough to explain what the night had been like for him. He opened his mouth several times when Sarah finally finished his sentence.

"Yes, Sir... it was."

***

He sped away, annoyed with himself for having fallen for Sarah. Her words came back to him, 'no foreseeable Master in my future.' He reminded himself that she was his trainer, nothing more. Only a week ago he had been thinking about Ciara in the same way. What the hell was wrong with him? He had never been so irresolute in his life and his indecision irked him.

Back at his condo, he packed a small bag, becoming more irate as the seconds ticked by. He paced his kitchen for several minutes and finally slammed his bag down on the counter and threw himself into his large chair. He needed to get his shit together and focus. He forced himself to slow his breathing and envision Ciara's chestnut-colored eyes and meek smile. *Sarah.* He clenched his jaw tight. Seduce consent. Breath play. *Sarah.* He fisted his hair and grunted. Gain Ciara's her trust. Take it slow. Remind her that limits are meant to be pushed and reassure her. *Sarah.* Throwing his hands up, he cursed the air.

Sarah. He smiled and laughed at himself. Even in his turmoil about his feelings for her, she brought him peace. Shaking his head, he gathered his bag and left.

Traffic had delayed his arrival only giving him more time to think about the upcoming scene and eating away at what little calm he had.

When Kerian opened the door, he promptly slapped Sawyer on the back and gave him an enormous smile. "Domly One!"

Sawyer's eyes immediately scanned the room for Ciara.

"She's in the dungeon. I permitted her and Julia to engage in a bit of playtime before your arrival. We had expected you earlier, but perhaps if we go down there right this instant we might be able to see their spectacular finish."

Sawyer smiled stupidly like a teenager getting ready to watch his first porn movie and dropped his bag where he stood. "What are we waiting for?"

Sneaking in quietly, the Doms stood just out of sight as Julia plunged into Ciara with a strap-on dildo attached to her slim hips and her dark-brown hair a fantastic sweaty mess all around her face.

"Christ, Kerian, you're one lucky man," he whispered.

"Yes, I am, but thank you for noticing," Kerian lifted his eyebrows proudly.

Ciara held her legs wide for Julia and was completely open to the intense fucking that she was being given, and had the most hypnotic look of orgasmic delight on her face. And the smell. Good, God. Sweat, perfume and pussy. It was glorious and filthy, and Sawyer became erect so quickly, he feared he would pass out from the lack of blood flow to his vital organs. He stumbled from dizziness and nearly knocked Kerian over.

"Christ, man!" Kerian huffed as he steadied Sawyer, breaking the women's concentration.

He felt like an asshole for having interrupted their breath-taking scene with his juvenile reaction. "I'm sorry, ladies," he sheepishly grinned. "You just look so damned tasty. It's all a Dom can do not to pass out from lack of blood in his brain."

The two women and Kerian all laughed loudly. When Ciara looked at him, he felt the familiar pull to her that he had felt the previous weekend. She was so damned gorgeous. He inhaled their mixed sex, and arousal and excitement rioted within him.

Kerian climbed on the bed and his face spread into a depraved smile. "Shall we finish them off?"

"Hell yes."

***

Late breakfast was being served while Sawyer and Ciara chatted in whispered tones, their bodies pressed tightly together. He was anxious to tell her of his endeavors at the club. He almost ruined the surprise and spoke of his new found liking for breath play, but luckily Kerian politely interrupted before he spilled the beans. Ciara sat quietly, enthralled with his every word. He stroked her hair and decided on breaking tradition by feeding her. She seemed to be uncomfortable with it initially, but quickly eased into her new role of being pampered. It was what her Master wanted, after all, and what Sawyer wanted, Sawyer got.

During brunch discussions, Sawyer was shocked to hear that an outing was planned. It was to be a lesson on proper Master/slave behavior in a public setting for him and a refresher for Ciara.

She dressed in something sexy yet appropriate and handed a short leash to him. He looked at it suspiciously. He wasn't fond of the idea of a woman wearing a harness of any kind, most especially not in public. Not particularly because he cared what people would think, but because he felt it was degrading. A collar, yes, but a leash?

"Does Kerian normally make you wear this out in public?" he asked, his face twisting into an unwitting sour frown.

"Master Morrison, this leash is a symbol of my commitment to the life I have chosen. The restraints I wear don't need to be connected to anything to make me stay. I am bound to this life as a slave because I choose to be."

He shook his head and let out an audible sigh. "You're so bright and expressive, Angel. And also very knowledgeable for being a trainee."

She bowed her head gracefully, the blush on her cheeks clear to see. "Thank you, Master, but the title of trainee is soon coming to an end."

"That's what I've been told. Are you excited for your transition?"

"Yes, as well as nervous. What about you?" she peered up at him.

"What about me?"

Her mouth popped open and she looked mildly dazed. "Nothing, Master. I didn't mean to speak out of turn."

"I don't know what you mean. You weren't."

Ciara shook her head, "Your casualness catches me off guard every time. I just mean aren't you nervous about your training ending?"

Sawyer huffed and grinned at her. There was no doubt he was much less strict than Kerian and he couldn't imagine how difficult that was for Ciara to acclimate to. "Absolutely. There's so much more for me to learn. Though I have to admit I hope my training isn't nearly as long as yours. Six months seems exceedingly long."

"Normal slave training averages three to four months, but the time frame is customized to each slave and their needs. Master K felt that I was a particularly hard nut to crack and so my training has been a bit longer."

As obedient and docile as Ciara was, he couldn't imagine her being difficult to train. "You? A hard nut to crack, huh?"

While putting on a black, pin-striped, low-cut blazer, she explained. "Yes, I was very insolent in the beginning. One half of my mind wanted the change, but the other half resisted it. It was a constant battle for me to accept Master K's rules and punishment. But once I accepted who I really was and let the inner slave who was begging to come out of me free, things seemed to fall into place. I had to let my walls and defenses down, too. Training has been the most arduous thing I've ever done in my life. Even more demanding than earning my Master's Degree and that was grueling," her eyes widened and she smiled. "As for my body, it liked what was happening all along and kept telling my brain to stop being so overactive."

And luckily for Sawyer, he was reaping the benefits of her 'arduous' training.

Finally dressed, she took the end of the leash and attached it to a gold bracelet around her wrist. She then looped the end of the leash around his wrist so that it was barely visible.

"You see, even in public, no one will know except you and me. Like a precious hidden secret only shared between the two of us," she smiled.

"And I still have control of you."

"Yes, Master. Complete control."

***

Seated in an upscale restaurant on the edge of Denver, the two couples ordered their lunch meals, everyone around them oblivious of their Master/slave secret. It was euphoric. The way Kerian, Julia and Ciara interacted with one another was captivating to watch. Their connection was profound, and the love passing between them was palpable. They were their own little family unit and it warmed Sawyer's heart. It also saddened him to think of Ciara on her own and away from the people who clearly loved her. The vanilla world was cold and harsh, and unkind to women like her. Most of all, they were judgmental and unwilling to accept something they didn't understand; like Sonya had been. Who would care for her and guide her once her training was over? To think of her without a Master was unacceptable. He gave her a secret smile, his unspoken thoughts kept to himself.

"Ciara is going to start working at a publishing company as a junior editor at the end of the month, Mr. Morrison. We're very proud of her," Kerian stated as he looked to Julia.

"Yes. We're so very proud of our sweet girl," she chimed in, longingly gazing at Ciara.

"Thank you, Master and Mistress," her eyes shined.

"I'm proud of you as well. Beauty and intelligence are two of the finest qualities a woman can possess, Angel, and you have them in spades."

"Well said, Sawyer. Let's have a toast to Precious," Kerian lifted his glass. "Our lives are forever changed because of her presence and will never be the same without her. May she be cherished and loved a for thousand lifetimes," he choked out.

Ciara's eyes darted to him and a pained expression flashed in her eyes. Julia, too, stifled a cry.

"May I be excused, Master?" Julia squeaked out, nearly sobbing.

Kerian nodded, removed her leash, and she quickly exited the table. Dropping her head, Ciara scanned the tabletop and let out a soft whimper. When she did, Kerian wrapped an arm around her shoulders and tucked her into his body protectively.

"Precious…" he whispered in her ear. "Go find your Mistress. Comfort her."

She looked to Sawyer for his permission and his heart went out to her. She didn't need his permission anymore than Kerian wanted to let her go. He was only an onlooker, a bystander and an intruder in their lives. He quickly unsnapped the leash and nodded.

When she disappeared into the restroom, Kerian sat mutely solemn, picking at an imaginary loose thread on his tie.

Seeing the sadness in all their eyes, Sawyer couldn't help but ask, "Kerian, why not just add Ciara to your family and ask her to be your slave indefinitely?"

When he looked up, a fierce yearning shone brightly in his middle-aged eyes. "Because it's not my place as her trainer to make a selfish offer like that. She's undergone a life-changing transformation and become attached to Julia and me. It's to be expected. She is a true slave at heart and she would never deny her Master, but I do not want her to fear the unknown or to stay out of some sense of obligation. Do I want her to remain under my protection and to live with us? Absolutely, but I cannot take that which is not mine to take."

He turned his face away to hide his hurt but Sawyer could feel it thick in the air all around them. Now he knew why Sarah would never offer herself to him and why their union could never be. He dropped his head, too, both the resilient Doms silently dealing with their sorrow the only way they knew how. At that moment he made his decision. Knowing that Sarah would never offer herself to him and regardless of how he felt about her, he would offer his Mastery to Ciara once their training was over. That is, if she still wanted anything to do with him after the impending scene that was looming in the very near future.

***

Lying in bed with Ciara before dinner, he rubbed circles on her back as they spoke of things to come. She knew a final test was being planned but not the details. Her anxiousness was bubbling over and he did his best to soothe her.

"It will all work out, Angel," he told her as she rested her head on his chest. "You're a very special woman, Ciara."

She tipped her head up to look at him and smiled, and it was hard to miss the look of optimism in her eyes. He wondered what she was thinking and if it was him that she wanted for a lifelong Master. Or perhaps someone else. She had been exposed to many men over her six months of training and surely there were others who were vying for her slavery. They'd be dense not to.

"I don't think you fully know the power you have over men."

"Nor do you realize the power you have over women."

"Oh, I know," he narrowed his eyes mysteriously.

Ella Dominguez

"You're coming into your Dominant skin, Sawyer Morrison, and your confidence has grown exponentially in the short time you've been away from me. You must have one amazing trainer."

Sarah. His heart clenched. "Yes, she is, just as your trainers are. We've been very lucky to have been placed in their knowing hands."

The same sadness that was in Ciara's eyes at the restaurant filled her eyes again. "Yes. I can't imagine my life away from Master K and Mistress J. I'll be lost without them."

"No, you won't. You'll walk a new path, with a new Master."

She looked at him doubtfully but managed a smile. "I can only hope."

***

During dinner, the conversation focused on Ciara's training and everything she had been taught. It was intriguing. She was not only instructed on how to speak, act and think in ways that were pleasing, but endured total power exchange. When he heard about the behavior modification sessions she had been put through, he had new-found respect for her. He couldn't imagine having to be put through such strict and sometimes harsh tests of one's will.

He quickly felt information overload when he heard of the stringent rules that she adhered to and he wondered if he could live up to the task of being her Master. He suddenly looked at Kerian in a whole new light and was in awe of his skill and patience.

When he learned that Ciara had also been submitted to aversion training that included spanking, cropping, and clamping to 'encourage' her compliance, he felt heartsick. There was no way he was going to do those things to her except for pleasure. He could barely stomach the spanking he had to give Sarah, for fuck's sake. He was no sadist and he needed to make that clear.

When the conversation paused, he asked his question. "Are you a masochist, Ciara?"

The question seemed to surprise everyone at the table but she answered without hesitation.

"No, Master."

He relaxed, but another question lingered. "Then how does doing all those things mentioned work effectively for someone who is a masochist?"

Ciara looked to Kerian who responded. "If the slave being trained enjoys pain, punishment may need to be in the form of psychological or emotional in order to create the unpleasant effects that punishment necessitates."

So in addition to doling out pain as punishment, he had to consider how to mentally punish his would be submissive or slave? He rubbed his palm over his face and tipped his chair back on two legs. What a daunting thought. Ciara sat staring at him with an acute sense of disappointment in her eyes, and he touched her arm to ease her anxiety.

"No worries; I'm no sadist, Angel."

She bowed her head and acted as if she was embarrassed. "I didn't mean to... what I mean is... even if you were, it wouldn't be my place to judge you. I would accept you no matter what your preferences are."

Kerian quickly chimed in. "Precious, your heart and attitude are in the right place, but you cannot accept a Master who you will not be compatible with. You are no masochist and you are not expected to be. Don't you ever allow a man to try and change the perfect slave that you are or to change that which is in your heart," he stated firmly, pounding a fist on the table.

It was easy to read Kerian's emotions as they played on his face. He would accept nothing less than the perfect Master for his precious Ciara.

"Back me up, Sawyer," he barked, catching him off guard and making him almost tip backwards in the tilted chair. He brought the chair down onto all four legs and cleared his throat.

Ella Dominguez

"Absolutely, Ciara. Nothing and no one can change what is in your heart, no matter how much you think you may want that person, or want to be wanted by them."

Dylan and Isabel popped into his head unexpectedly. His sadistic needs to her masochistic wants; did they even know how lucky they were to find each other? It certainly wasn't lost on Sawyer how fortunate he was that Ciara didn't crave pain. What if she had been a masochist? He didn't want to think about that.

Shit. What if Sarah had been? How would his training have gone then? Come to think of it, Isabel and Dylan probably wouldn't have chosen her to train him if she had been. This was all too much to think about. Again, he rubbed his hand over his face and sighed deeply. He was brought back by Kerian's deep and mocking laugh.

"It's a lot to take in, isn't it?"

"If ever there was an understatement – that was it."

***

While Ciara showered, Sawyer's phone alarm beeped, notifying him of his 9:00 p.m. appointment. He smiled and reached for it, but his joy quickly faded when he remembered that Sarah wouldn't be at the other end of town thinking of him while she played with herself. He touched the screen anyway and brought up her image. Those eyes... my God. The way they were staring at him in the photograph... the same way she looked at him when she was waiting for his command. And how they sparkled when she came. Or the way they got all sleepy and needy looking while she sucked him off. He swallowed hard and powered down his phone.

Ciara. It was about her this weekend, not Sarah and her beautiful blue eyes. Just then Ciara came out wrapped in only a towel, all wet hair and big, brown, lusty eyes. And submissive as fuck.

Christ, man! He heard Kerian's voice ringing in his ears. No shit. He needed to seriously make up his fucking mind. Why couldn't he just have both of them? His own version of a

211

mini-harem with an enormously obnoxious, canopied bed and all? Or maybe they could all move to Utah and he could become a bigamist and they could be sister-wives. Was that such an unreasonable thought?

"What are you thinking about, Master?" Ciara asked him.

Mortified of his inner thoughts, he blushed and he couldn't believe that he had actually fucking blushed. He shook his head and mentally kicked himself in the balls for being such a ridiculous, dithering pussy.

"Nothing, Angel. Let's lie down."

Ciara's hands roamed over his body, seeking out his pleasure points and finding them rapidly. He reached a hand out, gliding his fingers over the angel wing on her left shoulder blade and the same spot that Kerian had set aflame only an hour earlier. He had demonstrated his skills with fire play and Sawyer had watched with intense interest as his Angel seemed to enjoy what was being done to her. It was ironic to think about his dark Angel on fire and it was arousing to bear witness to.

Ciara's hand came to rest on his cock as she lay next to him, her free hand resting on his abdomen. She focused all her attention on his shaft as she stroked him into complete hardness. Her thumb glided over the head of his dick and he grunted, leaned his head back and closed his eyes. Her grip tightened and her hand moved slowly up and down, fiery sensations filling his lower belly. With his eyes still shut, he felt her warm, wet mouth on him, the sucking pressure almost too much to take. He didn't want to open his eyes. Her mouth felt so good and the sloppy wet sounds were too delicious, and he was content to just imagine what she looked like pleasuring him like this.

"Mmmmaster..." her soft, feminine voice broke through.

He didn't want to come just yet. Not just yet. He just wanted more of her mouth. She had the kind of touch and mouth that a man could get used to. Yes, he could most definitely spend a lifetime with that mouth at his beck and call. She began to hum some unrecognizable song while bobbing up and down, and the buzzing sensation on his shaft nearly made him shoot his wad. He abruptly sat up, tugged her hair, dragging her mouth away from him.

"I'm not ready to come," he told her when she looked up at him confused. "You first, Angel."

***

Sunday afternoon had arrived so rapidly, Sawyer felt ill-prepared and frankly, sick to his stomach. All that practice and this is what it came down to. His nerves were frayed and while Ciara dressed for lunch he contemplated backing out. Ciara trusted him; he could see it in her eyes and he didn't want to lose that.

Moving to the window, he placed a hand on the cold glass. The night had brought a heavy layer of frost and the ice-covered view outside was stunning. Winter was closing in on them and he couldn't wait for the first snowfall. *Sarah.* He smiled. Just the thought of her brought him peace.

He recalled the note and retrieved it.

"I write this in hopes of putting your mind at ease for your upcoming scene.

I started out in BDSM wanting to be controlled and owned. I wanted to be made to forget everything about who I had been. But when my Master gave me those things and we gave into our desires, I lost sight of all that and so did he. We became animal, instinct, nature. We became what we were meant to be — Dominant and submissive. And so will you. And when you do, nothing less than a woman's complete surrender will quench your thirst and that's okay to admit. You are a Dominant, Sawyer. It's who you are. I have no doubts about your abilities so go forward and accept Ciara's gift of submission and push her limits gently,

*knowing that no matter what the outcome is, you've
done what you were meant to do – to dominate.
    xxSarah"*

    Sarah's written words were exactly what he needed. He
closed his eyes and imagined her bright and eager face the
first time he met her. It was her submissiveness that day that
had urged him to go through with training and it was her
words now that pushed him to go through with the scene.
What would he do without her in his life? Could Ciara ever
fulfill the need that Sarah had? He didn't dare think that far in
advance. Right here and right now is all that mattered. He
squared his shoulders, ready to begin the next stage of his
journey.

Chapter 17

"Are you ready, Master Morrison?"

Sawyer smiled. Ciara's question reminded him of Dylan's question the first day he began his training, though his title was different now. "Yes, I'm ready. Are you?"

"Yes..." she grinned. "But... I can't help but feel like this is some sort of test. I know you can't tell me and that's fine, but I promise to be completely open to whatever you have planned for me."

She had no idea what she was agreeing to and again, he waffled. But only briefly this time because he knew there was no backing out and this wasn't only a test for her, but for him. Still, her trust meant everything to him. Absolutely fucking everything. The way she was looking at him... how could he even consider doing the one thing that she feared the most?

Brusquely he pulled her to him and held her face between his hands. "I just want you know that I would never *ever* hurt you."

Confused by his remark, she smiled awkwardly.

In an instant he made an executive decision about the scene. He glanced at his watch. Sarah would be here any moment.

"Wait for me in the library, Angel. I have to take care of something."

He strode confidently to Kerian's office and knocked before entering. When he came into the room, Julia was sitting on her knees in an elegant display pose with her back straight and her weight balanced between her hips evenly. The way her knees were bent and legs spread apart at shoulder width, he and Kerian had a perfect view of her exposed and waxed genitals through her crotchless, black lace panties. Her hands rested with palms up on the top of her thighs gracefully and Sawyer was momentarily stunned into silence by her beauty, but quickly recovered when Kerian caught him ogling the Korean beauty.

"There's a change in plans," he stated resolutely, his voice emphasizing that there was going to be no negotiating. Kerian's brows went up and he stood, but said nothing. "I would like Julia to be present for the scene as opposed to Sarah."

"Mr. Morrison, I…" Kerian began to interrupt.

"This isn't a request. I insist. Respectfully."

Kerian's eyes narrowed and he walked around to the front of his desk, seating himself on the edge. "Can I at least get an explanation as to why you want both my slaves present?"

"Ciara doesn't know Sarah. From what I understand, they've never even met, so it would be imprudent to assume that she would be comforted by Sarah's presence simply because she's a submissive. I understand why you can't be present, however, Julia does not hold the same power that you do. They are equals and therefore she will be at ease with her."

The faintest of smiles tipped the corners of Kerian's mouth and he dropped his head, nodding in agreement. Without raising his head, he asked, "But what about your comfort level? I thought Sarah was going to be in attendance not only for Ciara, but for you."

Yes, it was true, but this wasn't about his needs and he knew that. This was about Ciara and helping her to let go of her fears. "It would be selfish of me to have Sarah there when Julia is clearly a better choice for Ciara."

"Very well. Julia…" he raised his head and waved to her. "Join Ciara. Is everything set up?"

"It will be shortly. I'm waiting for Sarah to assist me."

A few minutes later and right on time, Sarah arrived, carrying a camera bag and looking divine in a white, cotton knitted cap and thigh length sweater wrapped around her thick waist.

"You look lovely," Sawyer kissed her forehead.

"Thank you, Sir. Shall we set up?" she beamed, her demeanor exuding enthusiasm.

"Yes, but first I need to speak with you." He guided her past the foyer into a small alcove that doubled as the coat room. "I've decided to have Julia as back up..." he paused to let his words sink in. He expected to see some kind of reaction, something, but she stood stoically unflinching, even unblinking. "Snowflake?" he asked, worried she had gone catatonic on him.

"I heard you. Would you still like me to help you set up?"

"Of course. Thank you. I didn't come to this decision lightly. I just thought..."

"There's no need to explain yourself, Sir. I know that your decisions are final and I would never question them," she cut in.

Her voice was calm and even, but there it was, that *something* he had hoped he wouldn't see; hurt. It flashed briefly in her eyes and her mouth twitched only the slightest. Anyone else would've missed it, but he saw it and he almost wished he didn't know her so well. He sighed heavily and rubbed the palm of his hand over his face.

"Let's set up," he turned away from her, unable to take the silence and her unblinking stare.

In the dungeon, Sarah acclimated herself and found the equipment he had requested, including a cane, double pinwheel, nipple clamps and silk scarf. Sawyer watched as she moved around the dungeon gracefully and laid out the lubricant and condoms next to the bed that he had chosen for his scene. She was adorable when she was focused and it was difficult not to get aroused by her. Sarah looked up at him and did a double take when she caught him staring at her heatedly.

"Sir? Is something wrong?"

He cleared his throat and shook his head, mildly ashamed for having been thinking illicit thoughts about her when it was Ciara he should be concentrating on.

She promptly went back to setting up the camera on a tripod while he searched for the perfect songs on his phone.

He needed it to be sexy, somber and slow. When he made his choice, he walked over and smelled several different sticks of incense trying to find the appropriate one.

Sarah slid next to him and picked up a lavender stick. "Lavender helps reduce anxiety levels," she said softly, inhaling deeply. "This might be beneficial for the both of you."

As usual, Sarah's knowledge astounded him. Was there anything she didn't know? "Good choice," he wrapped his hand around her waist. He leaned down to kiss the top of her head but she gently pulled away from him, the warmth of her body replaced by a cold chill. Her action left him feeling unwanted and irritated. He shook his head and brought the stick to his nose. Yes, it did have a calming effect.

"Everything looks to be in order, Sir. I've put her asthma medication just within reach should she need it… but…" she looked up and smiled as she moved to the door, "…she won't. Everything will be fine. Good luck, Sir. I'll send the girls in."

She turned to walk away, but Sawyer calling out to her halted her exit. When she faced him, he lifted one side of his mouth in a half-smile.

"Sarah… thank you. For the note. For everything. I couldn't go through with this if it wasn't for your help and encouragement."

Her breathing became shallow and her electric blue eyes bordered with tears. She gulped hard but held her equanimity steadily. "Thank you, Sir, for letting me be a part of this," she forced a smile before turning to leave.

Sawyer rubbed his palm over his face and pushed the vision of Sarah out of his mind. It was show time. No more pussing around. The prolonged anticipation of the day had been almost unbearable and he rolled his neck as he took a deep breath in then blew it out. He was as ready as he was ever going to be.

He quickly lit the incense and dimmed the lights for a romantic setting, and cued *Waiting Game* by Banks on the mp3 player. Ciara and Julia both entered quietly as he was dressing down. He turned to face them and motioned for Ciara to come to him.

"Come to me, Angel, let me undress you. Julia, please seat yourself on the bed."

Ciara moved slowly and purposefully seductively toward him, each of her steps an invitation to dominate her; an invitation he was more than willing and eager to accept. When she was within reach, he casually removed the cherry-red satin robe that she was wearing, letting it fall to her feet. Underneath, she wore a black velvet corset cinched to an unfathomable tightness making her waist look a good six inches smaller and a matching thong. He stood back and took in her image. She looked too good to take it off. He kneeled and slipped her panties down inch-by-inch. When he stood and looked down into her toffee-colored eyes, a sense of urgency filled him that he was powerless to resist and something intense flared though his entrancement. He was Dominant. She was submissive. This was his destiny.

He led her to bed and laid her down, showering her body with kisses as he whispered his desire for her. He touched the top of her thighs and his caress was a command that she willingly obeyed as she opened her legs to him. He reached for the cane and a flame flickered in Ciara's eyes that radiated a vitality that drew him in. She wanted this. She wanted him.

He rose up on his knees and began to flick the cane over every spot he had placed a kiss, the tops of her breasts, thighs and mound. He was careful not to deliver too harsh of strikes, mindful of his movements. He had only experimented with it twice on Sarah the previous week when they rehearsed and he replayed that scene in his head as he carried on. Ciara's response was so completely different than Sarah's. She lay compliantly still, panting quietly, whereas Sarah had moaned loudly and writhed beneath him, but both obedient and willing. He flicked and slapped the bamboo against her skin for several minutes, pausing only to kiss her. Time had slowed and he had no idea how much time had passed. Seconds, minutes… hours? When her panting became ragged and harsh, he laid the cane down to thumb her clit.

"I want to hear you, Angel," he told her, his voice a deep, raspy whisper.

Her mouth parted and a soft moan came out, followed by a louder one when he began to circle his thumb around faster and press down more firmly. She was wet… so very wet. He loved how her body responded to him. His brain became clouded with lust and he gripped his shaft with his free hand to try and satiate the ache throbbing in him and put the condom on.

"Yes, like that…" he growled as he began to stroke himself.

He was so hard and she was so wet, he wanted to plunge into her and fuck her. Instead, he maintained his cool exterior as he slipped his two fingers into her. He quickly found what he was looking for and began to tug at her G-spot roughly in a come-hither motion. Ciara immediately began to wriggle and grunt noisily. Yes, that's what he wanted to hear. Not quiet panting, loud moaning. His thumb found her clit again and he double assaulted her pussy by flicking her clit while finger fucking her. Her body began to quiver and he yanked his fingers out, leaving her a wet, squirming mess.

As the song *Fail for You* by Luke Sital-Singh began, he grabbed his next tool – the double pinwheel. He lay next to her and glided it over her pebbled nipples and her back arched into him, the wheel sinking deeply into her tender flesh and leaving a spectacular imprint on her areola. After several minutes with the wheel, he set it aside. He hovered his body over Ciara and held her head between his two large hands, their faces only inches apart.

"Right now, you belong to me. Is that understood?" Ciara's eyes became like liquid and she nodded eagerly. "Say it," he whispered against her lips.

"I belong to you."

He smiled a wicked, debauched smile and slipped his tongue into her mouth to remind himself what her arousal tasted like. He savored it and etched it into his memory.

His feelings of excitement began to intensify and everything around him took on a clean brightness when he reached for the blind fold. The moment was drawing nearer and he could feel the air around him begin to change like it had when he was with Sarah.

He wrapped the scarf around her eyes so that she couldn't see what was coming. He wanted her to feel his hands around her throat while only hearing his soft words of reassurance and to be without sight so that she could focus only on his voice.

With the silk securely over her eyes, he reached for her medication and looked to Julia and nodded. When she moved next to Ciara, he handed her the inhaler. Next, he grabbed the nipple clamps and gently eased them onto each of her breasts, twisting them down slowly. He wanted the sensation in her breasts to be a distracter to what was about to take place.

He moved between her legs, kneeling with her feet planted next to his thighs. Just then *Better in the Dark* by Say Lou Lou began and it couldn't have been a more appropriate time or song for the occasion. He began to massage her body while alternately fingering her and adjusting the clamps down. He could sense Ciara's relaxation and trust, and the sexual magnetism that she was putting off made him feel confident. Her reactions to his touch made it clear that he was doing all the right things to her body.

As casually as he could manage, he ghosted his hand up the center of her belly, between her breasts and paused at the base of her neck. He eyed her suprasternal notch longingly and stroked it with his index finger. It was such an erotic part of a woman's body. He licked his lips and smiled. If he was still a whiskey man it would be the perfect spot to do body shots from. Then again, it made no difference what the liquid was so long as he could lap it up from that deliciously small, dipped space on her neck. Perhaps another day he would indulge that fantasy.

Redirecting his focus, he thrust his fingers back into her to take her attention off his impending action. Centimeter-by-centimeter, he moved his hand to its soft target and stopped when he felt the beat of her heart against his fingertips. Ciara was so caught up in her near-orgasmic moaning, she didn't even realize where his hand had come to rest until he ever so gently squeezed.

Suddenly her body jerked, her hands came up to his, and her breathing hitched as realization of what her test was hit her.

He moved on top of her and leaned into her ear. "It's me, Angel. It's Sawyer." He tightened his fingers a hairbreadth more and she began to claw at his hand and thrash her head.

"No Master... please...not this!" she cried out.

The panicked look on her face caused his heart to thump madly in his chest. Her fear was tangible and harrowing to watch. He ached for her and just wanted to make it all stop. He eased his grip back down, but left his hand stationary.

Looking up at Julia, she appeared to be just as distressed as Ciara. Despite being horrified at seeing her lover and friend suffering, she placed a delicate kiss on Ciara's cheek and spoke soothingly into her ear.

"I'm here, too, my precious girl. It's me, Mistress J."

Ciara's movements slowed only minimally, but her clawing ceased when Julia licked a tear that had rolled down her cheek.

Sawyer spoke softly into Ciara's ear. "Do you remember what I told you earlier, Angel?" Her breathing was still loud and harsh, but she nodded woodenly. "What did I tell you?"

She swallowed loudly and moistened her lips. "That you would never hurt me," she began to weep.

"That's right. And I never will. I'm not hurting you now, am I?" She sucked back her tears and shook her head. "No, I'm not..." he continued, his tone serenely patient. "You know that Kerian and Julia would never allow any harm to come to you, don't you?"

Both her tears and rapid breathing began to slowly subside. "No. They wouldn't," she acknowledged.

Sawyer glanced up at Julia who had tears running down her cheeks, all the while stroking Ciara's hair.

"Mistress J..." Ciara choked out.

"I'm here Precious. I'm right here next to you."

"Where's Master K? I want him..." she began to cry again.

Julia gave him a withering pointed stare and shook her head as if pleading for him to stop. And he almost did. Her tears were too much. But her anxiety was unwarranted and he wanted to free her from it. He began to loosen his grip to ease her pain, but he knew that he couldn't back out now, not when she was so close to being unchained from her fears.

"Master K is waiting for us just outside my precious girl," Julia murmured against her cheek.

"Let it go, Ciara," he said softly, tightening his grip again.

Her breathing halted briefly and was quickly replaced by rapid panting again, and Sawyer began to worry that the medication might be needed after all. God, he hoped it wouldn't come to that. He wracked his brain for the words to pacify her aching.

"I have your medication right here, Angel, but you don't need it. Slow your breathing down and match it to mine and Mistress J's. Can you hear how slow we're breathing? Can you feel my breath on your ear?" he reassured her, his fingers clenching tighter yet. When his words still didn't take hold of her, he began to feel a sinking anguish. But he couldn't give up yet. No... not just yet. He would give it one more go, only one more, and if she still remained panicked, he would just have to release her.

"The only way we can move forward is if you trust me. You once told me that the excitement was all in the limits and pushing them. Do you remember that?" Ciara continued to cry, but nodded. "Another wise person told me that life gets boring when you stay within limits that you already know and to never be afraid to try that which you fear. Do you know who that was? Master K. He's here with you in spirit. Everyone who cares about you wants you to be free from this fear. Let it go, Angel... let go..."

The underlying sensuality of his words slowly began to captivate her and his voice finally had the effect he wanted when it began to lull her into a relaxed mood. Her tongue poked out to wet her lips and a faint pleasured moan fluttered out. Little-by-little her hands came down over her breasts, across her tummy, and finally rested at her sides. At long last she calmed and a smile worked its way onto her mouth. And there it was - freedom. Sawyer looked up to Julia, shocked at what he had just witnessed and had a hand in, and saw a smile on her face so wide it nearly knocked him over.

With the go ahead, he moved back between her legs and sunk into her slowly while continuing to apply pressure to her neck. Fully submerged in her wet depths, he tore off her blind fold so he could see her eyes. She squinted against the light, and with tears still trembling on her eyelids, she smiled when he and Julia came into focus.

He thrust into her vigorously and clutched her neck until he saw her eyes roll back and heard her breathing still. Watching her body closely and peering into her deep brown eyes, he gave his command.

"Spread your wings and fly, my dark Angel. Fly..."

Her pupils flared and just as he released his grip, he thrust into her deeply. When he did, Ciara inhaled sharply, her body shuddered and she screamed out.

"Oh. My. God!"

Sawyer tried to stifle his laugh, but couldn't, he was too damned happy. "No, Angel. It's Master Morrison."

***

It was Ciara's duty as a slave to clean her Master up after their encounter, but Sawyer was so proud of her, he decided to do the chore himself. With the help of Julia, of course, who was all too eager to assist. She was beaming with pride as well, and it was an absolute delight to watch the two women bubbling with excitement after their experience. Ciara must have thanked him at least a dozen times, if not more, post aftercare, but he felt as though he should be the one thanking her for giving him the pleasure of setting her free.

When they met Kerian in his office, Ciara threw herself into his arms and deep sobs racked her body. Kerian shot him a lethal look as he held her in his arms until he realized her tears were tears of joy. His face then softened and he took both women into his arms. A smothered cry could be heard from Julia and Sawyer quickly left them to their private and intimate moment.

Sitting in the library and replaying everything that had happened, a feeling of knowing began to creep up on him and crawl under his skin. He had every intention of asking Ciara to be his slave, but it was out of duty and honor that he was going to ask her, and those were the wrong reasons. The way she had run to Kerian, her heartfelt words asking for him during the scene, and the looks on all of their faces after she had so proudly overcome her fears... With sudden clarity, he knew what had to be done about Ciara.

As he sat quietly alone looking out the library window, he felt a warm hand on his back. He knew the familiar touch. Sarah. He turned to face her, anxious to tell her about everything that happened and how he had completed his task admirably, but was met not only by her eyes but by Kerian's.

"Shall we watch the video?" Kerian asked, motioning toward the door.

The fucking video. Sawyer had completely forgotten about it. It's a good thing too or else he might not have done so well during the scene.

Once in Kerian's office everyone sat down for the show. Even though the scene had a positive outcome, he didn't particularly feel like reliving the moment and watching himself fuck and choke Ciara, most especially not in front of Sarah.

Becoming Sir

He pulled his chair back a bit and kept his eyes trained on a spot on the wall while it played. He could hear his words and Ciara's whimpering and he felt nauseated. Out of morbid curiosity, his eyes darted to the television screen, but he quickly averted his eyes elsewhere. Hell no. A person wasn't meant to see their own dick on 1080P. Christ, he could see every single one of his scars in high-definition.

As he chewed the corner of his lip tensely, Sarah glanced over at him. He thought he saw something in her eyes, but the room was too dark to make out what the emotion was.

When it was over, Kerian flicked the light on and proceeded to slap Sawyer on the back.

"Well done, Mr. Morrison. That was quite a show. I'd like to point out your errors, but there are none that I can find. Except maybe for your 'O face,' but it's not like we have any control over that sort of thing, is it?" he laughed obnoxiously.

Sarah's face reddened and so did the other women, and Sawyer felt like punching Kerian in his arrogant head for being such a tactless shit. He rolled his eyes and cleared his throat awkwardly trying to silence Kerian's mocking.

"Sarah has some things to discuss with you," he finally added when he had his fill of his own crass joke.

He and Sarah went into the foyer when he noticed she had their contract in her hands. He stared at it numbly wondering why the hell she had brought it along. She gripped it tightly but finally handed it over.

"Your training is complete, Sawyer. We won't be needing this any longer."

Her words sent his head spinning and he felt the screams of denial at the back of his throat. Widening his stance, he placed his hands on his hips and shot Sarah a penetrating look.

"I thought a decision like this needed to be made by all my trainers."

Her eyes immediately lowered to the floor and she whispered, "It wasn't my decision alone. The Youngs and Kerian all agree that you've made significant and rapid progress. Your selfless and brave actions today have proven to all of us that you're a true Dom, and that my services are no longer needed."

His dark eyes showed a tortured dullness of disbelief. There was no way he felt ready for his training to be over. Who the hell did Young and Kerian, and Sarah for that matter, think they were making a decision like that without first discussing it with him? Didn't he have a say in the matter? There was so much more to learn. So much more...

He shook his head regretfully and touched her chin, guiding her to look at him. How could she think that all that she had given him was a service? "You've provided me with more than just a service, Sarah. You've given me more than you can ever know... don't you know that?"

"Just because your training period is over doesn't mean that your learning is, Sir. This lifestyle is a never-ending lesson on life and love...learning your partner's desires and to trust... I can only hope I've provided more than a service to you, but I can't teach you anything that you don't already know. You're such a brilliant, kind, stern man... and so good..." Her eyes became glassy and for a moment he thought she would cry, but she rigidly held her composure. "...whoever you choose to be your submissive or slave will teach you the rest."

All at once Sawyer felt like he couldn't breathe. The scene, his upcoming discussion with Ciara about his reasons for not committing to her and now this... he felt as though the life was being choked out of him. How apropos considering what he had just done to Ciara.

The heartrending look on Sarah's face was tearing him apart. He had to get out of the room, fast. Dropping his hand to his side, he turned to walk away without saying anymore. What else was there to say? His feelings were too raw to discuss and he didn't want to say anything hurtful.

When he arrived in his suite, he slammed the door behind him and sank onto the bed, his hands fisting his own hair.

Didn't his time with Sarah mean anything to her? She had insisted on open and honest communication, and still he hadn't made his intentions perfectly clear. Even if he had, would she have accepted his offer of commitment? Of course not, he was only her trainee. All at once he could understand how Kerian felt at the thought of saying goodbye to Ciara.

His sense of loss was beyond tears and he fell back onto the bed. Only a few minutes passed before Ciara came in. She lay next to him and ran her hand over his face, sensing his turmoil.

"Why are you so upset, Master Morrison?"

He rolled onto his side to face her and propped himself up on one elbow. There was no point in prolonging the inevitable.

"I just want you to know that I had every intention of asking you to be my slave when my training was complete, which it is now, I've been told."

Ciara's brows drew together. "You *had* every intention? But you no longer do?"

"No, Angel, I don't."

Her mouth parted in surprise and she sat up on the edge of bed as she began to physically withdraw from him. It was painful to see her feeling rejected and he moved next to her, wrapping his arm around her shoulders.

"You're home is here, with your true family, and the true loves of your life – Kerian and Julia. I could never hold a flame to them, and I'm not even going to try."

Ciara gasped and shook her head. "No, Master. I can't stay here. Master K has made that very clear. I need to find another Master. I want you, Sawyer."

He smiled and felt a knot rise in his throat. "I'm truly honored that you would even consider me, but... Your heart doesn't belong to me any more than mine belongs to you. You know that to be true, don't you?"

Her eyes wet with tears and she scanned the palms of her hands. "But we can learn to love each other."

"Is that what you really want? Someone you've learned to love and chosen by default? Or someone you know without a doubt that you love?"

"But Master K has said that he cannot offer himself as a Master to me..." she began.

He drew her closer and put a finger to her mouth to quiet her. "Kerian will never offer himself to you out of tradition and respect for his role as a trainer, but some traditions are meant to be broken, Ciara. Like this one. I can honestly tell you that if you offer yourself to him, he will not deny you."

A shadow of alarm touched her face. "But what if he does?"

"He and Julia love you. This is where you're meant to be. If you don't ask, you're denying yourself what rightfully belongs to you – their love and protection."

"But what about you?" she asked sadly as she reached over and touched his mouth.

Again he felt the powerful physical pull to her. It would always be there. But his heart belonged to someone else and he didn't want to be with Ciara by default either. He wanted someone he knew without a doubt that he loved and that person was not Ciara.

"You and I are in quite a predicament, Angel. We've both fallen for our trainers."

She smiled understandingly and rested her head on his shoulder. "Then may I respectfully give you a piece of your own advice? Ask her to be yours, Sawyer, and take what is rightfully yours."

Chapter 18

Sarah stumbled to her front door and barely made it inside her house when the tears came. She had rigidly held them at bay on the long drive home but there was no denying them anymore. Throwing herself onto her bed, she could still smell Sawyer and her anguish peaked, shattering the last threads of the fragile control she had been holding onto for weeks.

Her mind was languid and without hope at the thought of being without him. But how could she have fallen for him so hard and so fast? Angry with herself, she bit her bottom lip until it throbbed like her pulse in hopes that it would snap her out of her agonizing maelstrom.

Damn her for agreeing to train him when she was still grieving for Doug. No, she was kidding herself. She had accepted his passing months before Sawyer, despite what she had tried to convince herself of. She would never be over his death, but she had avoided physical and intimate contact for her own selfish reasons – because she didn't want to suffer the loss of love again. And here she was, bereft and desolate over a trainee.

But Sawyer was no mere trainee, he was her other half. Like Doug had been. She had preached honest and open communication, and she had hidden her true feelings all along. And now it was too late. He was gone and she would never have him again.

Images of the video flashed in front of her closed eyes. She had done her best to watch it objectively, but she had damn near broke down seeing her Sir's hands wrapped around Ciara's throat as he took her. Was she selfish for wanting that pleasure and his hands only for herself? It was her own damned fault for having taught him how to do it. Why did she have to teach him the fetish which she held near to her heart? Because it was her duty. Her job. Her *service*. And she had done it admirably, too, hadn't she?

She rolled onto her back and a tormented choking cry escaped her throat. As a raw and primitive grief overwhelmed her, she screamed his name loudly, her squeaky voice echoing off the walls. Not giving a damn about being selfish anymore, she prayed he heard it on the other side of town and that he thought of her while he was passionately fucking Ciara, his slave.

Blinded by her tears, she closed her eyes, the pleasures of their night together still haunting her. She just wanted to sleep the rest of the day away and to forget about the wretched images of Ciara with Sawyer. Her Sir. Her Master.

***

When she woke, nightfall had already come. She looked at her clock and was stunned to see that it was nearly 10:00 p.m. She forced herself to shower and made herself eat, numbly going about the chores on auto-mode.

Lying near the door was her camera bag and the contract she had dropped on her way in. She inhaled deeply and did what had to be done. She removed the camera and promptly did what she had promised she would, and erased the footage of Sawyer's scene. She hesitated to do what came next, but swallowed hard and bit back the impending tears as she shredded the contract. It was the final act in her sad and pathetic theatrical performance for which she deserved some sort of award for having faked her lack of emotions so well.

Seated on the couch in her darkened living room, she let the silence wrap itself around her like a warm blanket. It was calming. She looked to a picture hanging on her wall of her and Doug and smiled. He was such a good man. Closing her eyes, she envisioned Sawyer and smiled. He was such a good man. He deserved only the best and she began to feel guilty for her thoughts from earlier. No, she didn't want him to think of her while he was with Ciara. Ciara deserved better than that. They deserved one another and to be loved completely and without reservation, and without the memories of past lovers haunting them. Ciara looked so beautiful when she

231

accepted Sawyer's touch and when she was finally free from her fears. Sarah hated to admit it, but Ciara and Sawyer were meant to be. Maybe someday, if she was lucky, she would find true love again.

Just as she leaned her head back, her phone rang. Picking it up, she was surprised to see Isabel's phone number on the screen. Wondering what the reason for such a late call would be, panic gripped her heart. Perhaps something had happened to Sawyer. A car accident. God, please, no. Not again.

"Is everything okay?" she blurted out as soon as she answered.

There was a moment of silence before Isabel answered. "Yes, of course. Why would you ask that?"

Sarah heaved a loud sigh of relief. "I just thought that maybe something had happened to…nevermind. Is everything okay with you?"

"Yes. I'm really good actually, just a little pukey. Anyway, I know it's late, but I really need your help with something. I wouldn't ask except that it's very important. Can you come over?"

There was a note of vagueness and nervousness in Isabel's normally silky voice and Sarah felt uneasy with her request. "Right now? What's so important?"

She sighed and shuffled her phone before answering. "Oh, Sarah, please don't ask. I'm a terrible liar so don't force me to make an excuse. What I need to discuss is… personal. I really don't want to speak about it over the phone."

Sarah couldn't deny that it was a welcome request. She needed the company to take her mind off of Sawyer and she was looking forward to seeing Isabel's growing baby bump. "Okay, okay. I'll leave right now."

"You're the best, Sarah. Thank you."

On her drive to the Youngs' residence, her thoughts were once again on Sawyer. It couldn't be helped. It would take time to get over him. A long time. He had worked his way into her heart and getting over him would be like grieving another lost lover.

She was so engrossed in her thoughts of the previous week and how glorious it had been, how the sleek caress of his body had felt against her and how his dominating words and touch had affected her, she didn't even realize when she parked in the Youngs' garage. She was promptly met by security who escorted her to the elevator and up to their living room suite.

As soon as the elevator doors opened, she was greeted by Isabel's warm hug. She looked bright with a healthy glow in her cheeks. Sarah hoped someday if she ever became pregnant, she would look as good.

She reached a hand out and touched Isabel's barely visible belly. It was warm and firm.

"You're so blessed, Isabel," she smiled at her.

Isabel laid her hand over Sarah's and smiled sympathetically at her, understanding shining in her honey-colored eyes. Her eyes blurred with tears at the look on Isabel's face and she felt the blood drain from her cheeks. She would not break down, she repeated over-and-over to herself.

Isabel pulled Sarah to her and hugged her tightly. "Oh, Sarah..."

"I'm okay, really. I'm just happy that Sawyer has found someone. Ciara is a lucky..."

Isa swiftly put her hand up to her mouth. "Please don't say anymore. Just come with me.

They climbed a spiral staircase to the Youngs' bedroom. She knew the path they were taking as she had walked it only a few weeks before; the night she had engaged in femplay with Isabel and Claire in the dungeon.

If she wasn't still reeling from the loss of Sawyer she would've been more concerned as to why she was being led there, but her mind was blank. The large bookshelf that disguised the room slid open and she stared wordlessly across at Sawyer who was standing on the other side, her heart pounding against her ribcage. She stood there, blank, amazed, even shaken at the look of utter longing in his mahogany eyes.

Becoming Sir

She hadn't even realized she stopped breathing until he reached out and traced his index finger across her bottom lip. When he did, she took in a quick breath, barely able to control the panting that ensued from his sexy and familiar touch. An unexpected warmth surged through her, the feeling not unlike that of a subspace high and dizziness overwhelmed her. Her knees weakened and for a moment, she thought she would faint as spots filled her vision, but Sawyer's strong arms steadied her.

"I wish I had this effect on all women," he smiled down at her, his lusty brown eyes revealing what she had been aching to see all night.

"Oh, you do," she breathed out.

"Snowflake..." he whispered, his mouth inching towards hers.

She knew she should've stopped him and asked what he was doing there, but she didn't want to. She didn't care. He was there and she was in his arms, and that was all that mattered. His nearness and smell set her brain and nethers on the spin cycle. It was so easy to get lost in the way he was looking at her. Yes... she wanted to get lost in those dangerous eyes... in his arms... in his past, present and future... and to climb into his dark headspace with him and experience all the wanton wickedness he could imagine.

His arms encircled her and his mouth covered hers hungrily, his caressing tongue and firm lips commanding her to submit to him, demanding her surrender. Like it had done the first time he kissed her like this. But why? What about Ciara?

Just as his mouth began to sear a path down her neck, she grudgingly pulled out of his reach even though she had no desire to back out of his embrace. When she did, she saw his domination flicker in his dark ravenous eyes. He hated being pulled away from and she feared what kind of punishment she might have brought on herself.

Ella Dominguez

He growled deep and primal as he stalked toward her slowly, his eyes mere slits. "The last five hours have been hell without you and I. Will. Not. Be. Denied."

"I would never..." she stammered out, both turned on and frightened at the look on his stubbly, princely face. "But... Ciara..."

His movement halted and he lifted an eyebrow at her. "What about her?"

"I assumed..."

"You should never assume, Sarah," he cut in. "And you should know that I wouldn't be here if I was with Ciara."

She shook her head, confused and not understanding his statement. It made no sense at all. She saw the look in his eyes on the video when he was with her. He wanted her. She wanted him.

"Look at me, Snowflake," he ordered when her eyes dropped to the floor. Complying, she met his impassioned gaze and waited for his explanation, hoping she wouldn't have to request one. "My heart belongs to you and only you. I came here tonight to offer myself to you. If you don't want me, I can accept that. But I want to hear from you that it's for no other reason than because you don't feel the same way about me that I do about you. I will not accept your denial because of some sense of obligation as my trainer or out of duty or honor. You preached of honest and open communication and now's the time to put your words to the test. Do you want me or don't you?" When he spoke, his dominance was unquestionable and irresistible.

Sarah dropped her chin to her chest. Of course she wanted him. Her heart belonged to him, too. She could hear Sawyer's uneven breathing and she raised her eyes. He looked so lost. She opened her mouth to profess her love, but his next statement came spilling out before she could speak.

"Your beauty captivated me from the first moment I saw you. Your intelligence and knowledge stimulated and motivated me. Your body satiated my deepest sexual desires...

235

but it was your submission that awakened my Dominant tendencies and ensnared me. Before you deny me, Sarah, I want you to know that when I dream, it's your face I see, and when all is dark, you are my light."

Her lips parted and her breath quickened when she looked into Sawyer's eyes. The steely intensity held within that deep brown gaze and his words undid her, and she fell to her knees at his feet, gripping his leg and sobbing against him. He was her Sir. Her Domly One. Her Master.

She loved him. Completely. And though she would always love Doug just as he would always love Serena, their love for each other was different and nothing less than intense and consuming. There was no competing with their lost loves; theirs was simply another love to add to their hearts.

Sawyer picked her up into his arms and sat her on the bed. Reaching into the inside of his blazer pocket, he pulled out a white leather collar with an ornate silver snowflake just below a D&O ring. Sarah gasped and tears filled her eyes again. She glided her fingers over the soft leather and cool metal buckle. It was the most beautiful collar she had ever laid eyes on.

"This was the reason it took me so long to see you tonight..." he whispered as he unbuckled it. "I had the Youngs' jeweler working feverishly to get it just right. Isabel helped me design it."

"It's exquisite, Sir."

He laid the collar out in his palm so she could read the burnt engraving on the inner leather. It contained four, simple yet touching words: "Beauty. Inspiration. Intelligence. Mine."

Taking her hand, he helped her to her knees in front of him. Just then, Isabel and Dylan came into the room, both of them smiling lovingly. Isabel walked over and played with Sawyer's phone and *All of Me* by John Legend began playing softly over the speakers. The words washed over her and she felt as if she was being surrounded by pure love. This was their own personal, intimate collaring ceremony and it couldn't be any more perfect.

Ella Dominguez

She gracefully tucked her feet beneath her, placed her hands in her lap and lowered her head. She couldn't believe her fortune. Only an hour ago she thought her fate with Sawyer was sealed. It all came down to honesty. If only she had been truthful with him, she wouldn't have had to suffer the way she did over the last five hours.

When she felt the leather slip around her and Sawyer's warm fingers fluttering over her neck as he secured the collar snugly, she deeply exhaled the breath she had been holding in. She was really his and he was really hers. Twice now she had the privilege of being collared, and for the second time, she felt whole.

Her left hand came up and touched the collar just to reassure herself that it was no dream. When she was satisfied, she tipped her head back to stare up at her new Master. "Thank you for finding your way back to me."

Leaning down, he held her firmly below her chin as he kissed her forehead, "No, Snowflake, thank you for blazing a trail so bright I could never get lost."

Moving directly in front of her, he pushed the hair from her eyes and touched the top of her head. His eyes were narrowed but a sinful smile flitted across his deliciously firm lips and Sarah's hands inched up his thighs in anticipation of sealing the deal.

"You belong to me now, Snowflake, and I belong to you. From this moment on, submit to me always and I promise, you'll be the only woman ever allowed to serve me."

Sawyer's absolute dominance crushed what little will Sarah had left as he stood glaring down at her. He was her alpha, she - his omega, and his name was forever emblazoned on her heart.

"Yes, Master. As you wish."

Epilogue

Winter was glorious. The previous night had brought eight inches of pristine snow and Sawyer felt energized by the cold gust of wind blowing past him and Sarah. Spring would soon be upon them and he just wanted to enjoy the snow while it lasted. He tucked her into him for warmth as they entered the Dark Asylum.

The heat and smell of sweat and sex hit them like a wall when they walked into the social area. Kerian was a shit like that. He loved the heat cranked up to some unbearable temperature just to watch everyone roast their asses off.

"Domly One!" he heard from across the room.

Kerian was waving them over. They removed their coats and made their way to him. Julia and Ciara were on display for all to see and the pride on Kerian's face was like a ray of sun shining in the dimly lit room. Tonight was the official collaring ceremony for him and Ciara and the energy in the room was thick in the air. The usual sounds of sexy debauchery could be heard in a back room and the familiar orgasmic scream of Isabel broke through the din.

"Are you nervous to be giving Ciara away?" Kerian directed his question at Sawyer.

"Not at all. I'm honored she's asked."

"And we're thrilled you've accepted." He gently pulled Sawyer aside and his mood grew serious. "I know I've thanked you already, but..." he took in a deep breath. "It doesn't seem like enough. I truly can't express my gratitude for what you've done for me and Julia. For Precious."

Sawyer placed his hand on Kerian's shoulder and gave him a firm, reassuring squeeze. "Well, I knew your old school ass wouldn't do anything about it," he kidded.

Kerian's brows raised but he remained serious. "You're right and I banish the thought of how our lives would've turned out if Precious hadn't offered herself to us. We would be lost..." he broke off midsentence.

He knew well how Kerian felt. He would be lost without Sarah. He glanced over Kerian's shoulder. She was watching him keenly and he lifted one side of his mouth. Her eyes brightened and she returned his smile.

"Everything is set for tonight," Kerian winked suggestively before he returned to his slaves.

Sawyer and Sarah seated themselves at the bar in anticipation of the ceremony and Dylan sauntered over with Isabel in tow. She waddled a few steps behind him, still shaky from whatever torture he had inflicted on her. She was a full five months pregnant and her belly was just as round as a mini-globe and her motherly breasts deliciously abundant. A wicked smile tipped Sawyer's mouth. He couldn't wait to plant his own seed in Sarah and get his hands on her milky tits. Soon... very soon.

He glanced at his watch and touched his pocket to make sure the ring was still there. Just after the ceremony he was going to surprise Sarah with his proposal. Kerian had the scene all set up. Sawyer would perform a little sensual sadism on her, cane her and bang that sweet ass of hers, then let her know that he was claiming her for the rest of their lives. It would be an epic proposal.

Following that was the Young's surprise gift to the club. Isabel had finally come into her father's estate and she and Dylan were donating a large sum of money to the club for some needed updates and additions. The rest of the money was going to various domestic abuse and children's charities. It was a nice gesture on their part and the closure that they both needed.

He looked back to Isabel who was trying to seat herself on a stool but failing miserably. Her petite figure wasn't meant to carry that kind of load. Dylan assisted her and Sawyer smiled. She was seriously the most adorable pregnant masochist he had ever laid eyes on. Then again, she was the only pregnant masochist he knew. He furrowed his eyebrows thinking about Young flogging her when she had a baby on board.

Isabel shook her head at him. "Please don't look at me like that. The endorphins are good for the baby, Master Morrison."

Dylan quickly chimed in, "Yeah and so is my man juice. It helps promote a positive outcome..." he quirked an eyebrow and laughed.

Here it comes - Dylan's lame wordplay.

"See what I did there? *Out*come? Positive out*cum*? Did you catch the double meaning? The baby's coming out and my cum is positive for it?" he explained as if they were all dense.

Yeah, yeah. Sawyer rolled his eyes and shrugged his shoulders in response.What did they know anyway? He'd never *ever* like the idea of Isabel being punished. He didn't care how much she liked it. Or needed it. But whatever. Punishment was all part of the D/s dynamic and had come to accept it. Anyway, it was their kink. Hell, he had his own fetishes to deal with. Like breath play. Seriously, who would've fucking known? And anal sex and caning... he shook his head and laughed at himself. Yeah, he was one kinky motherfucker with a dark past alright. And he was completely okay with that.

"Accept no one's definition of your life. Define yourself." - Unknown

Becoming Sir

Pimpin' Time

Made in the USA
Middletown, DE
04 August 2015